THE
FOURTH
HOUSE

JAMES P. BARKER

ISBN: 979-8-9992063-0-5 - KDP eBook
        979-8-9992063-1-2 - KDP paperback
        979-8-9992063-2-9 - Draft2Digital eBook
        979-8-9992063-3-6 - IngramSpark paperback

This is a work of fiction. Any resemblance to actual persons, living or dead—or somewhere in between—may be purely coincidental. In the liminal spaces between memory and myth, truth and illusion tend to blur. Reader discretion is advised.

Trigger warning: Hell yes. Come inside. Stay a while. But be warned: the light only reveals what the dark wants you to see. And once you do, you can't unsee it — because the only thing more unsettling than the first read is the second, when you face the darkness in a new light.

DEDICATION

For my parents, Mark and Beverley Barker. This novel was written between the long shadows of their deaths— one foot in grief, the other in the quiet inevitability of yet another goodbye. A story born in the liminal, where echoes linger and the past never truly rests.

Special thanks to the delightful Heidi Hertzog, who asked to write a sentence or two. I picked the spot in the story. She hit a home run. Perhaps you'll find where that ball landed on the page.

The more you look, the more you see.

CHAPTER 1

Tap. Tap. Tap.

Sunny stared at the sink with a hand over her mouth. A ring of rust surrounded the drain; water dripped rhythmically from the faucet. Those weren't the only things she saw, though.

Someone entering the restroom might think she was waiting for the queasy rush to come again. It always did. At the most inopportune times too. At least this time, she was alone. That warmth usually spread from her belly to her head. Sometimes, it turned her legs into uncontrollable, stumbling mush.

She would welcome it if she were among people she didn't know. That way, she wouldn't have to explain her frozen stupor to someone who thought she was lost in space. This wasn't something she could readily explain, nor was it something she wished to discuss. The episodes were short at first. Broken shards of fleeting images. Fragmented memories. Or some repressed thoughts, perhaps, but like experiencing a waking nightmare.

The attacks were always random and set in darkness with a distant light at the far end of the black. Lately, they had been more frequent, disturbing, and prolonged. And then there was that old Victorian mansion. When the sights came, it felt like her trachea was constricting, and she couldn't breathe. The pain was sharp, as if she was inhaling shards of glass.

Sunny wondered if this was what an asthma attack felt like. She dismissed any notion of an elephant sitting on her chest, a description given to her before. That was more like being crushed. This was more like choking on a hive of angry bees.

She didn't dare speak of the experience or what she saw to anyone. Her husband was to blame for that, as far as she was concerned. Nobody wanted their every experience, action, or thought psychoanalyzed. Especially under the guise of "understanding" it, for there was no explanation.

That quote from old Fritz Nietzsche came to mind. Those seen dancing were thought crazy by those who could not hear the music or something of the sort. All she knew for sure was that she wasn't one to risk dancing like nobody was watching, regardless of the music playing. At least she had control of that. The sickness, however . . .

Tap. Tap. Flush.

The swirling gurgle of a toilet sidetracked her train of thought. This was followed by the clacking of high heels on the tile as a woman exited the stall behind her.

"Oh, hey, you scared me. I didn't know anyone else was in here," said the woman as she turned on the faucet next to Sunny. "How's that course of yours—?" She stopped midsentence, noticing Sunny's stupor as she glanced in the mirror. "You going to get sick again?"

Sunny's hand dropped from her mouth and curled her blonde locks around her ear. How long had she been standing here like this? "False alarm. I'm fine now. Thanks for asking though, Angela."

Angela gave an exaggerated, doubtful sideways glance. She leaned close to the mirror, applying a fresh layer of ruby-red lipstick. "Girl, you better get something else in your tummy," she said before pressing her lips together and puckering up.

"Something other than the acrobat renting the space now?"

Angela dropped the lipstick into her purse and laughed.

"Looks like the landlord's about to hand out an eviction notice any moment now. Talk soon, hon, and you later, Rebecca," she said with a slight bend to Sunny's girth.

Angela's heels clattered away as Sunny viewed herself in the mirror. She brushed her hair away from her brown eyes and turned sideways. The door opened and then closed with a dull, echoing thud as her hand ran over her belly. The bathroom was otherwise silent except for the low hum of the lights overhead and the leaky faucet.

Tap. Tap. Tap.

Sunny needed to get moving to class. The familiar yet hypnotic dripping was threatening to trigger another spell. Thankfully, she saw no larvae falling to the floor in sync with the rhythmic tapping—at least not this time.

Navigating between these rows of students made Sunny feel like she was walking a tightrope in high heels. Rebecca using her umbilical cord for acrobatics didn't help matters. It left Sunny feeling like a Weeble. Thanks to her childhood, she knew Weebles wobble, but they don't fall down.

The students, with their laptops and tablets, seemed to spend more time looking down than looking at her. They weren't much younger than herself, though she didn't recall being so reliant on technology. One student repeatedly placed a pencil atop his chair, letting it roll down. He was always doing something to annoy her, so calling on him gave her some measure of satisfaction.

"Kyle," she said and waited for his response. Instead, he looked straight at her belly. "Can you give an example of an unproblematic belief? One that we don't question?"

Kyle swallowed hard, his eyes on Sunny's girth. "It's big and round."

"Hard to believe it was once flat," Sunny quipped to a round of laughter from the class. Kyle was blushing.

"The earth, I meant."

"Some might beg to differ."

Sunny grimaced with a hand to her belly again but did her best to hide the discomfort. Rebecca must be on the uneven bars, she imagined, as she wobbled back to the front of the class.

"What we believe defines not only us but also how others perceive us." Pausing for emphasis, she looked them over. "Beliefs are framed by society and most often by those closest to us. Including our very own families."

"Yeah. Until 'I Saw Mommy Kissing Santa Claus.'"

That was the Kyle Sunny knew, always getting a laugh from the students.

"Ah, but why do we deceive others? Or, better yet, ourselves? Any examples of a problematic belief? Preferably neither round nor flat."

Sitting alone, banished to the room's rear, the runt of the classroom litter raised his timid hand.

"Yes, Steven?"

Steven's eyes fluttered about the room before gazing at his desk's surface. He spoke to it instead of the class.

"My father told me once of this mansion, upstate, on a river—"

"Can you speak up?" someone asked.

Steven took a deep breath and began again, louder.

"My father told me a few years ago about this mansion farther upstate on a river. He used to photograph weddings there. The woman who turned it into an inn claimed it was haunted."

Snickering from several students drew Sunny's stern gaze.

"Class, be respectful." She nodded to Steven. "Please continue."

What he was about to tell the class would send more than a shiver down her spine.

"He thought she was crazy until one night, something happened that he couldn't explain," Steven said.

Sunny could feel the warmth rising from her chest to her neck and head. An uneasiness swelled from within; she didn't know whether this was a garden-variety hot flash or another of her spells.

"As he described it, the place was a big, gothic mansion with a round tower and white pillars from the porch to a balcony. He did some photography there a year before. He was in the area again, working on a weekend wedding shoot at a nearby property, when he stopped by. A full moon was in the sky, and these bugs—cicadas, I think—filled the air with 'the shrill chorus of a buzz saw,' he said. A beam from a distant lighthouse would go around, and as he stood outside the gate to the mansion, he watched it. As it passed through the tower's windows, he saw something flutter."

All eyes were on Steven as silence fell over the classroom. Feeling the warm rush within, Sunny sat on her desk. Her heartbeat sputtered at his description of the mansion, almost as if he had read her mind.

Steven took a sip from a water bottle, wiped his mouth, and continued. "Something made a noise, but nothing was there when he turned toward it. Just then, the clouds passed by the moon, and he had an eerie feeling. It grew darker for a moment, the cicadas falling silent as if something, or someone, was near. A woman's voice said, 'It's as if you can still see her, there in the window.'"

Sunny leaned closer, staring at Steven.

"When he turned back to the mansion, he saw a younger woman in a white dress. The brim of a white hat obscured her face as she walked toward him. Stories were going around then, and he told her, 'I don't think there's any such thing as ghosts.'"

Steven caught Sunny's gaze again and paused. Though he might be the runt of the class, the more he talked, the more convincing a storyteller he became.

"'Neither do I,' the woman said with a smile as she passed by him. My father looked back up to the window, then back to the road with a nervous gulp. The moon reappeared from behind the clouds. The bugs resumed singing their midnight music. But the woman? She was gone."

The class continued to stare in catacomb silence. One girl next to him leaned heavily on her tablet. It slid so close to the chair's edge it was a miracle she didn't topple to the floor.

"Pfft. That's it?" Kyle rolled his eyes with bitter disappointment.

"Kyle." Sunny's tone caused him to whip his head back.

"When my father got home a few days later, he rummaged through his closet to find the negatives he had taken there the year before. He found the one he was looking for. He held it to the light, and what he saw shook him. It was a female wearing a white dress visible in the same window. Afraid of what people might think, he never spoke of it to anyone else."

Sunny's hand covered her mouth, drawing a concerned look from Steven. He probably was thinking she might get sick like before when she had excused herself. Except it wasn't so much a physical reaction as a physiological one. His shared story sounded—no, *felt*—oddly familiar.

"So . . . who was in the window?" the girl next to Steven asked, oblivious to the fact that her tablet was about to plunge to the floor.

"My father swore it was the woman who passed by him that night," Steven said. "Except she had hanged herself in that room several weeks after he took the photo."

For Sunny, the last sentence stumbled out of Steven's mouth while he stared at her as if time had slowed to a standstill. The classroom grew darker as her heart raced. Everything grew black and silent. Then, she saw a distant flash of light, accompanied by the buzzing of flies. The light revealed the broken shards of nightmarish images in a strobe-light effect. The silhouette of a woman against a window. A pair of greenish-yellow feet with purplish toes dangling. Larvae falling to the floor—tap, tap, tap—as the drone of flies grew deafening.

Sunny was jolted from her spell when the girl beside Steven fell to the floor with a shriek. The throat-clenching feeling had come over her as if she were going to cough up broken glass. It subsided as she breathed heavily, in and out.

"Sorry," the girl next to Steven gasped, gathering her tablet and sitting back in her chair.

Sunny finally lowered her hand from her mouth with a nervous laugh. She swiped her hair back behind her ear—something she habitually did when nervous.

"And with that in mind, I look forward to your papers due next Tuesday," she said, regaining her composure and dismissing the class.

As students trickled out the door, a gush of warm June air rushed into the room. It smelled of fresh cut lawn with a hint of something decaying. Sunny wiped the blackboard, then dropped the eraser to the floor with a wince. Little Ms. Rebecca was up to her tricks again.

Steven knelt and picked it up, handing it to her as she grasped her belly.

"I think she's telling me she's going to be a kickboxer," Sunny said, playing it off with a nervous laugh. "Is that what you're doing your paper on? Ghosts?"

"I was thinking that, or reincarnation," he said, catching Sunny wincing again.

"In that case, maybe she was a kickboxer in a previous life," she said with a grimace.

"Are you OK, Mrs. Johnson?"

"Me? I was hoping to make it through the summer session. But it's my husband you should be worried about." She grabbed her cell phone from her purse and dialed a number. "Ready or not, Rebecca's rounding third base and heading for home!"

CHAPTER 2

Sunny stared out the passenger window at the moon in the early evening sky.

"Relax," she told her husband as he drove. "Breathe easy. In and out. You're doing good. Everything is going to be OK."

Beads of sweat cascaded from his messy, gray-tinged hair.

She turned the car stereo on. A hauntingly atmospheric Radiohead tune, "How to Disappear Completely," filled the cabin.

Looking at Taylor, she wondered if this was how he felt as he loosened his tie. Watching him had her stifling a round of giggles with her hand.

"What?" The car's tires chirped as Taylor shifted gears.

Sunny couldn't contain it anymore. She was moaning between teary-eyed laughter and gasps for breath as she attempted to complete a sentence.

"I'm . . . the one . . . about to give birth, but you're the . . . hot mess!"

Her laughter simmered into a long, drawn-out sigh, and she looked back out the window to the moon. "Relax. Breathe easy. In and out. You're going to be OK." She leaned the seat back as far as it would go.

"Speaking of hot messes, I vividly recall the last time I heard this," Taylor replied.

"I should hope so. It was only nine months ago."

"It's why we're here, isn't it?"

"It's why we're *all* here." Another moan broke Sunny's smile.

The memory came over her with not-so-random images. Taylor tossing her onto the bed. His piercing eyes. How she gasped and moaned with each thrust. Nibbling at his ear as she clenched the sheets. All this came to her as the same song played on the radio. It wasn't the least bit romantic, but neither were they as a couple.

Passion, yes. Romance? That was for daydreamers with their heads in the clouds.

The sex that night had felt like an out-of-body experience, which was why the song resonated so much. She should have paid more attention to the lyrics; they were always the last thing she picked up on. She tended to focus on the music and the atmosphere it created instead.

Hearing this song now, its sparse, haunting lyrics crept up on her and hit her out of nowhere. Maybe it was a lingering feeling from Steven's story. It might be a coincidence that it was playing now, but it was problematic because she felt her mood shift. The smile she had worn moments ago faded completely.

The song—or so she believed, at least—was about being a ghost.

"Earth to Sunny?" Taylor asked.

"I'm fine. God . . ."

"I beg your pardon. No, you're not."

She followed his glance to her feet resting on the dashboard with her legs spread. They both laughed.

"Like you didn't have a hand in this."

"Uh, a little more than a hand," Taylor said, grabbing her hand and kissing it.

"Emphasis on 'little.'"

"Walked into that one." He paused, and his tone became serious. "I'm just a little worried about these . . . *thoughts* you've been having."

Sunny let go of his hand and gazed out her window. It was funny how the moon seemed to be chasing them. It symbolized femininity and fertility. Or so she recalled reading somewhere in her undergrad courses. As Kyle would say, it was big and round too. It also represented the unconscious. Darkness. Secrets. Emotions. Even eternity.

Not to mention that one only saw the "sunny" side of the moon, leaving the dark side a mystery.

"I know it's rare, but some people do experience prenatal depression. Although even rarer—"

"We've been through this, Dr. Johnson. I don't have postpartum depression or psychosis. I haven't even had her yet, for crying out loud."

"It's not called that anymore."

"Then what's it called?" she asked, growing agitated.

"It's peripartum."

Sunny fell into silence.

"The American Psychiatric Association recognizes depression, or psychosis, associated with having a baby may begin during the pregnancy—not just after birth. In other words, like I was saying, it's not unusual—"

The look she gave him cut him off before her words did.

"It's just hormones," she rationalized. "Most pregnant women experience bizarre dreams or random thoughts, some terrifying. They're stress induced. And it doesn't help matters when those around them who should be understanding create conflict instead."

The silence between them swelled with the music from the car stereo. A crescendo of discordant strings and Thom Yorke's hauntingly emotional vocals gave Sunny goose bumps. It also reinforced their relationship. At times, it too was dissonant, lacking harmony.

"Can I have my husband back now, please?" she asked with a feigned smile.

What she couldn't fake were the painful wails that soon followed.

"We'll be there momentarily," said a tall man to Sunny's the right of Sunny.

The royal-blue smock he wore showed hair creeping up his neck from his back. The thought of that being the last thing she saw before giving birth made her cringe. To her left, Taylor kept pace with the gurney she was on.

Sunny controlled her breathing as much as she could. Considering she was on her back with her legs bent at an angle, it was an achievement. Her light-blue gown, however, wasn't the warmest garment for a cold sweat. Or was she trembling from the growing unease with what little talk there was? It was hard to read faces covered with masks, after all.

Still, she had the feeling something wasn't right. The pace at which they were moving down the hall had an urgency to it. It was cold, impersonal, and joyless for what was to be one of the happiest moments of her life.

Taylor slowed to a stop and turned into a room.

"Where is he—?" Sunny asked, attempting to sit up with a moan when the gurney burst through double swinging doors.

"Please lie still," a nurse dressed in blue said with all the warmth of the sterile room they were now in.

Equipment beeped and pinged in a pattern of threes. The rhythm had Sunny imagining larvae falling to the floor, hitting it with the same beat.

"He had to go put on some blues. He'll be right back," the nurse said, surprising her with a soft hand on her shoulder. "Your baby's breech. We're preparing you for a cesarean."

That would explain Sunny's feeling that Rebecca had been doing a routine on the uneven parallel bars earlier. Rebecca had gotten herself upside down and needed help nailing the dismount. As if Sunny weren't nervous enough about having her first child, it would be nontraditional. This was something she hadn't expected at all.

Relax. Breathe easy. In and out. You're going to be OK.

One of the nurses prepped an oxygen mask. A small tear escaped from the corner of Sunny's eye and rolled to her ear.

"Sounds like the eviction notice was served," Sunny said, trying to maintain a sense of humor to ward off the jitters. A blank look was all she received in return as the activity picked up around her. "Inside joke. Literally." Her voice cracked, trying to hold the fear in as the mask was strapped over her mouth and nose.

Without forewarning, another nurse pulled her gown up and made several short strokes with buzzing clippers. Was this typical? She'd seen videos of births with the mothers unshaven. This felt too systematic. Like men in the army getting buzzed for sanitation. It only added to her trepidation.

The nurse nodded to the anesthetist, who readied a needle.

"Good evening. We're going to administer general anesthesia. The procedure should be—"

"I want to be awake."

Taylor appeared by her side, dressed in a light-blue smock, mask, and cap, and took hold of her hand.

"Relax. Breathe easy. In and out," he said, stroking her hair. "You're doing good. Everything is going to be OK."

"But I want to be awake for her birth!"

The anesthetist hovered over her, blocking out some of the overhead lights. "You'll be a little foggy when you awaken. There will be a slight prick. Try counting backward from ten once you feel something cool."

His mask moved with what appeared to be a reassuring smile underneath. It reminded Sunny of a frightful trip to the dentist years ago. Of course, this was a little bigger than having wisdom teeth pulled.

"Be sure to call my parents."

"I will," Taylor said, letting go of her hand. "See you two in a bit."

Sunny winced at the sharp pierce into the skin of her forearm. A coolness spread.

This must be what it feels like to grow numb.

"Ten . . . nine . . . eight . . ."

It was not much longer before she disappeared completely. Lucky number seven. That's when everything started to go black. As it did, the beeps and pings of the equipment sounded like chimes.

CHAPTER 3

Sunny tried to open her eyes. Everything was glaring and blurry as if she had fallen asleep and awoken at the beach. She squeezed her eyes closed and groaned. Her mouth felt stuffed with cotton, reminding her again of her trip to the dentist years ago. She tried to generate saliva. Her throat felt like coarse sandpaper, and her head ached as if she had lost a fight with a jackhammer.

She lay still with her eyes closed, listening to the beating of her heart.

Fine. I'll just lie here.

Her hand roamed over her flat stomach, and she understood where she was.

"Becca?"

Sunny attempted to prop herself up, then plopped back down, defeated. She smacked her tongue to the roof of her mouth several times. The image of a fish out of water, flopping and gasping for air, came to mind.

She tried to open her eyes again.

Whatever room she was in, it was bright. She blinked, and her body rebooted as she tried to get this operating system named Sunny back up and running.

Objects began to take shape. She focused on a nearby chair. Her hand caressed her stomach, exploring it before dropping to her pelvis. It then ran over a scar that felt odd the more she touched it. Then, with a grunt, she propped herself up, her eyes continuing to squint and blink as she looked down at her body.

"What the . . .?"

There was a scar but no staples or stitches. It was completely healed.

The shaved area was now a blooming field of pubic hair at least half an inch long. She was slow to sit up.

She pulled the sheet away from the rest of her body. None of it looked familiar. She tried to recall her last memory. Nothing came but the sound of musical chimes and a distant light.

Her eyes came to focus on a cluster of objects on the wall next to her bed: a montage of photos. She recalled the one of her and Taylor from two years before when they were on a trip to New York City.

One photo showed her in a light-blue gown with a precious little bundle of joy resting atop her chest. In the picture, her blonde hair was matted to her face, and her baggy, exhausted eyes gazed at Rebecca shortly after her birth.

She touched the photo, and the blurriness stormed back with tears.

The door burst open. An older nurse with penciled-in eyebrows pushed a wheelchair into the room.

"Just in time." She motioned for Sunny to sit. "You've been quite the sleepyhead."

Sunny brushed her hair away from her face. The air smelled like mothballs doused with an old, oriental perfume. A mortician might use it to make the smell of formaldehyde a little more bearable.

"Where am I?" Her voice was gravelly and coarse.

The nurse helped Sunny from bed.

"Why, the same place you were the last time you asked," she said, patting Sunny's hand. "It's not unusual to have difficulty remembering things for a while."

Sunny slid from the bed to the wheelchair, careful not to inhale the dreadful perfume. Who would find such an aroma attractive? Then the name came to her: Morticia. Of course, this nurse looked like Morticia Addams. It was odd how the brain made such random associations.

"Where's Rebecca?" she asked Nurse Morticia.

"Your husband has made arrangements," the mortician-smelling nurse said.

She wheeled Sunny into a white hallway and past a large, open room. There, several other patients milled about, some like zombies.

A painting sat on an easel in one corner by a window that looked more fitting for a prison. Sunny adjusted her eyes as she was pushed closer. The picture became clearer, leaving her to wonder if she was seeing things.

From what little she knew from art history, it was an expressionist painting. The colors were vivid, and the object they formed was gothic and familiar. A round tower on one side of a mansion with pillars rising from the porch to a balcony overhead. It was set against water, a description that she remembered vaguely.

But the painting itself? If van Gogh was the impressionist who severed an ear, whoever painted this frenzied nightmare must have lopped both off.

Despite its frantic composition, she recognized it as the place that appeared in her broken shards of memories.

"That painting?" she asked, confused. "It looks familiar."

"It should," Nurse Morticia said with a smile. "You painted it."

Sunny's heart skipped when the nurse wheeled her into another, smaller room. It was claustrophobic and full of equipment, and she recognized its purpose.

The mental fog she had awoken with dissipated at the sight of the bed and its many straps awaiting her. Most people believed electroconvulsive therapy didn't exist anymore, but it had made something of a silent comeback in modern medicine. Sunny shook her head, fearful of her memory disappearing completely. Even worse, she was confused about why this was happening.

Two technicians, who might have been twins in identical blue scrubs and face masks, assisted her from the wheelchair onto the bed. That's when she saw him, standing to the left of the entrance so she wouldn't notice him when she came in. She had never felt so betrayed, and all Taylor could do was shift his uneasy gaze to the floor.

"Hello, Sunny. Do you remember me?" asked a petite Asian woman.

Sunny shook her head no.

"My name is Dr. Kim. I'm your anesthetist."

The last three words sparked a moment of déjà vu. Sunny remembered a different anesthetist right before Rebecca was born.

One of the technicians took her left arm and placed it on the armrest. Another put an oxygen sensor on her index finger. A third wrapped a blood pressure monitoring cuff around her right arm. A fourth began attaching sticky electrodes to her chest; they were cold on her bare skin.

When she tried shifting her torso, the electrodes felt like bugs crawling toward her neck.

With a flick of a switch, the heart monitors next to Sunny's bed sprang to life with a rhythmic beep, beep, beep.

"After I administer the anesthesia, we'll give you a muscle relaxant. Your right arm will be isolated from it," Dr. Kim said. Sunny's confused eyes darted about the room while the technicians affixed electrodes to her head. "We will secure your other arm and legs as a precaution."

Tears cascaded from the corners of Sunny's eyes. "Why? Why are you doing this?" she asked Taylor.

"You gave consent," Taylor said.

His words provided no comfort. She could not recall doing so. "I just want to see Becca." Her voice cracked with raw emotion.

Dr. Kim held up a needle. "I'm just going to put a tiny IV needle in your hand. Once you feel the small prick, start counting backward from ten. You'll be asleep for a few minutes while you have your treatment and then wake up immediately."

"Please," Sunny said. The technician twins held her down, stymying a short struggle to resist.

She stared at Taylor, wincing as the needle penetrated her skin. Her eyes never left him despite their heaviness under the weight of the anesthesia. Everything grew dark around her, but she didn't bother to count backward this time. Instead, she focused on the steady beeps.

There was no feeling of warmth coming up from her belly, nor was there any nausea. The last thing she saw before the proverbial lights went out wasn't Taylor. It was a darkness broken by a roaming, distant yet bright white light coming through a window. It was from a remote lighthouse, warning her of danger ahead.

The lighthouse's beam exposed yellowish-green feet with purple toes in its path. Larvae fell to the floor, landing in sync with the monitor's beeps.

Sunny's last thought as the light passed and the darkness came to swallow her whole was how odd the beeps sounded, almost like the chiming of a music box.

Dr. Kim injected the muscle relaxant into Sunny's IV; moments later, her buckled hand began to tremble. "Minor fasciculations," the doctor said with a nod to one of the technicians standing behind the chair.

The technician cupped Sunny's jaw. Widening her mouth, he placed a rubber guard between her teeth.

The beep of the heart monitor continued as a technician put the oxygen mask over Sunny's nose and mouth. Her eyes were still open with their unblinking gaze on Taylor, who was stirred by Dr. Kim's calling, "Dr. Johnson?" He sauntered to a cart next to Sunny, took the electrodes, rubbed their ends together, and placed one on each side of her head.

One of the technicians pressed a button on a piece of equipment. Sunny's body tensed up, her free arm launching upward. Her hand grasped at thin air before it was restrained. Her body trembled and buckled—nothing dramatic, more like a restless body trying to sleep.

After holding the electrodes to her head for thirty seconds, Taylor pulled them away. Sunny's fidgeting slowed to a stop, her eyes still looking off to where he had been sitting minutes ago.

For a moment, he wondered if he was doing the right thing by subjecting her to this treatment. She had already been through so much, and he doubted she would ever forgive him.

The thought was quickly dismissed. This was best for her; she was halfway home with only nine treatments left over the next month.

Chapter 4

The discharge coordinator's arm waved enthusiastically in the air, flagging a vehicle. Sunny wondered if the coordinator was as excited for her to leave as she was. Sitting in a wheelchair underneath the hospital's carport, she couldn't wait to escape this place.

The same ordeal seemed to happen at every hospital she'd ever been to. The patient rode in a wheelchair to the exit as if they were feeble and helpless. Yet here she was, about to return to the real world. It reminded her of the mandatory attendance at her high school graduation rehearsal. If one couldn't walk across the stage when their name was called, if they couldn't receive their diploma, shake hands, and exit without practicing, those thirteen years couldn't have been worth much. And neither was this so-called therapy.

Despite this, Sunny could hardly contain her excitement. Her father had come to pick her up rather than Taylor, though, honestly, she was more excited to see Becca again. At the same time, she was nervous too. She had been here at least a month, maybe two. Her memory was still foggy, though she was assured it would improve with time.

As far as she was concerned, she might as well have been there for an eternity. Those first months were crucial for a mother's learning and bonding with her newborn. Also, as a first-time mother, losing precious time together saddened and panicked her. How would Becca respond to her? How would she react in turn?

Sunny also knew that seeing Rebecca would have to wait. As much as she would have loved to have her come with her grandfather, there was no way he was driving all this way with a baby. Trying to imagine him making an emergency stop to change Becca's diaper gave her a laugh. It subsided when she caught the nurse looking down at her.

She must think I'll need a round-trip ticket.

"It's a beautiful day to be going home, isn't it?" the discharge coordinator said.

"Not really," she said, surprising the nurse. "Home is that way." She pointed a finger in the opposite direction. Across a lake, cumulonimbus clouds rose like dark tombstones on the horizon.

"Oh, that doesn't look very nice at all," the discharge coordinator said as a streak of chain lightning split the sky.

"No offense, but anywhere is nicer than being here," Sunny said. She rose from the wheelchair as the car pulled up to the curb.

George, her father, labored out of the driver's side and limped around the car's front end. He held himself steady with a hand on its hood along the way.

Sunny fetched her suitcase from next to the nurse and turned to greet her father. She was then stopped dead in her tracks. Confusion turned to concern, followed by sadness as she covered her mouth. It was his left leg. Something was wrong with it. It was so much slimmer than his right underneath his dark-green pants.

"Dad? What . . . what happened?"

George stuck his leg out and pulled his pant leg up a few inches to reveal a slick metal rod protruding from his shoe. Sunny almost lost it right then and there; as strong as she'd been through her own "dilemma," she wasn't prepared for this.

"This thing? Most folks put the pedal to the metal. I guess you could say I put the metal to the pedal."

"When?" she asked breathlessly, her confusion growing.

"A couple of months ago," he said, his arms opening wide.

Sunny dropped the suitcase to the ground and fell into them, trying not to cry. "Why didn't you say something?"

"Because I didn't want my little girl to worry, not with all she was going through herself." He pulled away and looked at her as she wiped tears with an awkward laugh.

"I'm not so little anymore, Dad."

"No. But you'll always be my little gal."

He picked the suitcase up, opened the rear door, and placed it inside.

"And here are these." The discharge coordinator handed Sunny three canvases. "Don't want to forget about your work in therapy."

Sunny recognized the painting of the mansion. The second painting appeared to be little more than a small crescent moon in the upper portion of an otherwise blank canvas. The third had the word *Lies* scrawled in three-inch red letters at the bottom.

"Guess I didn't get very far with the other ones."

"Oh, let me get these out of the way," George said as he took a pair of old work boots from the back seat. "Got room in the trunk." He limped past Sunny, stopping with a befuddled look at her artwork.

"I managed to do a little painting between sessions and climbing the walls," Sunny said.

George continued to the car's trunk and popped it open. He tossed the boots inside and closed it with a dull thud.

The discharge coordinator stepped back and turned to him, much to Sunny's chagrin. "Her husband has coordinated all her follow-ups. If there aren't any questions . . . ?"

A crack of thunder punctuated the uneasy silence.

"Thank you. I'm sure she'll be just fine," he said before limping around the front of the vehicle and heaving himself in.

Sunny took in the fall foliage colors: a blur of oranges, reds, and yellows against a backdrop of gray. Windswept rain streaked the passenger window as the car zoomed down the road. She twisted a rubber bracelet around her wrist. *Sunny* was engraved on one side and *Rebecca* on the other. Her leg jackhammered away at the floor mat with frustration and anxiety.

"Thank you," she said, annoyed.

"For what?"

"Picking me up. And for that, back there."

"Was it her telling me instead of you? Or her mentioning him?"

Sunny gave a half-chuckled response. "Both."

George chewed it over. A farmer by trade, he was a cowboy at heart with his laconic replies, and she could feel one coming. "As you said, you're not so little anymore. But by the looks of it, you need a restroom stop."

Sunny noticed him glancing at her leg bouncing up and down. He adjusted the rearview mirror with a sun-dried, leathery hand. She turned to follow his gaze as he trained his weary, crow-footed hawk eyes on it. Behind them, an empty infant car seat with a price tag still on it.

"You know how your ma is. Got that. Crib. Clothes..."

"She shouldn't have," Sunny said, turning back around.

"Why wouldn't she?"

"Is this all really necessary?"

Sunny turned her attention back out the window. The trees with their fall foliage were gone, replaced by a sea of brown cornstalks waving in the wind.

"I just want my life back."

George couldn't help but chuckle. "Can put that notion to pasture if you want to be a mother."

An awkward silence followed as he glanced out the driver's-side window at a scarecrow in the middle of a cornfield.

That must be where I got that distant look out the window from, she thought, looking at him. Gosh, he's getting old. He should be retired by now, in his early seventies. As he always said, "Farming ain't a living; it's a way of life. At least until they plant *you* in the ground." It made her wonder for the first time how much longer he might live. The thought spurred more anxiety and sadness as they passed a tree barren of leaves already.

If anybody on this little green-and-blue ball spinning around the sun knew about the pasture, it was her father. His name might as well be John Deere, minus the ingenuity.

Dad was hardly the innovator type, but he'd spent most of his life working the land—and the land worked him in return. It wouldn't be long before it got the best of him.

George caught her sullen at the thought and returned a smile and a double pat on her thigh. This, followed by a tight squeeze above her knee, always got them laughing. Who knew such a simple little gesture like that could make her leg involuntarily kick out? It also could make everything right in the world, if only for the moment.

She loved that most about him. His impeccable timing in saying or doing the right thing at the right moment. Whether cracking a joke or imparting wisdom, times like these lived forever in her heart. Moments involving secrets and half-truths, like his leg amputation, broke it.

"I just wish you would have told me."

"What good would that have done?"

"That's not the point," she said, staring out the window.

"There's no use worrying about something you don't have any control over, Sunny."

"What if it's the result of something hereditary? Shouldn't I have the right to—?"

"No!"

Sunny flinched. It was rare for her father to speak in such a tone. There was no mistaking his no for her right to know, but she noticed he already regretted it by his heavy sigh. That meant only one thing: a speech was a-comin'.

"Can I give you a piece of advice? From father to daughter?" He didn't wait for her permission. "You're still young. You've got practically your entire life in front of you. Don't go squandering it worrying about the future. And don't waste it dwelling too much on what's happened in the past."

Sunny knew these were wise words. She also anticipated a poignant truth was coming when he turned to her. His blue eyes pleaded louder than his voice.

"Try to spend as much of your life as possible living in the present."

She nodded and turned her attention back out the window. The anticipation got the best of her leg again, and it bounced up and down. The landscape was familiar now. She reminded herself that they weren't far from home—at least, not far from the house she grew up in.

It was a weird experience to return home married but without her husband. She had mixed feelings. On the one hand, she was happy to be out of that place, but she was still upset about the circumstances. Not to mention the "arrangement" Taylor had made for her to have some form of supervision for a while. Even so, her father was right; she looked forward to moving on and putting the past behind her.

Well, it was a start. The contradiction even made her smile.

George pulled the driver's-side visor down as an orange sliver of sun beamed through the windshield. His hand reached for the rearview mirror again, adjusting it. The reflection moved from the infant car seat to the painting beside it.

Sunny noticed he spent the rest of the ride home quiet, glancing at the gothic image in her painting. If she hadn't known better, she'd have thought he seemed troubled by it.

CHAPTER 5

George's car rumbled past an old cemetery and turned into a crushed-stone driveway. Sunny eyed a wooden piece of lawn art of a woman wearing a dress and bending over. The modest farmhouse behind it had seen its last fresh coat of paint the year she was born.

"Where's yours?" Sunny asked, nodding at the lawn ornament.

"Huh? That is mine."

"That's Mom. Your rump's in overalls."

The car rolled to a stop, and George parked it near the barn. "Exactly. She's my sweetie." With a cautious step, he opened his door and put his foot onto the crushed stone.

Sunny sprang out of the passenger side, opened the rear door, and grabbed her suitcase. George took the paintings, giving the mansion a long look. She closed the door with a thud, breaking his trance before barreling her way to the front door. "Come on; I'll get those later!"

With an uncertain shake of his head and a weary sigh, George returned the paintings to the car's back seat.

The old, rickety front door flew open, and Sunny burst into the house. She stopped and took in the entirety of the living room. The scraped hardwood flooring. The folksy dark-blue, maroon, and country-white color scheme. Several cow-related ornaments adorning the shelves and bookcases. Nothing had changed much since her last visit, far too long ago.

"Oh, honey! We've missed you so," Martha said from the dining room.

Her flabby arms opened wide, threatening to swallow Sunny, who froze. The image of her arm shooting up into the air reminded her of the coordinator waving for her father. It was another broken shard of memory, like the rest. It might have been humorous in any other moment if it weren't for the uneasy, cold feeling it left behind. She was thankful the warmth of Martha's embrace replaced it.

While holding her mother, Sunny's eyes fell on her father as he entered. As was customary, he placed his keys on a hanging placard with the phrase HOME IS WHERE YOUR STORY BEGINS painted on it. Like everything else, its color was a dark blue on a country-white background. She closed her tear-filled eyes and pursed her lips. Being here and seeing them felt good, yet it wasn't home anymore.

She suddenly longed for different circumstances and the simpler times of her youth.

"I bet she's grown like a weed," she said, her voice drained of emotion.

Martha pulled away with a crooked glance at George. He held a blue curtain open as he peered out the window.

"Why don't you get yourself settled? Taylor will be here any minute now," he said, letting the curtain fall back into place.

Sunny darted to another window with long, determined strides. She whipped the curtain back and wilted at the sight of Taylor's slick black German car barreling down the road. He had devised a name for the two-ton black beast quicker than he'd decided on one for his six-pound-seven-ounce daughter. That was months ago. He raced past the cemetery, slowing and turning into the driveway. It was the first time she'd pondered which was more important to him.

The curtain fell to Sunny's side as she let it go. Her head dipped with her chin to her chest, a deflated balloon. The warmth and excitement she had experienced moments ago were gone. In their place were cold, swift breaths of anxiety.

"Oh, Sunny. He's only trying to—" Martha stopped at the thump of a car door closing.

"Then why doesn't he listen to me?" She paced back and forth. "He's a psychiatrist. That's what they're supposed to do, after all."

George limped forward with an uneasy step. "He's your husband, not your doctor."

"All the more reason for him to believe me."

"Maybe you should meet him halfway"—he paused as the doorbell rang—"and trust him."

Sunny stormed down a hallway and slammed a door.

Martha, shoulders heaving with a sigh, shuffled to the front door and opened it. She gave Taylor an awkward smile.

"Come in, sweetie," she said, greeting him with a brief hug. Pulling away, she noticed he was holding something. He held out an old porcelain baby doll with a pale, expressionless face.

Martha took it and brushed its disheveled brown hair from one eye that was stuck open. "It's Miss Carmella. Sunny's had this forever."

"I didn't want it to get mixed up with Rebecca's stuff," Taylor said.

Martha passed in front of George and opened a door. The light from the living room revealed part of a crib inside the darkened room. She carefully placed the doll in it, paused momentarily, then turned and walked out. She closed the door behind her with a somber silence.

"So, what's next?" George asked.

"She'll continue with her medication, several more weeks of outpatient therapy—" Taylor stopped, seeing

George rubbing his neck and looking doubtful. "Did something happen?"

"Well . . . Sunny's as you might expect," Martha said, glancing down the hall.

Sunny was sitting in a chair and clutching its armrests, a silhouette against the window and the pink sky outside. It was the calm before the storm. A rumble of thunder in the distance echoed through the room, portending what was to come. Her leg began bouncing up and down again as she waited for the inevitable entrance of Dr. Johnson. She smoothed a hand over her leg to steady it and noticed how loose her clothes were now.

Peripartum psychosis. It was more like a postpartum fashion crisis, with none of her clothes seeming to fit. Maternity clothes were too big for her now, but her old clothes were far too tight. Size-wise, she was in the middle of nowhere. It should be the least of her worries, but she welcomed the momentary distraction.

Sitting in this room, she couldn't remember the last time she was here. Ten years ago, perhaps, she thought as she glanced around. This was where she used to come to escape everything. There was the old grandfather clock in the corner, standing tall. Its constant tick-tock was soothing and sparked daydreams out the window.

The present scene was far from that. Dark clouds overtook the sun, turning it into eerie blood-red as it shone through the window.

Sunny scanned the various portraits on the wall of her mother, her father, and herself from over the years. They were all drenched in the fading sunlight. One photo was of her being held by her mother at several months of age. It reminded her that she would add to this collection with one of Rebecca and herself before long. The thought of Taylor being in the photo didn't even cross her mind—at least not until the sun on the portraits dimmed with the passing clouds.

The respite from him had been nice, however long it had lasted. She was not surprised the dark skies and lousy weather had arrived with him. The door opened, casting the dim light from the hallway upon her. Taylor entered and closed the door behind him, placing a hand on her shoulder.

Holding it, she felt how cold it was and ran her thumb gently over his skin as if to warm it.

Where was this tender touch at the hospital?

She couldn't help but associate its frigidness with the cold feelings of that place. It was as if he lacked warmth throughout, and she questioned whether things would be the same again.

"I want to try something," Taylor said, giving Sunny her answer quicker than anticipated, and she let go of his hand.

"Why? So you can use whatever I say against me?" Sunny wasn't sure if her mood had resulted from him coming in or from herself. She was naïve, believing she might find some peace here again.

Tick-tock went the clock that once sounded soothing. Now, it was mocking her. Each shift of its pendulum was an omen of what he was about to do. To her relief, the clock lacked a little bird coming out to deride her further with its routine.

"No. So you won't go through all that again."

Sunny retrieved a small yellow notepad she often used for jotting down thoughts. She flipped through several sheets and found the laundry list of symptoms. "Hallucinations, anxiety, paranoia—"

"Suicidal thoughts?" Taylor asked, cutting her off. "Did you write that one down too?"

She shook her head, looking for a way to escape. Her attention was stuck in neutral, spinning its wheels. What she needed was to be careful talking to Taylor. Conversations were like walking blindfolded through a field of booby traps and land mines. Worse yet, he would lead her where he wanted her to go: right into one of them.

"Then who was the woman? And don't tell me some apparition."

Try as she might to escape the moment, Sunny snapped her attention sharply back to Taylor with steely eyes.

"The only ghosts are the ones that live inside our heads." She realized how silly that must have sounded within seconds, though she was sure he knew what she meant. "It's what can't be explained that frightens me."

"Like delusions of a murder conspiracy?"

"Delusions are beliefs. These are like thoughts, except they're not mine. I saw these things as if they happened to someone else."

"Listen to what you are saying."

Sunny's face twisted with disgust. Trapped, and she knew it. How could anyone listen to what he was saying in that tone? All that was lacking were *crazy*, *deranged*, and *lunatic* in subtitles. She envisioned them scrolling under his head, like closed captions on television.

"It's not normal—"

"To suggest that I might hurt myself or Rebecca. That's what's crazy!" The last word drifted on the air, riding a wave of silence like a feather for a moment. Twirling down to the ground, it went into a death spiral.

"It's not normal, especially for someone teaching psychology. And in college, no less," Taylor said with his words landing more softly. "I'm not suggesting anything other than that your impulsive thoughts of harming *me* are real, are they not?"

Sunny ran her hands through her hair. She didn't even know what he was talking about—impulsive thoughts of harming him being real? What was that supposed to mean? "They're not . . . *thoughts,*" she finally said, causing the walls to close in on her further. Trying to explain what she couldn't understand was like giving Chinese finger cuffs to a child. The more they pulled, the tighter the trap became.

"Let's find an explanation together. It's what we both want, isn't it?"

With an indignant huff, Sunny pushed herself up from the chair and plopped down on a nearby couch. Her hands fidgeted as she looked at the ceiling. This was her way of doing the opposite of pulling away and easing the pressure.

Taylor pulled a small mini-cassette recorder from his blazer pocket and placed it on a coffee table. "I'm going to count from ten to one," he said, pressing the record button before dimming the lamplight.

Sunny shifted her weight on the couch. "I vividly recall the last time I heard this."

Hiding his smirk, Taylor began yet another countdown. "Ten. Nine. Eight. Seven. Six. Block out everything but my voice."

Sunny's eyelids grew heavier by the moment as the grandfather clock ticked the time away. A blazing sliver of orange sunlight faded on its glass façade. Darkness drifted around them; the storm clouds were creeping closer.

"Five. Four. Three. Two. One."

Taylor leaned forward, resting his chin on his hands and his elbows on his knees. "Let's go back to the point when you're happiest. Can you tell me what's happening?"

Sunny's hand glided over her belly, the tension melting from her stern face with a smile. "I've just learned that I'm pregnant."

"Good," Taylor said with a small smile in return. "Have you any fears about becoming a mother?"

"Not knowing what to do, feeling helpless. Overwhelmed. Not bonding with my child."

Taylor reached for her face, stroking a strand of blonde hair away from her mouth. Leaning closer to the lamplight, he pulled a pen and a small notepad from his blazer pocket. "Excellent. Let us go to a time when you're afraid. A time when your current symptoms are present. Can you tell me where you are?"

Sunny curled into a defensive, fetal-like position, pulling her sweater tighter. Her face twitched into a frown.

"A large house. By water. Many rooms are here, but people only stay briefly before moving on."

Taylor scribbled "psychiatric center" onto his notepad. Sunny's head turned from side to side as if she were examining the room.

"I've been here . . . *before*."

Taylor sat up straight, watching Sunny's eyes rapidly rolling under their lids. "Go on."

"There's a hallway. Doors on both sides. Several of them. A man is there. Deceitful. A handprint on a door drips. It's . . . It's . . ." She frowned, trying to determine what exactly it was. "It's . . . blood. And there's a moon on the door. But not a full one. It's a crescent moon."

Taylor shifted in his seat, jotting down the descriptions. "What can you tell me about the man?"

"He thinks I'm sick."

"Do you know him?"

Sunny's voice was distant and morose. "I thought I did."

Taylor's head dipped. "Can you describe him?"

"I cannot." Sunny sat up. "He's on the other side of the door."

Taylor stiffened as she stood and shuffled past him, murmuring in a trancelike state. "I'm not crazy, despite what they say; please don't let them take my baby away." Her voice was tinged with sadness as if speaking of events in the here and now. "I can never go back there."

"Where?"

"That place."

"You won't have to as long as you continue improving."

An anxiousness filled Sunny's throat. She looked desperately toward the window. "But no one will believe—"

"It's all right. It's in the past. It's safe now."

Sunny began to hyperventilate. She shook her head. "No! No, it's not!"

She jolted as if struck. Her eyes rolled back into her head. She reached a hand outward, grasping thin air, then clutched her throat and gasped.

Taylor shot up from his chair. "Sunny!"

Her arms fell limp to her side, and she stared motionless at the door with her head cocked at an angle.

"The man, he's yelling." She banged her hands against the door and then slumped to the floor. There, she curled silently into a ball.

Taylor waited several moments before asking, "What's happening now?"

"I hear music playing. It's faint. It sounds so far away." She hummed "Dream Sweet, My Darling" before falling silent.

Taylor took a hesitant step forward. "Sunny," he said. "What happened in the hospital?"

Sunny's distant, blank eyes stared through him.

"What happened in the hospital?"

Her voice was low and devoid of emotion when she answered. "It's a different place. A different time. It's not where I am. It's *what* I am."

A flash of lightning illuminated the room with white light. The grandfather clock shuddered with a tick and a tock, back and forth, accompanied by rain against the window.

"What *are* you?" Taylor asked timidly.

Thunder cracked nearby, echoing through the valley. "Dead."

The thunder tapered into a long, drawn-out roll as Sunny grabbed Taylor's arm, her voice euphoric. "I can still see her!"

Taylor yanked his arm away and stuffed the notepad into his blazer pocket with venom.

"Can I have my wife back, please?"

Sunny fumbled for words, confused. Though unsure of what had happened, she knew where this was heading.

"There you go, using whatever I say against me."

Taylor scooped up the mini-cassette recorder and pointed it at her. It was like he was taunting her with evidence, and then he bit his tongue and stuffed it into his blazer pocket.

"What else do I have to do?"

With no reply, she raced out of the room, past a startled George and Martha and into the baby's room.

CHAPTER 6

Sunny stood over the crib and looked down at Rebecca. This was all new to her; she didn't know what to do, and Rebecca was fast asleep on her belly.

So peaceful, so precious. She wanted to hold her and never let her go but didn't wish to disturb her sleep. Sunny's heart started to flutter. The warmth and tingling rose from her belly to her head while her legs were so light she felt as if she could float away at any moment.

It wasn't one of those moments proceeded by nausea. This was when a mother finally saw the child she was separated from, her memories foggy at best. So much so that she thought she could use . . . a lighthouse.

A light beam cut through the darkness and revealed a woman's silhouette, appearing to float in midair. Try as Sunny might, she couldn't stop it creeping into her consciousness. It was gone in a flash, as was the tingling sensation that ran down her spine.

That was one of those moments, and she was thankful it was short-lived. She took a deep breath, but that dreadful feeling still lingered. She wasn't sure which was worse: not knowing what was happening to her or not knowing why.

Maybe it was her overactive imagination making associations again. After all, she associated forgotten memories with fog. Foggy conditions can call for a lighthouse, depending on where one is. It might even be a clue. Steven said his father had been taking photos on a river upstate. She frowned. She could not think of any lighthouses nearby, let alone upstate. Yet the light she had seen in these broken shards of memories appeared to have been from one.

A slight noise from the crib caught Sunny's attention. "Look who's awake!"

She reached into the crib, took hold of Rebecca, and lifted her, wrapping a blanket around her as if she'd done it a million times.

"Do you remember me? It's been so long, but Mommy's here now."

Cradling Rebecca in the dark room with only the hallway light filtering in, she noticed a shadow fall over them from Taylor standing in the doorway. She moved to the door and closed it in his face.

"What just happened?" Martha asked.

Taylor shook his head. "You're sure there isn't any history of this in either of your families?"

George limped into the room, rubbing his neck again with a yawn. "What was all that commotion? And what 'history'?"

"Maybe a bit of the blues," Martha said, looking at a confused George. "I s'pose, but not this, no."

Taylor pondered, eyes darting from the closed door back to Martha and George. "It's better that she has outpatient therapy." He moved toward the window. "I can't keep doing this."

"But," Martha said with a worried look at George, "you're only trying to help her. I just don't . . . I don't understand this."

Taylor pressed his lips together as he labored over his choice of words. "I should never have tried to help her in the first place. Doctors lose objectivity when dealing with loved ones. Of course, I want what's best for her. But when the line between spouse and patient blurs. . . . The fact is, she's never going to forgive me. Not for taking Rebecca from her. I'm not her husband anymore." Nodding to the room with its closed door, he continued, "I'm just a doctor on the other side of a door she doesn't want to open. Can you understand that much?"

Martha held a hand over her quivering mouth. George put his arm around her, rubbing his hand up and down her shoulder.

"I apologize I didn't get here sooner. If you don't mind, I better pick up the rest tomorrow. Give her one last night . . ." He finished the sentence with a wary voice. "The sooner she accepts the reality of it . . ."

"It'll be easier on all of us if you come early before she's awake," George said.

Taylor nodded and shuffled to the front door, pausing with a hand on the doorknob. "Sometimes I think she's just trying to get back at me. To hurt me. Other times . . ." He opened the door. "Other times, I wish that was the truth."

He stepped out and closed the door slowly behind him.

Moonlight through the window faded on and off Sunny's face as she lay in bed. She drifted between wakefulness and sleep, humming "Dream Sweet, My Darling" as she rocked Rebecca's crib.

Her humming faded, and her hand slipped off the crib. She turned on her side, teetering on the cusp of sleep.

"What happened in the hospital?" Taylor's voice echoed through her restless mind.

"Please don't do this," Sunny said, backing away from him, her hand taking hold of a heavy object. "You're not taking her from me!"

She slammed the object against his head.

Whether it was the dream or Rebecca's crying that awoke her, she did not know. She shot straight into a sitting position and drew deep breaths with her hands over her mouth. It was another fragment of a broken memory. She held up her shaking hands and looked at her palms. "I hit him."

I'm not suggesting anything other than your impulsive thoughts of harming me are real, are they not?

"I hit him at the hospital," she said, bewildered.

Another cry from Rebecca alerted her to the crib.

"Shh . . . shh, Mommy's here."

Sunny picked Rebecca up. She closed her eyes and inhaled the scent of her baby-fine hair. It was mesmerizing, nothing like what she expected. Not a baby powder aroma or the scent of cleanliness. It was hard to describe; she'd never smelled anything like it, and it had the most calming effect. Imagining her mother having had the same experience made her smile.

When she opened her eyes a moment later, the hallway light shone around the edges of the bedroom door. The shuffling of footsteps came closer. The commotion must have awoken her mother.

"Is everything OK?" Martha asked, knocking on the door.

"It was just a bad dream."

"Oh. Did you take your medicine?"

Sunny sighed. "Yes, I took my medicine."

A few orange plastic prescription bottles sat on a nearby dresser. Sometimes, she wondered what the doctors were thinking. No doubt her psychotropic medications had side effects. Even less doubt they ran the gamut from insomnia to tremors and confusion.

"Well, let us know if you need anything, honey."

"I will. Night."

The shadow retreated from under the door. Sunny listened to her mother shuffling back down the hall. A moment later, the light around her doorway's edges succumbed to darkness again. The rain pelting the window was the only sound now, at least until her parents' voices carried from a floor register. After placing Rebecca in the crib, she knelt and hovered above the brown metal register vent. Muffled voices echoed from within.

Years ago, when she was twelve, she'd figured out how to pull the entire register covering off to hide things in the air duct. This, however, was a first; she had never eavesdropped on her parents' conversations before.

She opened the register's damper with a turn of the small metal dial on the side of the louvers and placed her ear closer. The voices were tinny but clear enough to make out the conversation.

"It should never have come to this," her father said. The floorboards creaked with every dull thud of his artificial leg. Sunny could picture him pacing back and forth as she listened.

"We can't even be honest with ourselves, let alone Taylor," Martha said. Sunny knew she must be wringing her hands. It was a nervous habit she had seen countless times growing up.

As she lay on the floor, her foot kicked something unexpectedly. She glanced at several stacked boxes in a nook next to the closet.

"I can't say I wish to be around when she realizes what's happened," her father said with a tinge of fear. "She'll probably end up with another stay at the center."

"Taylor's trying to do the right thing for everyone."

Sunny's hand shot to her mouth, covering a gasp.

"The right thing. Humpf. We're damned if we do, damned if we don't at this juncture."

Sunny jumped to her feet, her gaze fixed on the register. The anxious dread came again. But this was different. It was of being in the dark about whatever they were discussing, and it brought on a distinct sense of nausea.

Her eyes drifted to the boxes. She opened the flap on the one at the top of the stack. Inside were baby clothes, all folded up.

Why was Becca's stuff all boxed up? Unless she was going someplace, she realized with creeping dread. Her frantic eyes pinballed from the boxes to Rebecca, the register, the window, and the door. They finally rested before her, finding an answer in the form of her suitcase.

Rebecca was going away after all . . . with her.

CHAPTER 7

Windshield wipers swooshed back and forth at a frantic pace in a downpour. The car's headlights were on as it idled in a dimly lit parking lot next to a closed roadside diner.

Inside the car, Sunny bounced a fussy Rebecca on her arm. After turning the headlights off with her free hand, she redirected the air to the windows to clear the fog. She then turned the engine off. If only Rebecca had a button. Unfortunately, she didn't even come with a manual. The breadth of Sunny's sigh signaled this would be a long night.

"C'mon, Becca. Please."

Pushing her closer to her breast didn't work. With her head hung low, Sunny pulled her shirt closed.

"I don't even know what I'm doing . . . where I'm going. Or where I am at the moment."

Wherever she was, the driving conditions were unsuitable. She made a quick stop at a twenty-four-hour convenience store for gas and a large cup of coffee. Unfortunately, it wasn't doing much good at this hour. She checked her phone: 1:24 a.m. No wonder her eyes were struggling to stay open.

As she sat with the steady rain drumming on the car, she pondered whether this was still considered running away from home. Technically, that hadn't been her home for the better part of a decade. Regardless, leaving the way she did hadn't felt right, and it would cause her parents more grief.

Don't worry about things you don't have control over, her father had told her. It seemed fitting here too, having it work both ways. They shouldn't worry about her either. Besides, it wasn't like she could turn back now. What would she say? That she decided to go for a midnight snack to the middle of nowhere an hour and a half away with the baby?

With a couple of six-packs of crunchy miniature doughnuts, she had enough to eat for a bit. She knew she needed something for Rebecca and that she'd have to make another stop soon. How long before they realized she was gone? Before people started looking for her? She felt overwhelmed.

Damned if you do, damned if you don't.

What she wanted right now was to sleep. Her life had been thrown nothing but curve balls since she became pregnant. Then came the unhittable knuckleballs upon

Rebecca's birth. After that, she couldn't remember her last night of good sleep.

At this point, she'd gladly be struck by a pitch if it meant coming out of the game for at least a quick nap. But, with a baby, she knew that to be nothing more than a dream. Oh, the irony. There was hope, however. Rebecca had settled into a deep sleep. She told herself she'd get some shut-eye and return to the road before daybreak.

She made herself as comfortable as possible in the front seat. As she finally settled in, a passing car's high beams engulfed everything in a bright white light.

Her last thought before the sandman and his cloak of darkness got the best of her: the passing beam wasn't unlike that of a lighthouse.

CHAPTER 8

Martha pulled open the curtains, greeted by dense fog glowing from the full moon hovering in the early morning sky. She leaned closer to the window. It was still too dark to discern anything beyond three feet of the garage door lights.

"I don't know how he made it here through this fog," she said. She poured a cup of hot black coffee before shuffling across the kitchen and handing it to George.

"There's my cup of rise 'n' shine," George said. A suppressed yelp followed as he took the mug and turned it to carry by its handle. "Shall we get the show on the road?"

Martha led the charge around the corner to where Taylor waited near the bedroom door.

"Just try not to wake her," George said. "I don't have enough liquor on hand."

"I brought a sedative, just in case."

"I was speakin' for myself."

"It shouldn't be necessary," Martha said. The two looked at her, confused. "I gave her a little something with her medicine to help her sleep. I figured it'd help us sleep too. She was up late, tossing and turning with bad dreams."

George shrugged and took a sip of his coffee. "She wasn't the only one," he muttered to himself.

Martha grabbed the doorknob and twisted it slowly. The bedroom flooded with light from the hallway as she pushed the door open.

The coffee mug slipped from George's hands. The deep black rise 'n' shine within spilled and splattered onto the laminate flooring. The cup shattered, pieces bouncing in every direction.

Martha gasped. The boxes were gone, the crib was empty, and no sign of Sunny was to be had.

Taylor sidestepped the mess on his way into the room and looked around.

George limped from the hallway to the living room. He focused on the dark-blue-and-white placard on the wall near the front door. *Home is where your horrors begin*, he thought, instead of its message of warmth. Then he noticed a note hanging on one of the hooks.

"For crying out . . . I don't believe it," he said. "The show is already on the road."

The keys were gone, replaced with a hand-scrawled note:

I took your advice too.

CHAPTER 9

Sunny's hand dangled over the empty Styrofoam cup. Its former contents were nothing more than a dark brown spot on the floorboard's gray mat.

Three quick knocks against the driver's window stirred Sunny from her slumber. Sprawled out on the front seat, she lifted her head. Groggy and confused, she shielded her eyes from the brightness through the car's windows. She sat up and glanced around the interior, oblivious to the glowing fog outside. Flashes of blue, red, and orange lights illuminated the bank of white behind her.

She drew a horrified breath as she looked down at the blanket she was lying on. A small, motionless hand protruded from underneath, its color a dull, lifeless white.

"Becca?" she gasped.

She pulled the blanket back. The old porcelain doll, Miss Carmella, stared blankly at her with one eye half closed.

Confused, Sunny wondered how her doll had gotten there.

The last time she recalled seeing the doll was before Rebecca was born. It was an heirloom, or so she considered it to be, to pass down to her daughter. Of course, she didn't remember it in the room last night. Then again, she'd hurriedly packed everything and left in a rush.

Her heart pounded in those moments of confusion. Then it struck her.

Where was Rebecca?

Finally, Rebecca's cries ended Sunny's bewilderment. She turned to the baby in the car seat behind her.

"Hold on, honey."

Sunny ran her hands through her messy hair. She was about to check the time on her phone when knuckles banged against the driver's window again, startling her. A dark, blurry figure stood outside. She rolled the window down and was greeted by a state trooper's friendly blue eyes. They pinballed the inside of the car, landing on the doll.

"Cute. You normally sleep like that?"

Sunny noticed the tinge of white hair at the trooper's sideburns and a purple tie matching the band around his hat. His uniform reminded her of the man with the yellow hat in *Curious George*. But instead of all yellow, he was wearing almost all gray instead.

Before she could reply, her cell phone rang, setting off a fresh round of cries from Rebecca.

The racket had her struggling to understand why a trooper would knock on her window. Then, a sudden realization left her frozen with a crushing thought. She had not only overslept, but they'd already managed to find her.

"You going to get that?" the trooper asked.

"No." Sunny glanced at her cell phone as Taylor's name and number appeared. "I mean, no, I don't normally sleep like this. They can leave a message."

The trooper's eyes darted around again. This time, they landed on the orange pill bottle in Sunny's purse.

"It was raining pretty hard last night. I pulled over and fell asleep."

"Are you heading back from the St. Lawrence?"

"The St. Lawrence?"

"The river. The Thousand Islands?" the trooper asked. He saw the confusion on Sunny's face. "The Thousand Islands in the St. Lawrence River?" He nodded to the painting in the back seat. "That's from up around Alexandria Bay, is it not?"

Sunny's brow creased as she turned, following his nod to the canvas next to Rebecca. "Oh yes. How'd you know?" Sometimes, there were benefits to playing dumb.

"Went a few times when I was younger. A neighbor had a summer place in that area."

"Do you think I did it justice? I love to stay there—"

"Stay? At that place?"

The way he asked had Sunny gripping her steering wheel tight. She hadn't meant to sound that dumb. Instead, the subtitles flashed in neon again as if asking, *Are you crazy?*

"The Thousand Islands, in general," she said. "Though I'm sure that place in the painting can't be any worse than some of the places I've stayed lately."

"Well, I suppose, unless you were dead. It used to be a funeral home."

A funeral home?

Sunny gave the painting another look. "Are you sure it's the place you're thinking of? I thought it was an inn."

"A short-lived one, come to think of it. Ironic, huh?"

The trooper smiled, noticing her wedding ring. His eyes took another long stroll through the car's interior. Sunny noticed he saw her medication sticking halfway out of her purse before she could close it.

"So, is the honeymoon over, or does he hog all the blankets?"

"I beg your pardon?"

"Sorry. I'm politely asking why you're sleeping out here like this. Any marital problems, abuse, or something you might need help with?"

Sunny feigned a smile as Rebecca started a fresh round of crying.

"We're fine, really." It didn't take a body language expert to read the skepticism on his face. "I bet you get that all the time with babies crying in the back seat," she said, warier with each passing moment. "Kind of ironic, huh?"

The crackle of radio static from the trooper's dark-blue SUV drew his attention away from her. She hadn't realized it was parked sixty feet behind her father's car. Its red, blue, and orange lights flashed, disappearing in and out of the fog that looked to be lightening up.

"You, uh, going to get that?"

"Touché." The trooper smirked with a pat on her door. "Have a good day, ma'am," he said with a wave and returned to his vehicle.

Sunny turned in her seat and looked closely at the painting. It showed the rough shape of a man sitting on the front steps and a moon hovering over the mansion beside a body of water. Unfortunately, she couldn't recall the inspiration to paint it. She was unfamiliar with the place. Contrary to what she had said, she'd never been there. Nonetheless, knowing that it existed was a bit of a relief.

After waving to the trooper as he pulled away, she focused her attention from the mirror to the orange bottle in her purse, picked it up, and tossed it out her window.

"Sunny one, crazy nothing."

She took her phone, opened its map app, and typed "Alexandria Bay." The location popped up, showing her coordinates. They appeared to be several hours from the pulsating little blue dot that represented her location. After all that, she hadn't made it as far as she had thought.

"I must have been driving in circles, Becca," she said, disappointed.

From her position, she could ride there from Irondequoit Bay across Lake Ontario with a boat if she only had one.

Taking the thruway to Syracuse and I-81 would get her to Alexandria Bay in two straight lines. Still, running into more state troopers was more likely on the main thoroughfares. Also, there was no longer an option to pay cash for the thruway toll. Everything was electronic, which meant photos of license plates. That, in turn, meant she could be tracked while on the thruway, and inquiring minds would know which exit she got off.

It was also possible to drive along the shore of the lake. With that route, she could pass through little hamlets most people never knew existed. The shortest distance between two points was always under construction. A professor had once said that, and it proved true here too. Along the shore would take longer, but it was safer, with more places to stop.

Of course, with the lake and river as big as they were, there had to be several lighthouses along the way too.

"Becca, we have a destination." She glanced in the rearview mirror and smiled. Her little angel had already fallen asleep again.

The phone's sudden vibration elicited a groan. A text message from "Hubby" appeared over the map: "Stay where you are." A pulsating red dot appeared on the map, "Hubby" hovering over it and moving in her direction.

"Shit!"

Gripping the steering wheel in a near panic, she sat still for several moments, thinking. She opened her Find My Phone app and tapped "Hubby" with a thumb hovering over "Stop sharing location."

As Sunny was biting her lower lip deep in thought, a yellow Labrador retriever crossed in front of her car, heading toward the edge of the parking lot. She opened the car door and stepped out, determined to coax it closer.

"Here, boy!" she called out. "Come here!" She returned to the car for the small pack of doughnuts, a yellow notepad, and a pen from her purse. "Want a treat?" she asked the dog, ripping the doughnut's packaging open.

The Lab approached with a hesitant step. It was a little shaggy and missing tags on its collar but appeared healthy otherwise.

Sunny held up a doughnut. The Lab smacked its tongue and stepped closer. She looked at the map again.

The red dot moved nearer as she scribbled the directions onto her notepad.

"Here—" she started. Then, with a closer look, "Girl, got something for you." She tossed the doughnut to the dog, who chewed it up. "Want another? You gotta come here quick. I don't have much time."

The Lab eagerly wagged her tail as she approached. Sunny rubbed her head and gave her another doughnut. "Wait right here," she said as she went around to the back of the car, popped the trunk, and pondered the old boots.

Now beside her, the Lab nudged her hand. "Good girl! You can have the rest now, but I have a favor to ask in return. OK?"

The dog's tongue unraveled out of the side of her mouth with anticipation. It had no idea it would soon become an accomplice to Sunny's disappearing completely.

CHAPTER 10

T he first thing Sunny thought while driving along the river was how beautiful it was. The fall colors were closer to their peak this far north. The orange, yellow, and red leaves dazzled against the drizzly gray mist snaking its way over the land. Her second thought was how difficult this place would be to find if the mist got any worse. The third thought was how long she could go without eating. The scenery was nothing more than a distraction from the constant growl of her stomach.

As for Rebecca, she seemed to be holding up well and slept most of the five-plus hours on the road. The last two and a half hours had flown by, going down roads off NY-12E and circling back. It was the main highway along the St. Lawrence River and seemed about as off the beaten path as possible.

After persuading the dog with the doughnuts, Sunny had not given much thought to Taylor other than a brief giggle. She imagined the moment he would finally figure "it" out. From then on, she was a woman on a mission to find this former funeral home turned inn. It was near; driving close to the water and Alexandria Bay, she could sense it.

Some stretches between the many left turns she was making were long. The area was much more rural than she'd expected. Yet quaint little villages and towns populated it. Cape Vincent, where she currently was, wasn't far from Clayton. She recalled that the latter was once voted the coolest small town in America by some magazine.

She had made a left turn that went some distance to a lighthouse. Tibbetts Point, it was called, where the St. Lawrence River met Lake Ontario, a hair west of Cape Vincent. Though the inn didn't appear to be nearby, she didn't mind the scenic drive.

So many historic homes dotted the shores here. A white bed and breakfast, Maple Grove, seemed straight from a southern plantation. A long, rolling green front lawn overlooking the river gave it additional charm. Nearby, another house had a similar style with an even larger front yard.

The road she drove down was on the shore's edge and lined with towering poplar trees. Most of the homes appeared to have been built in the 1800s. From what she could tell, the trees looked as though they were at least that old as well.

On her way down the road and into the little village, she passed a place with a historical marker. THE STONE HOUSE had been built in 1815 by J. D. Le Ray de Chaumont. According to the plaque, it had sheltered Canadian rebels during the Patriot War of 1838.

After passing a few cemeteries on the outskirts of the village, Sunny began making left turns off 12E. Poplar Tree Bay Road, Carleton Drive, Carleton Road, and Sunset Point Road brought no luck. The farther she drove, the more she realized how steeped the region was in history. No wonder it was such a tourist destination. It was also the perfect place for her to blend in and go unnoticed while digging around for information.

Before she knew it, she'd passed through Clayton, and Alexandria Bay was not far ahead of her. Doubt set in with every fruitless turn she made. Then, a sign caught her attention: SEARCHLIGHT ROAD. Sunny followed it, the car winding down its tree-laden path. After a short drive, she came alongside an ornate wrought-iron fence. Its iron bars were the blackest of blacks, capped with a fleur-de-lis motif.

She parked the car and took Rebecca for a walk along the wall. She was unsure how far it went. The mist was so thick here she had to use her free hand to feel her way. She held Rebecca close with a blanket covering her. After feeling her way along, she surmised that there were two gates, an entrance and an exit. Both closed.

The air seemed heavy for mid-October—not the cool, crisp weather one might expect this time of year when leaves crunched underfoot. Instead, a slight condensation on the iron bars left her hand cold and wet as she touched them. An occasional damp, yellowed leaf spiraled its way to the ground. Otherwise, everything seemed unnatural in its stillness, except the mist. It was alive, slithering around objects, making them appear and disappear. One's mind was left to its own devices to fill in the blanks. A tree here, part of the iron fence there. And something big and dark beyond them.

Her heart pounded with every step on the slick cobblestone walk along the fence. She tried to imagine what the dark mass of the building in the fog might look like. They soon came to a smaller walkway entrance between two columns of dark red brick. The gate here was open enough for them to squeeze through. Sunny's eyes were wide as the mist revealed a clearing in the trees. There, creeping ivy covered a large brick tower. A few steps closer, its tall, bow windows came into view.

An incredulous smile crossed her face. She knew at once. "It's real, Becca," she said, sliding through the gate and making her way forward.

The mist dissipated, unveiling a second-floor balcony above a wraparound porch. The mansion looked like it was grinning at her with a broken smile; the closer she came, the older it looked. Dark red brickwork seemed in fair shape, but the elements had had their way with the rest. The wood-and-fish-scale shingles on the gables were robbed of their color. In some areas, they appeared downright diseased with blotches of blackness.

The wraparound porches on both sides of the main entrance were missing several white balusters. The intricately designed soffits and trim were weathered, making the mansion appear tired and ornery.

A sudden breeze gave her a chill. "Becca, should we peek in the windows?"

She climbed onto the porch. Its floorboards groaned with every step as she approached the nearest window. A cloudy haze on its glass gave the impression of cataracts. Sunny rubbed the window free of the cloudiness and looked inside.

She almost jumped out of her skin at a female voice behind her.

"I thought nobody would ever show."

Sunny whirled around so fast that Rebecca let out a startled cry. Her heart exploded in her ears. She stood frozen with terror. It was fright and flight in her case, except her legs wouldn't budge. There, on the other wraparound porch, stood a woman.

Or was she a . . .?

But that was only a story Steven's father had told him. Who knew what liberties he took in its retelling? After all, she believed what she'd said to Taylor: the only ghosts were the ones inside our minds. Though it wasn't her thesis, misinformation was why problematic beliefs existed among so many. It needed to be part of the discussion.

Yet here was this woman who seemed to have come out of nowhere. Who was this person, and why were they expecting someone?

The question explained why Sunny felt so threatened: she was on the lam, and people would be looking for her. Once again, how schemas helped the mind organize, interpret, and make sense of information in milliseconds amazed her.

Besides, this woman, who couldn't be much older than herself, looked like a librarian. She also appeared to be just as surprised to see Sunny. With a long blue sweater over a white slip, she seemed to be about as harmful as a librarian too.

"I didn't mean to startle you," the woman said, clasping her hands together at Rebecca's crying. "Are you not answering the ad for help?"

Sunny came to, bouncing Rebecca on her hip. She looked away to the hazy window, embarrassed by all her initial thoughts.

"I'm sorry," the woman said, crossing the porch to Sunny, who peered through the window, trying to get a glimpse inside. "I'm Nadeen. I'm renovating—"

Sunny's mouth twitched into a frown. She felt a mini-stupor coming on.

Nadeen.

She knew that name from somewhere. Hearing it now made her stomach clench with an emptiness more than just hunger. Was she one of the nurses at that place? An old classmate?

Her eyes watered and her vision began to blur before she dismissed the confusion. That so-called therapy had left her with moments like these that came out of nowhere.

"You *own* this?" Sunny finally asked, incredulous.

Nadeen smiled with raised eyebrows. "To be honest, I think it owns me at this point. It's a surprise for my fiancé." She reached out to Rebecca and wiped a tear from her cheek with a gentle touch before pulling her hand back. "She has your eyes."

Sunny eased into a smile. "This is Rebecca. I'm Sunny," she said. A sudden weariness overcame her. Providing their names while unsure whether this stranger would help or hinder them hadn't been smart.

"Well, Sunny, if that's what you're here for, let me give you the dime tour. Welcome to the once-and-future Searchlight Bed and Breakfast."

Nadeen waved her arm, signaling to Sunny to open the stained-glass front door.

With a doorknob twist and push, the door creaked open to reveal a bright, spacious foyer. What had once been a grand entrance was now littered with paper bags and debris. It was as if someone had been here and abruptly left. Black walnut paneling and hand-carved wood-lined dual staircases rose at both ends of the room. Dull and covered with layers of dust, they curved toward each other on the second floor.

A large chandelier hung above the foyer and staircases. Shrouded in strands of spiderwebs, it looked decorated for this time of year. There were too many lamps to count, and the wallpaper bled yellow while time had tinted its peeled portions brown.

The ground floor was green marble with rustic gold and deep plum hues—at least what she could see. It was in serious need of polishing.

The interior looked exquisite and lackluster all at once. Illegible graffiti—unfamiliar symbols and gibberish—streaked across one wall. Broken glass crackled underfoot. It was a giant buffet of Gilded Age excess picked over, with the remains left to rot.

What struck her after the visuals was the musty, sour milk stench. The smell reminded her of a visit to her paternal grandparents during the summer when she was eight years old. They had been in their eighties and were having difficulty caring for themselves, let alone their home. The odor of time wasted away in rooms with closed curtains. The walls would sweat the same yellowish streaks in the humidity. It was overbearing and made worse by their refusal to open a window. Sunny used to believe the odors stalked her from room to room. There was no escaping them. Now, twenty years later, she was being assaulted by the same haunting smells. There was no running from them here either as she stood in the middle of the foyer, breathing them in.

Still, she could envision the mansion as a place where people came to vacation. Or for a short visit before they went to their final destination to rest in peace. The question was, what had happened here? And, more importantly, why had it made her life so restless recently? As she strolled through the foyer, these thoughts and others tiptoed into her head.

"I liked the idea of this as a gift for my fiancé. He's into historical architecture and things of that nature. I thought renovating it would be something we could do together," Nadeen said. With a hopeful smile, she added, "And turn it back into a hip bed and breakfast."

Sunny passed through an archway into another room. Inside, white sheets were draped over several pieces of furniture. The same dark wood design was incorporated into large, built-in bookcases with many old, hardcover books.

"This is the reading parlor, with all the charm of a gentleman's smoking room."

Sunny touched one of the white sheets. "May I?"

"Of course."

Sunny whipped the sheet back to reveal a well-worn antique Victorian leather couch. "Wow, look at that, Becca." It needed some tender loving care like everything else, but it was impressive.

Sunny restored the sheet to its place. "Someone mentioned this was once a funeral home," she said. She fingered a book from a shelf, blew the dust off its pages, and watched it dissipate before Nadeen's curious gaze.

"I'm afraid to ask what else you may have heard," Nadeen said, her eyes dropping to the floor.

Sunny returned the book to the shelf and wandered into the neighboring room. She ran her fingers along an organ resting against a wall to no effect.

"It's an old pipe organ. It works by pumping the pedals. It's from the funeral home days when this was a viewing room," Nadeen said, motioning to a staircase in the foyer.

Sunny grasped the marble finial atop the first stair railing, only to have it come off in her hand. "Sorry! I'll—" she began to say, trying to place it back. Finally, she got it to rest in place.

Nadeen laughed. "Did I mention it needs work?"

As they ascended the staircase, Sunny stopped to shift Rebecca into her other arm. With her free hand, she yanked her sagging pants up. What she wouldn't do for a pair of leggings or yoga pants, postpartum fashion crisis or not.

"There are eleven bedrooms—six in each wing, three on either side of the hallway. Two on the other side with the tower, which has a room too," Nadeen said as they approached the second floor.

Sunny looked down both sides and saw decorative candle wall sconces between the rooms. Her sense of déjà vu was overwhelming; she chose to go straight to the tower.

A large house. By water. Many rooms are here, but people only stay briefly before moving on.

Although she couldn't recall when or where, she knew she had spoken those words before. Nadeen was talking, but her voice was drowned out by a distant chorus of droning flies.

With another step forward, her heart rose in her throat. *Lub-dub. Lub-dub.* Her mouth was suddenly dry, making it difficult to swallow.

There's a hallway. Doors on both sides. Several of them.

As if in a trance, Sunny made her way down the hallway. She passed open doors on either side and headed straight to its end as if she knew exactly where she was going.

Lub-dub-dub. Lub-dub-dub. Her heart raced faster. Everything grew black. A faraway white light flashed as the flies droned on, growing louder.

God help me, it's happening again.

She focused on the tower room's door. Rebecca stirred in her arms while she struggled to make out the familiar shape on the door's surface.

She stopped before the door: the only one closed in the entire hallway. There, she gawked at the decorative crescent moon carved into its wood.

A broken piece of memory flashed in her mind. The bloody handprint on the crescent moon dripped fresh crimson down the front of the door. She reached out to where she had seen it, touching the moon.

"If there's one eyesore in this house, it's behind that door," Nadeen said.

"That *smell* . . ." Sunny's face twisted with disgust.

Tap. Tap. Tap. Larvae fall onto the floor, yellowish-green feet with purple toes dangling above them.

Rebecca's fussing brought Sunny back to the present with a quick yank of her hand away from the door.

"It's probably another dead bird trapped in the chimney flue—"

Sunny's hand jolted to her mouth, covering it and her nose. A single fly landed on it as the *lub-dub* of her heart slowed. She pulled her shaking hand away and watched the fly crawl on her skin before buzzing off.

"Are you OK?" Nadeen asked.

"I . . . I—" Sunny's legs buckled, and everything went black.

"We haven't had much to eat all day," Sunny said with her hand on her forehead, glancing around what appeared to be a kitchen. "I should have . . ." She stopped with the weight of Nadeen's gaze. "Gotten something."

Realizing she may have said too much, she turned her attention back to the interior of the adjacent room. She estimated the round room beyond the kitchen must have twelve sets of windows. Six windows were at least six feet high, with another set of smaller windows above them, about half their height, much like the ones on the second floor.

"I've never seen a turret before. It's bigger than most I've seen in photos."

"Technically, it's a tower. Turrets aren't built onto a foundation."

The sun peeked through the windows onto a cast-iron wood stove as Nadeen broke the moment of silence.

"Pardon my asking, but you're not from around here, are you?"

Sunny swiped a lock of her blonde hair behind her ear and looked away. How could she explain this without sounding crazy? "I was in a bad situation" was all she could muster as she wilted like a flower under Nadeen's silent gaze.

"I see. I'm not sure this would be much better."

Sunny's natural response would have been to roll her eyes and say, "If you only knew." Not wanting to dig the hole any deeper, she refrained, having learned that lesson from Taylor.

"What I mean is, there's no running water, electricity, heat.... I suppose if you could find some wood, you could burn it in the fireplace here." Nadeen gestured. "But, as you've seen, this place is far from being even a two-star flophouse."

Whatever the job required, it was clear it entailed staying here. Yet, regardless of the circumstances, she couldn't let the opportunity slip away. She could never return home. Not without finding the root of whatever she was experiencing. The answer was here, *somewhere*. She could feel it.

"I can help clean up, paint . . . you name it, and I will do it," she said without apprehension.

Nadeen strolled about the grand kitchen, eyeing the bare cupboards' glass doors. "I've become the insignificant other with as much time as I've been here." She stepped into the tower room and looked at its many windows.

Sunny admired a certain grace about her, watching her place a hand on a covered piece of furniture.

"I also said I didn't think anyone would ever show." With a sigh, Nadeen turned back to Sunny. "If you can do without creature comforts for a while . . ."

"I'm already a step ahead of you," Sunny said, wondering if Taylor had caught on to her yet.

"I hope you have some old clothes. With this place as filthy as it is, you won't see me in much other than my 'renovation' uniform." Nadeen twirled, showing off her outfit.

"Old is all I've got," Sunny said. "It's a question of whether they still fit after having a baby, though what we can't do without for much longer is some food."

CHAPTER 11

Taylor's black car pulled into the roadside diner's empty parking lot. By the looks of it, it was one of those greasy spoons that opened at the crack of dawn and closed at three in the afternoon.

It was seven thirty in the evening. His cell phone battery was hovering around 10 percent. His patience was even lower.

The long stroke of his hand across his weary face did little to ease his nerves. Not knowing how long this ordeal might take or where it would lead didn't help either. He'd spent most of the last twelve hours searching for Sunny. The last thing he wanted to do was sit in a car, no matter how comfortable it was or how many modern conveniences it had. He turned the engine off and exited with his phone in hand. He checked the app for her location; the pulsating blue dot appeared less than a mile away. Strange. It was far off any road on the phone's screen.

"Goddamn it!" He paced back and forth in the parking lot. "I was just there!"

It wasn't like she could be parked in the middle of nowhere. Yet there was no sign of her car on the road. His chest rose and fell, seething with deep breaths as he closed his eyes for a moment. Then, a calm fell over him. He opened his eyes and punched numbers into his phone. Strolling around the parking lot, he looked up at the stars weaving in and out of view behind passing clouds. They were a moving tapestry in the nighttime sky as he waited for an answer to his call.

"George, no, no luck yet. I'm not sure if I should be looking for her or the car now. I've been all over this area, chasing her location. Sometimes she appears to be on the road. Then she's way out in the middle of nowhere, according to the map. Other times, the signal is gone before reappearing a while later. Whether she's still using the car or walking, there's no trace—"

Taylor stopped in his tracks, eyes latching onto something on the ground. He bent down and examined the object closer. It was a crumpled-up wrapper for miniature toasted-coconut doughnuts.

"No, I'm still here. More important, so was she. You haven't reported her missing to the authorities yet, have you?" He stuffed the wrapper into his blazer pocket and returned to the car. "No, let's not do that quite yet." He opened the car door and paused. "Because if a person doesn't want to be found, the authorities aren't required to do anything other than inform you of their well-being. Believe it or not, she has the right to go missing."

Taylor dropped into the driver's seat and ran his fingers through his hair.

"No, there's no rule to wait twenty-four hours to report a missing person; that's a myth." He swung his legs into the car and started the engine. "If we do, we'll have to explain why she's missing. If she were to find out, she might push us away for good."

Taylor pulled a pen from his blazer and jotted the names of the roads at the intersection down in his notebook.

"I have only a few minutes before my battery dies. Let's give her some more time before we do that. I'll look around a while longer and make up some signs to put up tomorrow. OK, sounds good."

He plugged the phone into a USB cord from his center console with the battery clinging to life at 3 percent. He opened the map app and saw the blue dot pulsating on the screen again.

"You could have just as easily stopped sharing your location. But you didn't, did you?" An epiphany came to him as he stared at the blue dot. "That there? That's not you." He smiled, realizing he was on to her.

Leaning back in the driver's seat, he shook his head in disbelief.

"This is how you disappear completely."

CHAPTER 12

Sunny pushed a grocery cart past the rain-splattered storefront. Its windows were fit for the season, decorated with pumpkins, skeletons, and witches. Flashes of lightning and the slow rumble of thunder added to the atmosphere.

As if that weren't enough, one of the cart's wheels squeaked and twitched in the throes of death. The least the store could do was give it its last rites. Or better yet, put the thing out of commission.

At least Rebecca wasn't fussy. Strapped in her car seat, she was unaffected by the constant jittering the wheel was causing. But, of course, had she eaten anything earlier, she would probably be wearing it by now.

There weren't many shoppers this Sunday evening, which was just as well. The fewer people Sunny encountered, the less stressed she would be. As she passed down one aisle, she spotted the beauty section and wheeled the cart over.

Several hair dye brands and colors graced the aisle, but natural midnight blue-black caught her eye. She snagged it for those days when you absolutely, positively need to look like someone else. After scanning the instructions and feeling desperate, she dropped it in the cart.

For a moment, Sunny felt like a fugitive on the run. She hadn't broken any law. Yet, knowing Taylor, he wouldn't stop until she was back in the psychiatric center. Giving up her blonde locks was better than twitching like this shopping cart's wheel from ECT.

She perused the variety of baby formulas for several moments. Unsure of which to choose, she dropped box after box of the ready-to-use kind into the cart. "Sorry, Becca, it's either this or mother's milk, straight from the tap." She added a couple of rubber nipples before heading down the next aisle.

With the house lacking basic amenities, she also needed simple, ready-to-eat food for herself. After finding some, she squeaked and jittered the cart down the aisle to the front of the store. A crack of thunder immediately followed a flash of lightning. The store shook, sending the market into complete darkness. She should pick up a flashlight too. *Now, there's a bright idea.*

A droll female clerk informed the shoppers, "The emergency lighting should come on in a moment or two." She then added with some doubt, "Or six."

The thunder managed to do what the cart's wheel couldn't. It got Rebecca fussing. *Loud.* "Sh . . . sh," Sunny said, pushing her back and forth in the dark. "At least nobody will recognize us like this. Huh, Becca?"

After a couple of minutes, one by one, the lights from the back of the store flickered to life. Sunny continued to push her cart back and forth when the bank of lights behind her fluttered. A middle-aged woman stared at her with the most otherworldly light-green eyes. Over her head, she wore a black shawl.

"Guess we don't have to worry about that happening back at Searchlight, huh, Becca?" Sunny fought with the cart's death-twitched wheels to the nearest register. Unbeknownst to her, the woman in black kept her distance as she followed.

"All set?"

Sunny looked up from placing items on the conveyor to a bubbly teen girl behind the counter. Tammy, her name tag read.

"Usually, I'd ask if you found everything OK," Tammy said. She chewed a wad of gum into submission, adding with a laugh, "But I know it's a little difficult in the dark."

"I should probably get used to it."

Sunny added another baby formula case to the conveyor. Her eyes passed over magazines on display. One headline in particular caught her attention: "Are You Haunted by a

Past Life?" She took the last one and recoiled with a startle. The woman with green eyes looked back at her through the space, then continued about her business. Sunny, left shaken, placed her palm against her chest.

"The way she was looking at me . . ."

"Oh, she's harmless. You know how some people are. Probably reminded her of someone." Tammy leaned over and peeked at the portable baby car seat. "What's your baby's name?"

Sunny blocked her view by reaching for several water bottles from a cooler at the foot of the conveyor belt. Usually, she would have been proud to show off her baby— what mother wouldn't? But these were anything but normal circumstances.

"These too. I forgot where I'm staying doesn't have running water." She added several thick candles along with a flashlight. "Or electricity." Thinking better of it, she added several more candles.

Tammy eased up on her gum chewing. Sunny couldn't help but notice. She immediately regretted saying anything and wanted to get out of there quickly. She rummaged through her purse and withdrew her debit card out of habit.

"Looks like you're going to have a séance," Tammy said, glancing at all the candles. "You're not staying at that old bed and breakfast, are you? The one that used to be a funeral home?"

Sunny ran her thumb over the raised lettering of Taylor's and her name on the card. The last thing she needed was to use anything from their joint account. The store's location would show up on the transaction, giving her away. Instead, she turned to her wad of twenty-dollar bills and flipped through them with a sigh. "Uh, no. Why?" she asked, handing Tammy a good portion of the money.

"Someone's always talking about fixing it up. My friends and I used to dare each other to spend the night there. Nobody made it fifty feet past the fence."

"I wouldn't want to be caught dead hanging around there either," Sunny said.

Tammy covered her mouth with a hand but couldn't stop the short, surprised laugh from escaping. "I see what you did there. That's a good one."

A cold, firm grip took hold of Sunny's arm, startling her. She turned. The woman with the sea-foam green eyes was staring at her. For a moment, Sunny feared the woman might have recognized her.

"The shadows. You see them too, don't you?" the woman asked as thunder rolled.

Sunny pulled her arm away and hurried to the exit. The grocery cart squeaked and jittered past the woman peering at Rebecca asleep.

"Ma'am, your change!" Tammy hollered, but Sunny was already halfway through the sliding doors.

Once outside, she ducked behind the Halloween decorations in the window. There, she peered at the woman and Tammy inside. She ducked out of sight, her face superimposed over a ghost-faced decoration in the window. Its eyes aligned with hers to eerie effect. After a moment, she hurried off as the woman approached the window.

Another flash of lightning streaked across the gloomy night sky. Its bright white light illuminated the woman watching from the window. Then, brake lights washed her face in red as Sunny's car roared to life and squealed away into a downpour.

Sunny held a lantern up to a window in one of the rooms, the candle within flickering from a draft. The distorted reflection of her face materialized on the glass as she drew closer. Water cascaded down from the pelting rain; her eyes followed it to the bottom of the windowsill. There, several dead flies rested undisturbed for who knew how long. Outside, occasional lightning revealed a bit of the murky shoreline and river.

The first night at Searchlight Bed and Breakfast was wet, gloomy, and uneventful, except for the incident at the grocery store. She still wasn't sure what to make of the woman and what she had said. Seeing her stare through the space where she had taken the magazine made it all the creepier. Not to mention the headline. One thing she didn't doubt: those eyes would haunt her for days to come.

A shaft of light in the distance stirred Sunny from these thoughts. Round and round it went, less than half a mile away. Her eyes lit up; this was a lighthouse. No, the lighthouse from her fleeting moments of . . . whatever they were.

Most people would think somebody crazy to spend the night in a place like this, but not her. She'd never been one to shy away from exploring things that went bump in the night. Furthermore, she'd always had a fascination with the dark and macabre—not so much the unsettling stuff but people's reaction to it.

Though she didn't believe in ghosts or the supernatural, she had read enough about the subjects. She'd also participated in enough studies to know there was an explanation for everything. Yet there were always a few outliers. The uncanny and the unexplainable. They created cognitive dissonance for some who could not find an explanation.

Stress builds when a person holds multiple contradictory beliefs, ideas, or values. Her students needed to grasp this before diving into the meat and potatoes of problematic versus unproblematic beliefs. The coupling of the two could become toxic and overwhelming for some. Combined, they often resulted in rationalizing the conflicting ideas until they were consistent with other stories people told themselves. This is why conspiracy theories become believable, as absurd as they might be.

Introducing her students to this dichotomy was a fun way to grab their attention and interest. Ghosts and the like were harmless examples. But the truth was that her students were exposed to these tendencies on a regular basis. She wanted to teach them to be critical thinkers in a world full of manipulators. Otherwise, they'd be fodder for scammers, deceit, and the growing presence of artificial intelligence. The best remedy was through education and the willingness to seek out the truth.

That was why she was here; she was putting into practice what she preached—seeking out the facts required to explore alternate perspectives. Only then could one come to a rational explanation based on logic. But Sunny's fears weren't manifested in the manner most people might experience. Instead, they were from not knowing what these events were. Broken shards of memories, she called them, that scared her. They were the ghosts inside her head that she couldn't explain, which was very much a concept she *did* believe in.

She turned from the window to Rebecca lying on the bed and checked her diaper with the lantern. "Of course not. You haven't been eating." Then, drawing the light to the floor, she rummaged through a bag. She found and shook one of the ready-to-use baby formula bottles. A smile spread as she looked back at Rebecca, finding her asleep.

"Our first adventure has you all tuckered out. Huh, Becca?"

Sprawled out on the bed beside Rebecca, Sunny tried deciphering the room's interior. Though flickering shadows, all she could see with the lantern were faint wallpaper patterns. Some peeled away in ample folds. Those farther from the light's radiance disappeared into darkness. She supposed it was time to call it a day and grabbed the astrology magazine from one of the bags. Fanning through its pages by the lantern light, she could already feel her eyes straining. She found her flashlight, turned it on, and read aloud a random passage as if Rebecca were awake.

"'The moon is associated with a person's emotions, memories, and moods. It is also associated with the mother, home, our roots, the fourth house, and the past.'" She rolled her eyes, unimpressed. "Where do they come up with this stuff?"

She turned toward Rebecca and watched her chest rise, fall, and then stop. The complete stillness lasted for several moments. She jolted up onto her elbows. Never had she experienced terror so absolute. The *lub-dub* of her heart threatened to explode her eardrums and steal her breath.

Here she was, a first-time mother without a phone. In an isolated house. Without power. And she was potentially dealing with a life-and-death situation.

"Becca?" was all she could manage in a cracked voice. Having to rush her to the nearest hospital would surely end her quest too soon either way. *Damned if you do, damned if you don't.* She suddenly felt guilty, thinking there was even a choice. Of course, she would rather face the consequences than allow her child to die. Even if it meant returning to that place. . . . Wouldn't she?

As she was about to scoop Rebecca up and rush her to the hospital, wherever that might be, the baby's chest moved again.

Sunny closed her eyes and exhaled the fear and helplessness that had built up in those few short moments. She wiped her brow with a shaky hand, imagining how vulnerable her child was with her, an adult. Another wave of guilt washed over her. What had been a long day was turning into the start of an even longer night.

Then she heard the distant cry of a baby. It was coming from somewhere else, somewhere beyond her room.

She pointed the flashlight toward the door. Its beam cast light onto it—just a regular door—then she turned it off. Shadows from the lantern danced their way into complete darkness around her. It could be the wind howling through some opening. A window, or a fireplace perhaps. But, no, no ... that was rationalizing. It could have been anything, including her imagination.

Sunny heaved herself from the bed with the lantern, wanting to save the flashlight's battery. She found her way to the door and opened it. Sticking her head out into the hallway, she looked both ways. To the right was the closed door. A brief sliver of light shone onto the hallway floor beneath the door. The lighthouse's rotating beam flashed by.

With the lantern held high, she crept down the hallway, her tense face shining orange from the candle's flame. In a few short steps, the crescent moon on the tower room's door materialized before her.

Sunny attempted to turn the doorknob, but the room was locked. She looked down at the floor as the lighthouse beam went around again. A shadow under the door of someone, or something, from within moved as the light passed. She knelt on the floor and peeked through the keyhole. Nothing was visible inside other than the heart of darkness itself. If this house had a soul, that is what it would look like. She immediately dismissed the thought as something one would read in an astrology magazine. Or hear from a gypsy in a grocery store on a dark and stormy night.

As the light made its way around again, something fluttered on the edge of her field of vision. *Something white.*

The sight immediately suggested Steven's story again.

The candle's flame thrashed from a strong draft before it snuffed out. Sunny was without the slightest hint of light. She waited calmly for the beam to come around again and breathed a sigh of relief when it did. A white curtain fluttered in the nighttime breeze through a broken window. *See? An explanation for everything.*

Yet that did little to explain the cry in the dark, which left her tossing and turning for the better part of the night.

CHAPTER 13

S unny awoke the following day to Rebecca making such a fuss that it sounded like a caterwaul. Her immediate thought was that it was what she had heard last night, except that it couldn't have been Becca. It was too distant, coming from somewhere else in the house. Thinking she must be hungry, Sunny picked her up and bounced her around, settling her down for the moment.

She looked out the window and marveled at the beautiful morning. The mist was gone, with partly sunny skies in its place and a layer of fog rolling over the river. The colors of the leaves on the trees were at their postcard-perfect peak. Off in the distance, she could make out the lighthouse, an ancient white sentinel standing tall against the blue sky.

"Look, Becca! That's where the light that kept shining all night came from."

Rebecca only fussed again, prompting Sunny to grab a bottle of formula and shake it vigorously. She retreated down the spiral staircase and into the kitchen. There, she tried to feed Rebecca again, only to have her keep turning away from the bottle.

"Honey, you have to eat something."

Nadeen's voice drifted in from the doorway, surprising Sunny, whose frustration was evident. "I thought someone was up," she said. "Have you tried nursing her?"

Tears welled in Sunny's eyes, and she looked away, ashamed. "She hasn't taken to it."

Not establishing a bond with her daughter after such an absence was one of her greatest fears. And here she was now, failing at such a necessity. "Those first months are so important," she said, turning away to hide her angst. "I wasn't there for her."

Nadeen clasped her hands together against her chest, raising them to her mouth with pity. "May I try?" She graciously took Rebecca and the bottle, looking the part of a seasoned professional.

"I didn't run away—more like I'm running *to* something. My family . . . they haven't been honest with me," Sunny said, withering as she watched Rebecca take to the bottle.

"Don't worry. I know it looks easy, but it's anything but. I've had plenty of practice. You will get the hang of it before long." Nadeen hesitated, then asked, "What haven't they been honest about?"

Sunny plopped herself into a chair at the table. "I'm not sure. It's not just that. There's no doubt they're already looking for me. The question is how long before we're recognized? A mother and baby will probably stick out like a sore thumb in this place."

Nadeen gave her a heartfelt look as Rebecca continued working on the bottle. "If that worries you, I'll watch her if you want to head into town."

"You would do that for me?"

"Of course. It's no trouble, honestly. Perhaps you could pick up a gallon or two of paint to start. What do you think of rustic gold for the foyer instead of the stained and peeling wallpaper?"

Sunny craned, looked to the foyer, and nodded. "Yeah, I like that."

"If I may ask that you please do one thing for me. Well, for yourself."

"Sure. Anything."

Nadeen smiled, trying not to appear overly concerned. "Let your family know you're safe. Please."

Sunny gave her a slight, unconvincing nod, realizing she may as well have said she'd think about it.

"Trust me. Being here as much as I am, I hold my fiancé's curiosity at bay by keeping tabs on him first."

CHAPTER 14

Sunny didn't know where she might find a paint store. She decided to try her luck by heading to Alexandria Bay, unsure if it had more to offer than Clayton. Both were places she could go unnoticed as another tourist visiting during the fall, and they seemed a good place to start.

Following the main road into the business district, she found a place on James Street. The hardware-type store seemed out of place among the bars, restaurants, and gift shops, but here she was. Keep a low profile. Blend in. Buy some paint.

Sunny imagined this stretch was teeming with tourists during the summer months. But in mid to late October, only a few people sprinkled the sidewalks here and there. It's hard to blend in with nobody else, but that also meant fewer eyes on her.

Once inside the store, she realized she was the only customer. That suited her just fine. A middle-aged gentleman sat behind the counter, smiling with a nod as she walked by. She was sure he could tell she wasn't from around here.

Scooping her blonde hair behind an ear, she roamed the aisles. Something close to rustic gold, preferably in a gallon can, should do the trick to start with. She bent to look at the lower shelf, tilting the cans and reading their labels. After putting them back, she stood up and glanced toward the counter. The man was gone, apparently having disappeared into thin air.

"Now there's a face I recognize," a voice said from behind her.

She spun around, surprised to see the man with an eager-to-please smile. A name tag pinned to his plain white dress shirt read Cliff. Below it, Store Manager.

"Enough to drive you crazy, huh?"

She now realized fewer shoppers meant she was the sole recipient of attention. Even worse, he recognized her. "I beg your pardon?" she finally asked, shaken.

"Why, the biggest selection around."

Sunny relaxed with a nervous laugh. "You're serious?"

"Of course not. But I made you laugh, didn't I? So, what can I help you with today?"

"Rustic gold paint. Do you have anything like that in a gallon?"

"Ah! We sure do—it is a popular color, especially for fall. Right over here." He led her down another aisle and pointed to several cans.

"Perfect. I'll take two."

Cliff grabbed two gallons and started back to the register. "Right this way. Will this be cash or—?"

"Shit!" Sunny said, searching through her purse.

"Sorry, we don't take deposits," Cliff deadpanned.

Sunny face-palmed herself and smiled at his joke. "Sorry, I forgot—*cash*. Cash, please."

"Cash it is. Care to join our mailing list?"

"No, thanks. Get your name on one, and next thing you know . . ."

"We don't share personal information if that's a concern."

Changing the topic, Sunny asked, "Might you know who owned the old bed and breakfast outside town? On Searchlight Road?" She could tell she'd caught him off guard by the look on his face. "There's a lighthouse on an island not far from it. It's right on the river."

Cliff lit up with surprise. "Did you buy it? The old funeral home? Gosh, that place has been empty for quite a while now."

"No, but I'm curious about its history."

"Most people are spooked." He lowered his voice as if others were eavesdropping. "The owner claimed it was haunted. Said she saw a ghost. She poured so much into the place," he said with a sympathetic shake of his head. "It was her who was haunted in the end—by its failure."

"So what happened?"

"She took her own life."

Somehow, Sunny wasn't surprised. "How?" she asked.

"Hung herself." Cliff handed the change to her.

Sunny stared at the coins in her hand, feeling it coming on again. The darkness. The flash of light. A tinge of nausea followed the bloody handprint across the crescent moon on the door.

"Did I count it wrong?"

She shook the thoughts free, but not the disturbed look on her face. "How long ago was this?" she asked, a hint of trepidation in her voice.

"Oh, it had to have been, what—twenty-five, thirty years ago? Don't know much other than she wasn't originally from here."

Neither was Sunny. The coincidence gave her a chill, and before she knew it, she felt the sickness creeping back. Her mouth went dry, and her lungs yearned for air. She needed to do something. Say something.

"Is there a town library?" she asked.

"Closed for renovations."

"A village historian?"

"Not an official one that I know of, at least not since the last one retired anyway. There's a museum around the block at the old Cornwall Store, run by the historical society. But it's closed for the season. The building isn't heated."

Sunny grabbed a gallon of paint with each hand, exhaling a disappointed sigh. "Well, thanks for the paint." She turned, making her way to the exit.

"Those places aren't what you're looking for, though."

She stopped and turned back to Cliff.

"The Antique Shoppe, down the street." He pointed to his right with a bony finger. "They have all that 'off-the-record' and 'hush-hush' stuff you're looking for."

As Sunny exited the store, she inhaled the fresh air and listened to a crow cawing from a nearby tree. She was upset with herself for not asking for the money to buy the paint, knowing she didn't have much of her own left. At least she had found someone who corroborated what little information she remembered from Steven's story. Yet the bits and pieces of new information made her queasy. *It will pass*, she told herself as she scuttled across the street to the car.

When she opened the trunk and placed the paint cans inside, she spotted her father's boots, minus their laces. A mischievous smile grew from ear to ear, easing her momentarily before fading. It wouldn't be long before Taylor figured it out if he hadn't already.

A rhythmic clank, clank, clank from somewhere nearby triggered more disturbing images. Larvae fell to the floor. Tap-tap-tap. One by one, the purple toes dangling above them. Sunny covered her mouth, trying to keep the warmth from spreading up from her belly.

She followed her ears and turned to her right. On the corner, a sign swayed back and forth in the crisp morning breeze: ARBOGAST'S NOSTALGIC ANTIQUE SHOPPE engraved in wood, with RE-ELECT ARBOGAST FOR MAYOR printed on an attached sign below it.

The plaque swung inside a yard, surrounded by a white picket fence. The house there seemed even more out of place than the store she'd just come from—a white, two-story colonial next to a big, three-story souvenir shop. Even the trees in the yard seemed ancient and incongruous.

The sign and its hypnotic, clanking rhythm seemed to be beckoning her. It was as if she'd been here before, returning for the first time in more years than she could remember. Or perhaps more than she had ever lived, at least in this lifetime.

Chapter 15

The air inside the Antique Shoppe dripped with musty nostalgia. Late morning sunlight filtered through the windows. Its golden hues landed on a humorless woman in her late fifties who absorbed it like a black hole. With dark, straight hair done up in a bun and plain features, she had all the warmth of a polar vortex. She flashed a saccharine smile as she handed a shopping bag to a customer.

"I'm sure she'll enjoy it," she said, waiting for the customer to leave the register. She then snuffed the sunshine out with a sharp pull of the curtain.

At the door, a well-dressed man of about sixty handed the customer a flower. "Don't forget to vote next week," he said with a rich, baritone voice and warm, friendly, yet tired eyes. They appeared as if their sparkle for life had been long sucked from his soul.

"Why, thank you, Morgan." The customer nodded and waved back at the register counter. "Thanks again, Evelyn," he said before exiting to the sound of bells jingling overhead.

As soon as the door closed, Evelyn's smile flatlined, her eyes falling on Morgan busying himself working on an old clock. The room felt frosty, as if a storm front was about to pass through. She cranked a lever on an antique cash register, popping it open.

"How many of those do you plan on giving away?" she asked.

"Are you going to remind me again that they don't grow on trees?" Morgan motioned to the window. "Perhaps I should go frolic among the fallen, dead leaves and hand those out instead?" he asked, straining to see the inside of the clock.

"Only if you're going to tell me, 'It's the thought that counts.'" She slammed the register drawer shut with an exclamation point.

Morgan reached inside his blazer and pulled out a penlight. Along with tweezers, he used it to adjust a lever inside the clock. Satisfied, he pocketed the light, pulled the clock's weights, and set its big hand back.

Cuckoo! Cuckoo!

A small bird announced its cry as it sprang from a door. Morgan then moved the big hand forward to the present time, 11:20.

The bells jingled over the door, drawing his attention as another customer entered. A female whose ethereal presence, bathed in sunlight as she entered, set the store aflame. The eye-piercing brightness surrounding her from the door's reflection of sun rays stunned him.

Time seemed to stand still the moment Sunny entered. The store fell silent, save for the bells. An older man wearing a blazer raised a hand to shield his eyes from the light's glare off the door behind her. He followed her every step as she passed him and headed straight for the wall, stopping to reach out and touch something on it.

"S-Something we can help you with, miss?" the man asked in a wary voice.

Sunny could see his eyes were wide, alert, yet anguished. She pulled her hand away from the wall and thoughtfully pressed it to her lips. "It's not . . . *finished*," she said in a dreamy voice before turning to him.

The room grew dark again, the passing clouds blotting out the sun as they came face to face. The flower he held out to her fell to the floor; its landing punctuated by the cash register ringing again. Sunny bent over and picked up the flower. Behind her, a framed painting of the bed and breakfast hung on the wall with an uncanny likeness to her artwork. With its frantic, expressionistic strokes of dark colors and shades of light, it was eerily *too* similar. She rose to meet the man who seemed transfixed by her presence.

"Finished?" he asked.

Using the red flower, Sunny pointed to the sky in the painting—"There should be a moon here"—and then, lowering it—"and a gentleman sitting on the steps here." She handed the flower back to him. "Is it an original piece?"

"I-I don't ever recall seeing another. Not like it, anyway." He took the flower with an awkward smile.

"Do you happen to know who painted it?"

"Evie, er, Evelyn. . . ." He glanced at Evelyn, who was busy behind the counter. "She received it as an anonymous donation years ago."

Sunny continued to study the painting, gazing over its colors, strokes, and incompleteness. "It's almost exactly like the one I painted. I'd love to show you if—"

"We don't buy from the public," he confessed with raised hands.

"I didn't mean to—"

"It's not that—I'm sure it's good." He glanced again at Evelyn. "I tell you what. Bring it by, and we'll . . . place it—on the wall here—and see if there's any interest. No harm in that, is there?" He reached out a hand. "My name is Morgan. And you are . . .?"

Sunny noticed him staring at the bracelet on her wrist. She pulled her hand back, covered the bracelet, and then turned away to scan the rest of the Antique Shoppe.

One section was full of books and another with lamps and hanging light fixtures. Knickknacks filled the store. Vintage bottles, clocks, porcelain figurines, dolls, and old wall-mounted coffee grinders were everywhere.

"I am interested in learning more about the town's *history*. Rebecca. My name is Rebecca," Sunny said, hoping it was the name he saw on her bracelet instead of her own.

"Well, Rebecca, it's a pleasure to meet you. We're big on hospitality and tourism here, you know."

"So I've noticed, but I was referring to the inn." Sunny nodded to the painting. "It must be fun around here come this time of year."

"I beg your pardon?" Morgan asked, perplexed.

"Witches, goblins, ghosts, and the like?"

Morgan took a tentative step back, scanning the store to find Evelyn busy with a young mother and her infant. "Well, we're an antique store that dabbles in local history, not the local Hitchin' Post." Noticing Sunny's confusion, he added, "Watering hole. Bar. All the same."

The baby suddenly cried. Sunny whirled to see the mother comforting her. She watched for a moment, Rebecca and herself coming to mind. The antique cuckoo clock's cry broke her spell. "I'm sorry. Is that time correct?"

"Indeed. I just set it ten minutes ago. Everything else here is like stepping back in time, however. Sort of the theme, here."

"I should be going," she said, backing up and bumping into a shelf. An antique doll fell onto its side with a high-pitched "Mama."

Sunny suddenly felt jittery—dark clouds billowed in the sky, a storm front approaching the village. Morgan accompanied her to the door, holding it open as she exited. "Stop back with your work soon!" He waved and closed the door, his eyes following her through the window until she drove off. He then returned to the counter, turned the dial on a safe with a shaky hand, and removed a cloth-covered box.

"Who was that?" Evelyn asked, startling him.

He put the box back into the safe while she perched in the doorway behind the counter. From there, she eagle-eyed the room. "Hmm? Oh, just a customer."

Evelyn spied the tilted doll, swooped in, and straightened it. Twice. She gave the room another inspection. Finding nobody else present, she lit a cigarette, inhaled, and blew smoke in his direction.

"She couldn't very well have been a customer if she didn't purchase anything, now, could she?"

Morgan busied himself with wiping the counter clean. "She was interested in the area's history. The kind you're more familiar with."

"What on God's little green earth are you flapping your gums about?"

"Looking for a title to go with the book you're writing too?" He considered *The Man Who Knew Too Much* an appropriate title but kept it to himself. She flicked a long cigarette ash onto the spot he had wiped clean moments before.

"Feisty, are we? I just thought she looked familiar is all." She turned on her heel and left him in a cloud of smoke.

Morgan drifted back to the painting on the wall. He stared at it and covered his mouth with a trembling hand. Evelyn wasn't the only one who thought that.

Chapter 16

The black car pulled up to the diner midafternoon. With unkempt hair and two days of stubble on his face, Taylor stepped out of it with a piece of paper in hand. He scanned the near-empty parking lot and saw a man with a broom and dustpan heading toward the diner's entrance.

"Excuse me. Do you work here?"

The friendly man gave him and his BMW the once-over before answering. "Yes, but we're closing. We're open from six to three."

"That's OK. I was going to ask if I could hang a missing person flyer on your entrance door."

The man glanced at the flyer: a photo of a misty-eyed Sunny in her blue hospital gown with Rebecca on her chest. Below the picture was a brief description, noting that Sunny had a birthmark on the back of her neck.

"I don't see why not. Here, take this." He held out the broom and the dustpan, which had an orange medication bottle in it. Taylor exchanged the flyer and tape dispenser for them.

As the man entered the diner and affixed the flyer inside the window, Taylor checked the map on his phone. The pulsating blue dot appeared right on top of the red dot. Taylor looked up at the man with confusion before something rubbed against his thigh. Before he could look down, the man opened the door with a smile. "There she is!"

"Where?" Taylor looked around, seeing nothing but a yellow Labrador retriever with a bandanna around its neck. It nosed his blazer, surprising him. He pulled the empty doughnut wrapper from his pocket; the Lab's tail wagged patiently for more.

"This here is Susie," the man said, exiting the diner. "She's a local stray. Usually comes around two or three times daily looking for handouts." He knelt and patted her head and neck, and then something under the bandanna grabbed his attention. "Say, Susie, what you got here?"

"Son of a . . ." Taylor muttered, already knowing what it was.

The man removed the bandana, then a bulge tied to a collar underneath, wrapped in well-worn laces.

"What in the Sam Hill . . .?" He unraveled the mess to find an iPhone. "Well, I'll be. Who on earth would do something like that?"

"My wife." Taylor exchanged the broom and dustpan for the tape, noticing the orange bottle for the first time. "Who's apparently off her medication," he said with a nod to the orange bottle.

"I found it in the corner of the parking lot." The man gave the bottle a shake before handing it and the cell phone over.

"Thank you," Taylor said, looking at the horizon in defeat. He rummaged through his wallet and handed the man a business card. "Would you let me know if anybody happens to mention her?"

"Will do." The man held the card far away from his eyes and tilted his head back. "Dr. Johnson." He flipped it over, surprised to find a hundred-dollar bill.

Taylor squatted to Susie the Lab and scratched her behind the ear. "Thank you, Ms. Susie. May you eat like a queen instead of a pauper." He nodded to the man before returning to his car, dialing a number as he climbed in. After several rings, George's voicemail answered.

"George, I have some info. I'll call you back this evening or tomorrow. We might want to start thinking about filing a missing person report. Talk soon."

After a long pause, he dropped his cell phone onto the passenger seat with a sigh. "Pretty creative." He grabbed his little tape recorder from the dashboard. "I'll give you that much," he said before pressing the play button.

What happened in the hospital?

He fast-forwarded the tape, hitting play again.

It's not where I am. It's what I am.

"I beg to differ. I know what you are all too well."

He turned his navigation map on, staring at it as he rubbed his thumb over her name on the orange medication bottle.

"Where you disappeared to is indeed the question."

CHAPTER 17

Upon returning to the mansion, Sunny was uncomfortable leaving her car in plain view. She roamed about and found a place off road behind some bushes about forty yards from the gates. There, it should remain unseen by anyone pulling up to the entrance. Walking beyond it and to the porch, it was still visible, but only if someone knew where to look. Satisfied, she spent the rest of the day peeling yellowed wallpaper in the foyer. Layers of grime and dust that had built up on the staircase rails also needed cleaning.

It didn't feel like much was accomplished by the look of things come evening. She reminded herself it had taken a decade or two of neglect for the place to get this way. One thing she was sure of was waking up the following day sore; she hadn't had this much physical activity in a few years. That didn't include how often she had to stop and keep her pants from slipping.

She climbed the stairs with Rebecca and stopped to look at the other woodwork. That and umpteen other things needed some attention too. That would all have to wait until tomorrow. At least she'd placed candles in the wall sconces and lit them. They filled the hallway with a soft amber glow, enough light to find one's way, at least. After her long day, she couldn't wait to climb into bed and unwind. But first, she blew each candle out on her way to the bedroom.

With Rebecca asleep beside her, her thoughts drifted to the Antique Shoppe. The couple operating it, Morgan and Evelyn, were peculiar. He seemed nice enough, though unhappy and lost in some way she could relate to. At least, that's what she read in his eyes. Of course, she hadn't formed much of an opinion of Evelyn, though she appeared a bit stiff, but Sunny reserved judgment for now.

That a painting almost identical to her work hung on the wall was unsettling. Sunny still couldn't recall painting hers back at that place. She had grown fond of calling the psychiatric center that, but her foggy memory otherwise only added to her anxiety.

Her gaze dropped to the painting, leaning against a nightstand. For the first time, she missed her cell phone. Sure, it was helpful, turning the Lab into an unwitting accomplice to her disappearing act. But she could have used it to photograph the work at the Antique Shoppe and compare the two. There was no denying that having seen one called to mind the other. She also believed that finding the person who painted it might provide a clue to the mystery haunting her.

Another thing crossed her mind: Why had Morgan made it a point to say they were an antique store and not the local Hitchin' Post? She assumed it was one of the town's watering holes, where tall tales were poured by the ounce. It contradicted what Cliff had said about all the town's "hush-hush" information. It left her a bit uncertain about Morgan.

Was it a result of her sarcastic emphasis on the word *history*? Or was she overthinking it? She tended to do that the longer she was awake and knew she'd better call it a day soon, especially after last night. As she grabbed her pen and yellow notepad from the nightstand, her eyes fell upon the photo of her and Rebecca.

Sadness and anger over having the moment erased from her memory overwhelmed her. Her eyes grew misty as she wondered how Taylor could do that to her or anyone, for that matter.

She could feel the dryness return to her mouth and drank several big gulps from a water bottle. After setting it on the nightstand, she flipped through the notepad. A moment later, she found her handwritten list of peripartum psychosis symptoms:

Hallucinations
Hearing voices
Delusions
Insomnia
Loss of appetite
Anxiety
Paranoia
Suicidal thoughts

In frustration, she tossed the notepad back onto the nightstand and was drawn to a drawer she hadn't noticed before. She attempted to pull it open, but it was either stuck or locked. If it was the latter, she was out of luck. Giving the drawer another good tug tipped the bottle over. Water spilled across the top of the nightstand and raced toward its edge.

"No!" she yelled in a frantic attempt to stop it with her hands. Instead, it flowed around and dripped onto her painting of the inn. Water streaked down the tower windows, turning its dark colors into a white blemish.

"Damn it!"

She pulled the drawer again, and its contents spilled onto the floor. Among the items were some old thank-you cards embossed with "Nadir Bed and Breakfast," a potpourri jar, and an old key.

A flash of lightning followed by distant, rolling thunder gave way to the sound of a baby crying again. Sunny froze with an ear cocked to the door. She could hear nothing but the rain pelting the window. What she heard was real though; it wasn't Becca, fast asleep beside her.

Sunny sprang off the bed and snatched the key from the floor. With lantern in hand, she headed for the hallway in her nightgown. Armed with only a candle, any fear was tempered more by curiosity than by courage.

As she entered the hallway, the lantern's flame bent to her left; the draft came from the tower room. With the lamp held high, she followed the dancing shadows on the wall until she came to the crescent moon on the door. She listened for a moment. No other sounds of a child crying came in the dark of night, and doubt crept back over her. Was she imagining things?

She twisted the key in the keyhole, and the confirmation clicks echoed through the hallway. As its door opened with a long, whiny creak, the room took its first musty breath in what must have been ages.

The lighthouse's beam sliced through the darkness as it made its way around. Sunny shielded her eyes as she crept to an opening along the curved wall. The lantern's flame bobbed and weaved, revealing a staircase entrance.

She backtracked toward the door with the moon and crept past it to the windows. Something foul wafted on the cold air, sparking dread anew. For the moment, she was grateful she hadn't brought the flashlight for fear of what she might have seen.

With the next step, a phantom in a white gown materialized from the darkness in midair.

Lub-dub-dub, her heartbeat pounded.

Sunny looked down at the ghost's green-and-purple feet and gasped. Larvae fell to the floor one at a time. Tap-tap-tap. Their rotting stench had to be the source of the stink, not some dead bird caught in the chimney flue as Nadeen had suggested.

Lub-dub-dub-dub. Her heart banged like a gong in her ears now.

Her eyes worked their way up the apparition's white dress and her arms. A decayed green hand grasped a lantern and held it up high. Sunny tried to scream, but all that came out was a whimper and choked breath.

The beam of light circled back through the windows, and the ghost was gone as quickly as it had appeared. In its place was the reflection of Sunny holding the lantern up. Confused, she stepped closer; a full-size mirror hanging on a wall in a downward slant came into view. She rubbed her face in disbelief, and the image in the mirror did the same. And the tapping of larvae was nothing more than water dripping from the ceiling onto the floor.

"Jesus Christ, Sunny!" she shrieked with a mixture of laughter and scorn. Once again, there was an explanation for everything.

She tracked the lantern light farther along the floor to a dead bird, little more than feathers and bones. Her imagination, primed by stories, had gotten the best of her. It was clear she'd drawn upon her short-term experience to fill in the blanks of ambiguous stimuli. Boy, she loved psychology. But how it left her feeling sometimes? Not so much.

Stress and sleeplessness compounded the problem. The conditions were ripe for her brain to play tricks on her. The low light. The movement of the shadows from the flickering candlelight. They all factored into the equation. Even her prior pondering about what Steven's father had seen that night versus what he had imagined had played a role in this.

The only difference? She knew ghosts didn't exist . . . except those living inside our heads. And this was a perfect example of how we fed them into existence with our minds.

Once again, the thought left her uneasy. But this time, she had a better understanding of why.

The idea of ghosts living in people's heads wasn't hers. She'd come across it while doing a senior seminar in psychology and existentialism. As part of the curriculum, she had read Robert Pirsig's *Zen and the Art of Motorcycle*

Maintenance. It had had a profound effect on her and was a favorite class. Thinking about it now, she recalled that Pirsig, too, had undergone electroconvulsive therapy.

History was littered with visionaries, for lack of a better word, who saw the world differently than most. Another example was John Nash, whose life had inspired the movie *A Beautiful Mind*. Pirsig and Nash were two examples of geniuses diagnosed with schizophrenia and treated with ECT. Yet how many people walked around like them but unscathed by such experiences? Who stayed quiet and kept unexplainable and problematic beliefs to themselves? But speak honestly about what you thought you saw . . .

These thoughts ran through Sunny's head as she stood staring at her reflection for she couldn't tell how long. It would have been longer had it not been for the scraping noise behind her in the dark. A cross between a baby babbling and a cry followed it. Even though her mind was searching for some credible source for the sound, her body had other ideas. The lantern trembled in her hand as she shielded her eyes from the lighthouse beam passing by again.

She followed the scraping in the dark with the candlelight nearing its wick's end. She changed directions several times before another prolonged cry gave her goose bumps.

The light revealed an old chifforobe, and she reached for its door with a shaky hand and pulled it. It screeched open, revealing cobwebs stretching across the space. She held the light closer, but there was nothing to see inside.

An ear-piercing cry from behind had her spinning with a yelp.

Two green eyes stared back at her from the dark. At first, they appeared to be the sea-foam green eyes of the lady in the grocery store. As the lighthouse beam passed again, it exposed a black cat. In heat, it let out another of its baby-babble-like cries before it scurried past her and into the hallway.

"I guess this room was already taken," Sunny said with an uneasy laugh.

Muffled metal clanging came from elsewhere in the room, along with a low whistle. Sunny paced the room slowly, holding her lantern aloft. A fireplace of elaborate stonework built into the wall came into view from the dark—the whistling and clanking coming from within.

Shining the lantern over the stonework, she found a lever she assumed was the flue. She pulled it closed, stopping the banging for a moment. It also appeared to do something else. One of the stone's edges popped out from its flush placement next to the others.

Sunny shone the light on the stones. Confused and frowning, she touched them all. The others seemed dense while the one protruding felt hollow to the touch. She knocked on it, producing an echo.

"What the . . .?"

She pried at the stone's edge; with a squeak from a hinge, a little secret compartment was revealed. Inside were several leather-bound books stacked together.

She took one, opened it, and flipped through its pages. The edges were tinted brown, and handwritten passages followed chronological dates, appearing to go back about thirty years. Sunny suddenly felt like she had struck gold; this was a diary! The books may even have belonged to someone who once owned this place.

The notion made her heart skip.

She opened each book and checked the recorded dates, then returned all except the earliest to the secret storage space before retreating to her bedroom. Tonight, she was going to do some late-night reading. With Rebecca snuggled beside her, she was about to dip her soul into a mystery.

Dream sweet, my darling, the moon's shining bright,
She watches your window, and whispers, "Goodnight."
The stars weave a blanket to cradle your sleep,
While shadows stretch closer, their secrets to keep.

Chapter 18

The first thing Sunny noted upon opening the diary was a lack of personal information. No "property of," no authorship, nobody to return to if found. Nothing. It was odd, considering it was leatherbound and looked expensive.

The next thing she noticed was blood on some of the pages. Fresh blood. She opened the palm of her right hand. It was bleeding from fingernail impressions cut deep into the skin. It took a moment for her to realize this was the hand she had used to clutch the lantern.

The third observation was that some pages had suffered water damage over the years. As she flipped through them, the stains on the pages grew more significant. Then they became smaller, reminiscent of flipbook animation. Portions of some pages were illegible as a result. Others were stuck together. She hoped those were all the boring parts.

She realized that, for the second time in the last week, she was about to spy on the lives of others. This triggered the not-so-random thought of her father's keychain holder: HOME IS WHERE YOUR STORY BEGINS. This was somebody's home too. For whatever reason, sights of past events were plaguing her and had led her here.

A somber thought then occurred. Whoever owned and penned what she was about to read, this home was where their story ended . . . and a mystery began.

May 10, 1994

Today was a day unlike any other. It started so dreary, gloomy, and hopeless. I had to close the curtains at one point to keep from staring out the window into the rain.

I felt sorry for Doris, coming here almost three weeks before the season's official start. She worked hard for this once-in-a-lifetime event, only to see it washed out. She must have seen me moping when she told me it wasn't the end of the world.

She grabbed my arm and asked in her bubbly voice if I had seen the guy who had arrived last night.

I thought she was trying to set me up again, but I wasn't sure and reminded her she was engaged. Sure enough, it worked. She called me Ms. Lonely Heart, giggling as she pulled me through several rooms. We poked our heads into each, searching for this knight in shining armor she had seen.

I admit, I was intrigued, if only by her giddy reaction.

It was very unlike Doris, months away from getting married, to fawn over someone else. Before we knew it, we were back in the foyer, gasping for air and with tears from laughing. That's when she pointed to the top of the left staircase and said, "Look!" as a tall gentleman disappeared. She asked if I had gotten a good look at him. I hadn't, and she assured me he was handsome, in a Humphrey Bogart sort of way. Then she burst into another round of giggles. Doris sure does have a love for classic films. The day before, she was referring to someone as Jimmy Stewart.

It was all I could do to refrain from rolling my eyes when she mentioned that he was "very much with a pulse." It was apparent she was referring to this place having been a funeral home in the past. I gasped, trying not to laugh too loud. We were trying to make people forget what this place used to be, not remind them. She said I would have a pulse, too, had I also seen him.

She is such a character. I don't know what I'll do without her once she's gone. I'm already missing her.

It was at that moment that sunlight fell upon both of us through the window. We stood there, watching with surprise as the sky cleared.

Grabbing my arm again, she pulled me along and told me she didn't want me to miss this sight too. Several couples were already milling about the dock when we got ready and met outside.

I had been hoping the handyman would have the other sign for Searchlight Bed and Breakfast in place by now. It would have greeted guests and visitors by boat, letting the river rats know we were here.

But alas, it had fallen by the wayside with several other things still left to do.

I couldn't believe how fast it cleared, though we weren't "in the clear" yet. Pink, whispery clouds overhead started to rain on us. Doris noted an odd sensation in the air and that my face was ablaze with a pink glow. I covered my brow from the sun, and the world seemed to fall silent and still just then. Even the slight breeze stopped blowing.

When she saw me shielding my eyes, she told me not to look directly at the sun and handed me this odd cardboard contraption. She might as well have given me an accordion, as I had absolutely no idea what to do with it.

When I asked her how to use it, a pair of hands grabbed it before she could answer. We both looked up to see her dashing, tall gentleman.

I'll be honest. I don't remember exactly what, if anything, was said when our eyes locked as both our hands held the contraption. I could see a bit of Humphrey Bogart in him. I might have been sold if he had a cigarette dangling from the corner of his mouth. But those big blue eyes . . . they hung there, waiting for me to say something.

And there I was, at a complete loss for words. A crooked smile spread from the corner of his mouth as he twirled an umbrella over his dark hair. I don't remember hearing any sound whatsoever. No birds. No boats. Nothing until Doris said she would get some refreshments and asked if we cared for anything. I don't know how long we were standing there wordless, but the eclipse had begun with the sky turning slightly darker. I told her she would miss it, but she ignored me, turned to the gentleman, and asked, "Bogie?"

I couldn't contain my laughter and apologized, telling him not to mind her, that she was being silly. When he said, "Ah, sure. Bogie will have whatever the ladies are having," that was the moment I realized I liked him. I rarely find someone so casual and going with the flow.

With that, Doris hurried off in the growing darkness, leaving Bogie and me fumbling for words. Well, at least me. He said, "You're missing one of these," and exchanged the umbrella for the viewer.

My hand brushed his at that moment, and it felt like a shock. Like . . . static electricity that made me weak in the knees.

A cigarette dangling from the corner of the mouth was no longer required. I was signed, sealed, and . . . well, nothing delivered with a kiss. But let it be known, here in my journal, that it did get a little flirty.

As I opened the umbrella and held it overhead, he stepped behind me and wrapped his arms around me so that the viewer was at my belly. He said to keep it there and look down into its opening as he took hold of the umbrella. Before looking into it, I glanced at the darkening sky. It was a deep blue in some areas. In others, shapeshifting clouds changed colors as the moon crossed before the sun.

"The sun, moon, and the stars. They're so beautiful," I said in awe.

I dipped my eyes to the opening in the viewer to watch the eclipse safely when he agreed, saying, "Especially seeing them all at once."

I was sure he didn't know it, but I could tell he wasn't looking at the sky when he said that.

"Something like this doesn't happen very often, does it?" I asked, a smile having eclipsed the frown I wore just a short while ago when the day seemed spoiled.

"Once in a lifetime, if one is fortunate," he said, his eyes never leaving me.

Doris returned to us, arriving with our drinks and a big smile. She apologized for taking so long. Knowing her, she most likely kept her distance to watch and see if there were any fireworks between us.

I don't recall much about the event besides the odd sensation over the cove. After that, everything just seemed to come to a stop, as if time stood still. I had no idea the moon's passing the sun would last as long as it did, but the total eclipse lasted maybe a few minutes. One could even feel the temperature drop during totality.

When it happened, people watching in the cove and a good two dozen boats on the river erupted in cheers. One of the boats lit fireworks, much to Doris's delight. It was quite a spectacle and gave me hope that Searchlight Bed and Breakfast's first summer season will be profitable. No doubt it has gotten off to a memorable start!

The same could be said of Bogie and I. This is where our story begins. To be continued . . .

CHAPTER 19

A paintbrush's stroke of midnight-blue trails on a canvas.

Sunny stared at the impressionistic picture of a couple huddled together, watching the eclipse under an umbrella. Whispery orangish-pink clouds floated in the sky above the cove. She stepped back to critique her work, the brush in one hand and a spoon in the other, and nodded her satisfaction. This would be a better piece to show Morgan since the one she had intended was now tainted.

To think, the genesis of this new painting had begun as just a crescent moon on an otherwise blank canvas. Ironically, something good had come from being at that place. She wasn't sure what to do with the other canvas, with *Lies* scrawled on it in red. This one, however, seemed to be completed from a premeditated thought. One she couldn't remember . . . not that she could remember painting any of them.

"What do you think, Becca?" she asked, picking up a can of tuna and scraping the remaining fish from the inside before setting it on the floor. Only a few cans remained. "Does that look like an eclipse or a crescent moon?"

The colors reflected a rippled effect on the river, broken by darker boats with highlights shining off them. Purple, pink, orange, and red fireworks hung like flowers blooming in the sky. That alone gave the impression that it was an eclipse, or so she hoped. She had never experienced one.

Looking back at Rebecca on the bed, Sunny was surprised to see daylight already breaking through the window. "How long have I been painting?" she asked aloud, having lost track of time. A pounding headache was coming on, worsened by the bright light. It was one of the many side effects of her electroconvulsive therapy. She tried rubbing her temples to ease it as the faint sound of music drifted in from outside the room. It was familiar, yet she couldn't quite make it out. It almost sounded like it was . . . chimes.

She grabbed Rebecca, entered the hallway, and ventured down the stairs. The sun's golden rays brightened the foyer, amplifying her headache. Halfway down, she was sure the music had been the old organ playing.

Whatever it was, it had stopped. Seeming unnerved by the silence, Rebecca began to fuss in her arms as she approached the old viewing room. Situated here, it didn't catch the morning sun through the windows. While Sunny welcomed the relief, the sudden change left her straining to see if anyone was there.

"Good morning," Nadeen said, greeting her from behind with a startle. "It's just me," she said, sensing her embarrassment.

"For a moment, I thought the black cat that has taken up residence here had run across the keys."

"Oh. You must have met Spook then."

"Spook?"

"That's what I call her. She comes and goes as she pleases."

"Talk about hearing things . . . and after my trip into town, I can understand why you haven't had any help."

"Oh, but who hasn't heard those silly stories?" Now Nadeen seemed embarrassed. "But, of course, you're not from around here."

Sunny felt the urge to tell Nadeen she'd been here before but refrained from sharing her déjà vu stories. That a prior owner, who had committed suicide, wasn't from here either. Sunny had enough trouble trying to explain as little as possible as it was.

"You have to understand. The stories the people around here tell are just part of the area's attraction," Nadeen said. "The story about George Boldt not setting foot on Heart Island after the death of his beloved wife in 1904? It's just that. A romanticized story, repeated so much over the last hundred-plus years, people believe it to be true."

This—*this*—was right up Sunny's alley and was another part of the equation in her thesis. Nadeen had unknowingly referred to the illusory truth effect: people tend to believe false information the more they are exposed to it.

"So what really happened?"

"Boldt told the local newspaper he purchased the Stratford Hotel in Philadelphia. It was his intention to spend four million dollars expanding it. That same year, his wife died. He ended up five million over budget on what became the Bellevue-Stratford Hotel. He owned much more than the castle around here too. He had to choose between finishing the castle and the most luxurious hotel in the nation. One was for business, the other for pleasure. Boldt may have been a romantic, but he was a businessman above all else."

From what little Sunny knew, she could see the mechanisms beneath the tall tale. "You said it's on Heart Island. That creates a bit of irony. But why mislead people? What purpose does it serve?"

"Tourism, of course." Nadeen rubbed imaginary dollar bills between her fingers. "It's the same with many guides on the tour boats. 'Zavikon Island has the shortest international bridge in the world,' they say. But it's within Canadian waters with the border several hundred feet away."

She looked out the window toward the river. "So many old villas date back to the Gilded Age when money flowed here from pockets deeper than the river. Those times are long gone. Many properties remain, mostly owned by seasonal residents from cities far from here. Other properties over the years were lost in fires under mysterious circumstances. Some say insurance policies. Taxes on the properties kept climbing, but the old money had long sailed elsewhere. All part of the cycle of life and death on the river. And with it comes an opportunity for rebirth. Tourism is the river's heartbeat now. I figured, why not be a part of that? Without the stories, of course."

"It's amazing what people will believe. It's like mass hypnosis, though not at a dangerous level. Yet, when the truth is so plain to see, some people still don't want to hear it."

"That bridge story has been perpetuated endlessly in the newspapers too. But, when it comes to 'ghosts,' I'm only familiar with the Isle of Pines." Nadeen nodded toward the river. "Nobody talks about it much. Meat Loaf, the famous singer, filmed an episode of *Ghost Hunters* there some years ago. Now that I'm thinking of it, I recall hearing something about the ghost of a former owner on Long Vue Island too."

Sunny walked into the kitchen, grabbed one of Rebecca's ready-to-use formulas, and shook it. "I'm not one to believe in ghosts, but people? They can be haunted."

"By . . .?"

"The past, of course," Sunny said, trying unsuccessfully to feed Rebecca.

"Yes, but *whose* past?"

Sunny shuddered at the thought and felt her legs go rubbery. *Lub-dub-dub.* Her heart joined in the chorus of side effects of electroconvulsive therapy. She recalled that these things were also happening while she was pregnant. That's when those shards of shattered memories started. But the question of "whose" past seemed to trigger them now.

She was becoming confused, trying to separate reality from the thoughts in her head. Not to mention the ghosts whispering in her ear at every turn. Not literal ghosts, of course, but of that sense of time and the past. Objects were closer than they appeared in a foggy rearview mirror. She wanted to wipe it away to see clearly, yet she was afraid to. The best she could do was sit, wait it out, and hope Nadeen didn't notice. Unfortunately, Rebecca seemed to have and began fussing.

"What I meant is, don't we all struggle with the decisions that others make sometimes?"

Rebecca's fussing became incessant, overwhelming Sunny. She raised a shaky hand and rubbed her brow.

"I-I'm sorry. I've been a little . . . detached. From Becca. It's all a bit too much at times."

"All part of being a new mother, unless . . . I'm sure it's nothing more than the baby blues." Nadeen held her arms out, took Rebecca, and bounced her. "Feel free to wander around. Get some fresh air if that will make you feel better."

"I could use some. I promised somebody I'd stop back in town. Do you mind?"

"No, not at all."

"You're sure?"

"Of course. We'll be fine. Just try not to mix the stories with reality. As you said, many don't want to hear any different despite what they know and see. They fear it will destroy the illusions they cling to."

CHAPTER 20

Sunny didn't take long to find a parking spot on James Street. One was available right in front of the Antique Shoppe. It would have been nice to park farther away and enjoy the walk in the sun on a warm mid-October day. Colorful leaves and their crunching underfoot were things she cherished about the season. However, she decided against lugging the canvas any farther than she had to. She retrieved the art from the back seat, covered with some brown paper bags taped together. She had tied some twine she found in the kitchen around it, thinking it added a nice touch.

Getting it through the door was no small task. Not to mention the fact that she was unaware that the "black hole" awaited like a bird of prey from her perch behind the counter.

"We don't buy from the public," Evelyn said, her gruffness surprising Sunny.

"You must be—"

"You've been here before."

"Why, yes, just yesterday," Sunny answered warily.

"No. Before."

Sunny wilted, unsure how to respond. First, it was the woman with the sea-foam green eyes in the grocery store. And now this, as if the phantom voice whispering in her ear, telling her the same thing wasn't enough.

The bells jangled over the entrance as Morgan entered with a surprised look at Sunny and Evelyn.

"I was telling her we don't buy from the public—" The shrill ring from a phone behind the counter interrupted Evelyn.

"We're not. We're going to sell it," Morgan said, beaming at Sunny. "Aren't we?"

Sunny returned a small, polite smile under the heavy gaze of Evelyn while the phone continued to ring.

"Would you be so kind as to answer that, Evie?" Morgan turned his attention to Sunny. "Let's have a look, shall we?"

Sunny held the covered painting up. "Something happened to the one I had in mind, but luckily, I found some inspiration for this one instead." She undid the twine-tied knot and unwrapped the paper. Her smile was full of anticipation but flatlined as Morgan gazed at it, lost for words. "Y-you don't like it, do you?"

Several long moments passed by before he spoke.

"That was . . . quite a day."

"I bet. A once-in-a-lifetime experience," Sunny said as Morgan turned away. "The owner of the bed and breakfast, did they—?"

"She was a piece of work herself," Evelyn said from behind the counter as she hung up the phone.

Sunny pivoted to her, surprised. "You knew her?"

"Everyone in this county knew of her," Evelyn said. Taking menacing delight, she added, "She was something of a visionary. She saw things that weren't there."

The shadows. You see them too, don't you?

Sunny did her best to brush away the thoughts. It wouldn't take much for the warmth to spread from her belly. Not with the green-eyed woman's words entering her consciousness. This was all becoming too surreal.

The bells jangling over the door's entrance broke the onset of another stupor as a customer entered. "I should be going," Sunny said, her throat tightening as an uneasy panic took hold of her. She rushed out the door, Evelyn watching her every step.

"She's up to something."

Morgan shook his head, still in a gray area somewhere between confusion and shock.

"Then she knows something."

He turned his attention back to the painting, tracing a finger around the edges of the eclipsed sun. "She's just a girl. And this is just—"

"A painting? I should hope so, for your sake."

Sunny hurried to the car, opened the door, and climbed in. Her hands clutched the steering wheel, and her chest rose and fell with heavy breaths. She was unsure what had just transpired, except that Evelyn gave her a case of the creeps. She had no gray area. She was a black hole, sucking the light from everything around her. The Antique Shoppe was its event horizon, where the light could never escape. No wonder Morgan seemed like a man trapped in a nightmare. The way they interacted with the tension between them, they had to be unhappily married.

Sunny took a deep breath and adjusted the rearview mirror. Her tired, unblinking, bloodshot eyes stared back.

Then came more broken fragments of memory, like pieces of a shattered mirror flying in the air. Taylor hypnotizing her. Taylor asking what had happened in the hospital. Her hitting him in the head with a heavy object.

One after the other, broken, disjointed shards fell to the ground. If only she could put the pieces together and see what they portrayed, they might provide a clue, if not an answer.

It's not where I am; it's what I am.

Sunny recalled saying this, but her memory faltered at its context. She continued staring into the mirror at the ghoulish phantom, hardly recognizing herself anymore. The stress and lack of sleep were taking their toll on her.

For the first time, her grit wavered. What if she were crazy? She ran the list of symptoms through her head again: Hallucinations. Hearing voices. Delusions. Loss of appetite. Anxiety. Paranoia. Insomnia. Suicidal thoughts. Sunny realized she could check off more than a few of these. Nevertheless, she couldn't understand—no, *believe*—all these coincidences were in her head.

She tilted the mirror back into its normal position and swept aside all those thoughts. In the mirror's reflection, Evelyn perched herself in the Antique Shoppe's window, staring back at her.

It was one thing for Sunny to behave the way she did, not knowing what was happening to her. But everyone else? The way they were reacting to her being here?

That was an entirely different story.

CHAPTER 21

George labored down a long hallway, making his way toward a staircase drowning in sunlight at its end. It was closer than the elevator, and he thought it would be quicker to use. He held a cane in his left hand and a stash of papers and tape in his right; each step on his artificial leg left him feeling like he'd taken ten.

Once he arrived at the stairs, he swapped the cane to his right hand and tackled them. His artificial leg thumped up each one as he leaned on its railing, stopping to huff every few steps.

On the ground floor, a door opened on his left. Students flooded the hallway, passing him like water around an old, mossy boulder in the middle of a creek. He veered to the wall as they rushed toward him from a lecture hall. After catching his breath for a moment, he stayed to the left and out of the sea of humanity coming his way. When the tide subsided, he found a bulletin board. There, he taped a copy of the missing person flyer, stepped back, and nodded in approval. Good enough.

Outside, it was a warm mid-October day with temperatures pushing near 80 degrees. It wouldn't take long to break a sweat. Moving down the promenade, he stopped to ask an occasional student if they knew or had seen Sunny. Most didn't, but a few were happy to take flyers after he mentioned she taught a few classes there.

A bench in the shade of a maple tree looked like an excellent place to take a break. He looked around, searching for someone, and then checked his watch when his cell phone rang.

"Taylor, I got your message. What's the news?"

"I found her phone attached to a stray dog."

George laughed in disbelief. "Oh, for heaven's sake. How on earth did she manage that? I can barely get one of those dang things into my pocket."

"It was bound with a couple of shoelaces."

"Oh, for crying out loud. My boots. I put them in the trunk."

George waved to Steven, approaching with a stack of flyers in one hand and a stapler in the other. "One of her students was kind enough to play chauffeur, seeing how she's got my four wheels. Unfortunately, I myself am running low on gas. Not used to doing so much walking since the surgery."

"George, there's something else. She's off her medication. A prescription bottle was found in a roadside diner parking lot about forty minutes away. Of course, she could be anywhere by now, but I have a lead."

"Go on, I'm all ears," George said after a lengthy pause.

"First, I want you to know I didn't report her missing. When the state trooper—"

"Trooper?"

"I came across a state trooper who chatted with Sunny the other morning. He was checking on a parked car in the fog next to a roadside diner. I told him she wasn't missing so much as she doesn't want to be found."

George choked back urgency. "Did he say how she was? Where she's headed?"

"This will sound a bit strange, but do you know anything about that place in her painting? The trooper said she told him she was returning from there."

George closed his eyes, swallowed hard, and rubbed his forehead in dismay. He pressed the phone's mic to his shirt and cupped it with a hand. "Can you hand a few more out around here?" he asked Steven. "My leg isn't quite up to it."

Steven headed off like a fish swimming against the tide, George watching as he stopped every few steps, handing a flyer to whomever he made eye contact with.

"Are you still there?" Taylor's muffled voice came over the phone.

"Yeah, still here." He didn't want to fill the air with silence, nor did he like the sound of it. "Let me call you back in a little bit." He ended the call without waiting for a response.

As he was deep in thought, the wave of students died down to a trickle, Steven still working his way upstream.

"So help me God, I hope I'm doing the right thing," George said, looking at his phone. With a deep breath, he made the phone call he wished he'd never have to make.

Chapter 22

The last thing Sheriff McCullough expected to receive a call about was the old abandoned funeral home between Clayton and Alexandria Bay.

He'd been a young deputy in the early 1990s when it reopened as a bed and breakfast. The business did well at first but nosedived after the first year, and the owner committed suicide. She had claimed it haunted, so, to nobody's surprise, there had been odd stories and tall tales ever since.

Taking one's own life gets much less attention and press than murder. After the suicide, the mansion changed hands a few times but had remained vacant for the last decade. Empty, that is, except for the thrill seekers. With nothing better to do, they stirred up trouble, partied there, and vandalized it.

It wasn't unusual in the area. Most river homes were empty from late fall to early spring. In 1937, Iroquois Island had been robbed of over $7,000 worth of valuables. Even Boldt Castle was looted in the years after Boldt stopped construction. It continued, long after the Bridge Authority assumed ownership in the 1970s.

The same happened with the reportedly haunted Wyckoff Villa on Carleton Island. The wife of its builder died five weeks before completion. The owner himself spent only one night there after it was finished before he too passed. In such cases, facts often became intertwined with overactive imaginations.

Besides the occasional stories, the sheriff hadn't heard much about the place. They were nothing out of the ordinary, but it had a peculiar reputation among the locals.

So, when the phone rang on an unseasonably warm and sunny Wednesday afternoon, he figured it was his wife. It wouldn't have been the first time she'd called and asked him to leave work early. But the voice on the other end belonged to an older man who sounded quite worried. He wanted to know how to handle a situation involving his daughter, who had left her husband.

"If she's left but isn't missing, then you should probably give her a reasonable amount of time to return. If she's missing, you'll need to come down—" He pursed his lips. Being cut off wasn't even on his bottom ten list of things he liked. But he was willing to give the man on the other end the benefit of the doubt, given the way he sounded.

"She took your car? Do you want to report it stolen then? That way, we can put a bulletin out for it and her . . ." He rolled his eyes. "There's a baby involved too?" McCullough sat up in his chair, searching his desk for a pen. "Well, if it's hers . . . You don't say. I see. That certainly changes things." He jotted the phone number down, noticing its area code was in Western New York. "Where are you calling from again?"

Swiveling in his chair, McCullough eyed a topographic map of New York on the wall. "Any specific reason you're calling here? You're a few hours away." He wiped a heavy hand down his puffy face. *Where on earth would this lead?* he wondered. The man on the other end mentioned the old Searchlight Bed and Breakfast.

"I'm all too familiar with it. I'll tell you what. I live out that way and will take a look and get back to you . . ." He scribbled the man's name under the phone number. "OK. I'll be in touch, George."

Sheriff McCullough hung up the phone, exhaled, and reached into his desk drawer. His fingers found the cool metal of a magnetic dart. Once, in another century, that drawer might have held a bottle of spirits for moments like these. A low chuckle rumbled in his chest. *Spirits.* His eyes drifted to the map on the wall. With a flick of his wrist, the dart sailed—spinning, twisting—before landing off target, swallowed by the imaginary cold, dark waters of Lake Ontario.

He thrust himself out of his chair and moved the dart from the lake to a point between Clayton and Alexandria Bay. He took a closer look at the sepia-toned 1890s map. The whole fiasco started with the owner claiming to have seen a ghost. He wondered for a moment if it too had involved a bottle.

If he were a gambling man, he'd bet dollars to doughnuts he wouldn't see much of anything. Nope. Nothing other than a large, dilapidated, old house on the river. And some empty, if not broken, bottles.

Hush now, don't stir, for the night's here to stay,
It carries your worries so far, far away.
But hold to your breath if the wind starts to call,
For not every voice means you're safe after all.

CHAPTER 23

After returning from her trip to the Antique Shoppe, Sunny picked up where she had left off the day before. She made the most of the remaining daylight hours, working and playing with Rebecca.

She cleaned the woodwork in the foyer and swabbed more than a few cobwebs. Most of the wood was in pretty good shape but buried underneath years of dust that took some elbow grease to rub off.

At this rate, she should be able to fit back into her old clothes from before her pregnancy. Besides, using an old shoelace for a belt on her pants had grown old. It also made her look one step closer to being homeless. Indeed, if someone were to see her here, it might cross their mind.

As the daylight waned, she lit the candles in the upstairs hallway. She also poured a bottle of baby formula into a bowl and left it out for Spook. That was when the dreaded tapping sound began again on the second floor outside her room. It was the last thing she wanted to deal with after a long day. But she figured it was better to deal with it now than have it keep her awake all night.

It didn't take long to determine the leak couldn't be from the roof; it wasn't raining outside. But even with the flashlight, she couldn't figure out where it was coming from. As a last resort, she decided to check the tower room.

She found a ladder in an upstairs closet and stood on it, pointing the flashlight at the ceiling. The light revealed a series of brown stains in an oblong circle, growing darker toward the center. That's where the leak was coming from.

Tap. Tap. Tap.

The water droplets were now larvae, falling to the floor. On their way, they passed the sickly greenish feet with the purple toes. But the ghoulish feet weren't dangling in midair; they were her own as she stood on the ladder, looking down. The tapping grew louder and became a dull thudding.

She shook the images from her head with a weary sigh and placed the flashlight onto a crossbeam. A necklace's pendant suddenly jerked before her face, swinging from its chain. From the light, she could see it was caught on a nail protruding from the wood. Her flashlight must have pushed the necklace over the edge of the plank.

She steadied the pendant with her hand, marveling at its craftsmanship.

A crescent moon of silver eclipsed a sun made of gold. Their half faces on each side raised, forming a whole with diamonds between the sun's rays meant to be stars. Sunny turned the pendant over and read aloud a message engraved on its back: "For my love."

Whomever it once belonged to and how it ended up on the crossbeam were a mystery. The pendant looked handmade and painstakingly so. And it was heavy, suggesting it was pure silver and gold.

The last bit of daylight shone through the tower windows as Sunny untangled the pendant's chain. Having freed it, she stepped down the ladder and headed toward her bedroom.

The day had begun with her dropping off the painting at the Antique Shoppe. It had ended, for now at least, with her finding this old pendant, giving her another reason to stop back there. In the meantime, she needed to let Nadeen know about the leak and see if she had any idea what might be causing it.

For now, she would join Rebecca in bed. She had listened to her happily babble while searching for the drip's source but found her sleeping now. She held the pendant for another look before exchanging it for the diary on the nightstand. Then she blew out the lantern flame and slid into bed, careful not to disturb Rebecca. Once settled, she turned the flashlight on and read.

July 18, 1994

The last two months have been perfect. The business at Searchlight has been fantastic, beyond what I would ever have expected for the first few months. There were a few days here and there in the middle of the week when we had several empty rooms, but come weekends, we've had to turn people away.

Slowly but surely, the reservations have been trickling in through early October. If this continues, we may be able to make a year-rounder out of it!

This evening, Bogie and I crossed the mini-bridge and strolled down the other side of the cove. The rows of apple trees masked the otherwise starry nighttime sky. We walked underneath them, hand in hand, the stars twinkling between the leaves as we gazed up at them.

I don't think I have ever laughed as hard as I did when we came to a clearing, and I pointed upward. "Look at all the—" I began to say when he slipped and landed on his behind with a shriek. Then, reaching underneath himself, he pulled out the remains of crushed apples. I said, "Apples on the ground," with perfect timing and another round of laughter.

He could only laugh as I teased him about making apple sauce at a time like this. I extended my hand to help him, but he pulled me down instead. I landed on top of him; my nose was an inch from his. Our eyes locked, and our laughter subsided to warm smiles.

"So it used to be a funeral home? For real? Kind of creepy, isn't it?" Bogie asked me.

My nod elicited an exaggerated shiver. I told him I shouldn't mention the caskets still in the attic. He seemed eager to know more when he asked why they weren't stored in the basement instead. He stared at me in silence for a moment, and his smile faltered after I told him the undertaker still resided there.

We both broke into laughter as he rolled his eyes.

"There is no basement due to the house's proximity to the water. But there is a coffin still up in the attic," I said, then asked if he wanted to see it.

"How about the sun, moon, and stars instead?" he replied, surprising me with a necklace I had never seen the likes of before.

It had a pendant of a silver crescent moon and a gold sun forming an eclipse. Diamonds surrounded the sun's rays and the moon's edge like stars in the night sky. He drew the necklace around my neck from behind and fastened it, smiling as it rested on my bosom.

I lifted it, surprised at its weight; it must be real silver and gold. I ran my thumb over the raised faces of the sun and moon.

"Something like this doesn't happen very often, does it?" I asked.

He started to tell me "Once in a lifetime" when I pounced on him with a kiss. Before long, we both fumbled to remove each other's clothes, Bogie lying me down on the grass.

I gasped with each thrust, my eyes opening to see the stars above before closing again. I nibbled his ear and scratched his back with my fingernails. For a moment, it felt like I had an out-of-body experience. I had to clench a handful of grass to believe I was still on the ground.

After we finished, Bogie apologized for not spending the night—he had an errand to run early in the morning. I assured him it was OK and that I didn't want to give Doris something to tease me about, seeing us together then.

While the night left me anxious to see him again, the tryst and its spontaneity had me wondering . . . Are we heading in the same direction or merely crossing one another's paths in a once-in-a-lifetime event?

July 19, 1994

I awoke with the oddest feelings this morning, ones I couldn't put my finger on. They just hovered there, crossing in and out of my mind between sleep and wakefulness.

First, I wondered how much time would pass before I saw Bogie again. Then I wondered if last night was for real or if I had romanticized something meant to be primal.

I suppose my insecurity was to blame for some of each. I enjoy Bogie's company; he's thoughtful, caring, articulate, humorous, and sensitive. Have I mentioned those eyes too? They can pull one in like a tractor beam. Yet I need clarification, thinking we rushed too fast into the physical aspect.

The events that unfolded felt organic and happened innocently enough. But there's the perception that he could have his pick of almost anyone, leaving me to wonder, why me? These doubts consumed my morning. So, when I was in town earlier today, I couldn't resist my curiosity when I saw a sign.

As I walked down Lower James Street near the dock, an old, weathered wooden sign on a small storefront caught my attention. Located at the corner of Miller Avenue, it read MADAME VANDERHILL'S SECOND SIGHT, engraved and painted in gold against forest green. A slight breeze blew it with a creaking rhythm.

This might sound silly, but I wouldn't have bothered if it weren't for the noise it made. It seemed like it was calling for my attention. I'm not exactly a believer in such things, but I thought it was something new to try on a whim. It might even put my restless mind at ease. I had no real idea what to expect, but the idea felt exhilarating. It gave me butterflies thinking about what might come of it.

I decided to mill about the gift store next door, waiting to see the reactions of anyone leaving. Picking over an assortment of souvenir T-shirts displayed in front of the shop, I saw a girl exiting with her friend. She covered her smile as she relayed the details of her reading. That was enough for me to make my way toward the Second Sight's entrance.

As I entered, an older lady, whom I presumed to be Madame Vanderhill, ushered me through a curtain of beads. Her speech was sparse, peppered with broken English and a heavy accent.

The air inside was rich and thick with the sweet-smelling smoke of burning incense. Mystic, new-age music played in the background, and the lights were dimmed. As one might imagine, it was something straight out of a movie and a bit clichéd. I was not impressed. Naive as I am, an air of authenticity would have made it more realistic than what was on display there. All those lit candles and melted wax were enough to start a crayon manufacturing plant. The only thing missing was a crystal ball.

I wasn't holding out hope as the woman sat me down at a table and left me there in the dark room's mystical ambiance. It all just felt so scripted. Of course, that changed when the real Madame Vanderhill entered the room.

She couldn't have been more than fifteen years old with straight, dark hair and the most haunting light-emerald-colored eyes. She very much reminded me of the striking Afghan girl on the cover of *National Geographic* years ago. They both had the same eyes.

Madame Vanderhill entered through the beaded doorway with the older woman. It may have been her daughter, for all I know. I wouldn't presume anything as she took the seat opposite me.

Confused, I turned to the older woman and said, "But she's only a child." The older woman turned and walked away, disappearing through the beads. I looked at Madame Vanderhill, who placed her smooth young hands on the table and spoke plain English.

"And children have nothing but the future to look forward to. The older one is, the more one reflects upon the past. Is this not true?" She then offered to record the reading for me on a cassette tape.

Even though I'm sure the events that transpired won't be forgotten, I've transcribed what she said. I'm doing so to understand and make sense of it as this was not what I expected. Besides, people thirty years from now probably won't even know what a cassette tape is.

After she started recording, she held her hands out, palms up, and waited for me to place mine on top of them. I hesitated, finally doing so, and she closed her emerald eyes. A long moment passed, and she asked, "You're searching for your mother?"

Although I'd never been to one of these before, I knew better than to offer confirmation or denial. Thankfully, her eyes were still closed; otherwise, she would have seen me rolling mine. No sooner had I done this than she opened them.

"I see Nadir, the fourth house. It is associated with a person's beginnings. Their home. Their nurturing parent, along with what's inherited from previous generations. Even past lives."

I resisted the urge to roll my eyes again, wondering what this was all about. But I couldn't refrain from saying under my breath, "I hope I don't see money going down the drain." We were not off to a good start. At that point, she squeezed my hands and continued with her mumbo jumbo.

"Subconscious self-images are formed here. Whether we felt acceptance or rejection from our parents."

I yanked my hands away, stood up, and readied to leave. I did not want to hear more of this malarkey. "This was a mistake," I said and turned to exit through the beads.

"Ah yes . . . the sun, moon, and stars."

It stopped me, and I sank back into the chair. She had my full attention now. At least until she closed her eyes and said, "You are with child." She was staring at my pendant when she opened her eyes again.

Of course. The sun, the moon, the stars . . . and a sucker sitting right before her. Played like the fool I am, I said, "No pun intended, but you have got to be kidding—"

"The six houses of the zodiac below the horizon symbolize a reality only in the imagination," she said, cutting me off. She shuffled large black tarot cards with a red eye on them, placing them in two groups on the table. The final card she left before me. She flipped it over; there was an astrological symbol on it that I couldn't decipher with my limited knowledge.

The mystical music playing in the background stopped then. The room grew eerily darker as Madame Vanderhill stared at the card.

"Nadir is the house of shadows. They tell us what we fear. They paint a picture of what we're afraid to feel. Especially with the end of matters."

"The end of what?" I was more confused and agitated than ever.

She pulled her hands from mine, stood up, and looked down as if ashamed. "I'm sorry. I've told you all I can."

Shocked, I wondered who would pay for such a thing as this. "What about romance? Love? Happily ever after? That's what I came in here for. So, if you're going to patronize me, can you at least humor me in the process?"

She ejected the cassette from the recorder and handed it to me. "You will see them. The shadows. Now that you are with child."

She walked through the beaded curtain without another word, leaving me stunned. This talk of houses, the end of matters, and shadows was like some cryptic jigsaw puzzle. It required more than a second sight on my part to put together. I felt blind, if not altogether blindsided.

And this "being with child." I can't be pregnant, can I?

I left, wondering what kind of person she mistook me for. Then, as I stepped out of the cold and darkness of the joyless ride I took, I realized the answer to my question. A tourist. They come here in droves. Seeking entertainment, they spend their money and then leave.

The more I thought about it, the more it made sense. As Second Sight's primary audience, they probably have certain expectations. Hence, the whole theatrical presentation. Otherwise, they might leave disappointed.

This was something for me to consider with Searchlight Bed and Breakfast. But still, the content itself fell flat with the lack of satisfaction. I suppose my curiosity got the best of me, and that oddest of feelings I awoke to this morning only grew tenfold.

That, and my purse was twenty-five dollars lighter.

July 20, 1994

The most horrible thing happened moments ago. It has shaken me so badly that I can hardly write.

I was sketching an idea for a new sign a little while ago and saw that I had written "Nadir Inn" in my absent-mindedness. I must have been daydreaming while doing so. But, when a soft lullaby played outside the door somewhere, I decided to investigate.

It sounded as if it were chiming a familiar tune, something from my childhood. I couldn't quite make it out as it seemed so distant, either in space or time. I went into the hallway and followed the melody to the tower room. The chiming stopped there, replaced by a creaking noise reminiscent of the Second Sight sign. Both had the same odd, rhythmic tempo.

I opened the door, and the room was pitch black as it was nighttime and not occupied.

Off on the distant St. Lawrence River, a lighthouse flashed its beam through the windows as it went around. The creaking continued in the darkness for several moments, and the light passed again.

As it cut through the room, I saw what appeared to be the silhouette of a figure floating in the air for the briefest of moments. The creaking was much louder now. The light moved so fast that I didn't have time to register what I saw. I thought I might have even imagined it. It was almost subliminal in its effect, but it was definitely of human form.

Rather than wait for the ray to pass around a third time, I flipped on the ceiling light. Before me, a woman in a white dress or nightgown swayed from the crossbeam with a noose tied around her neck.

I gasped, watching her limp body rock in time with the creaking back and forth. Then her arm jolted forward, her hand grasping at thin air.

Shielding my eyes, I shrieked so loud I feared guests might decide to check out or, even worse, ask me to check on the room. The woman and the creaking sound were gone when I looked again.

Yes. Gone. Just like that and without a trace. I have doubts about whether what I saw was real or if I had imagined it.

I called for Doris to hurry. She rushed up the stairs and asked what that horrible scream was. I knew then that I couldn't tell her the truth for fear of what she might think. Instead, I explained that when I opened the door to the room and flipped on the light, a bat had swooped down at me. That's not an unusual experience here on the river with the seasonal cottages. As it turned out, it was also perfectly understandable for a woman to scream at the sight of one too.

Had I told the truth . . . Well, I'm sure that wouldn't fly as well as the bat story.

I hope they understand my avoidance of the room in the future. I'd rather they think me to be afraid of a bat than batshit crazy.

CHAPTER 24

Sunny lay propped up in bed, Rebecca wrapped up next to her as she read aloud from the diary. "I couldn't make out her features, nor could I decipher the music . . ." Goose bumps spread across her arms as she stopped, her voice echoing in some far corner of her mind.

I hear music playing. It's faint. It sounds so far away.

She gave the door a disturbed glance, pushed the thought away, and continued to read. "But that dreadful creaking sound. It was unmistakable with the woman swaying from the crossbeam."

"The cheese just slid off her cracker," Sunny said, glancing at Rebecca.

It was impossible not to think of Taylor and herself in that one passage. The nibbling of his ear. The clutching of the grass. The out-of-body experience. The only thing missing was the somewhat discordant yet atmospheric Radiohead song playing.

No matter how much Sunny tried to push the coincidences away, they kept coming. Even worse, they were all starting to make her question her sanity. Once she began doing that, what right did she have to judge someone else?

That the owner had visited the same green-eyed woman was even more unnerving. It only gave credence to the fortune teller recognizing her. This ordeal was becoming both alarming and surreal. Could the shadows Madame Vanderhill referenced be the same as her broken shards of memories? And what exactly were they of? A past life?

Postulating this caused a wave of anxiety to billow up from within. She was adamant that there was some rational explanation for these irrational occurrences. Yet here she sat in bed, her brain working overtime to sort through what was real and what was her imagination. Her reality seemed caught somewhere between these two worlds.

As if on cue, the creaking began outside the bedroom.

Determined to find the cause of the noise, Sunny hoisted herself out of bed. With a bundled Rebecca, she snatched the lantern and entered the hallway. She rushed straight for the tower room and stopped at the crescent moon before her. It was aglow from the lantern light shaking in her hand, and the bowl of baby formula on the floor was empty.

She slowly pushed the door open; its hinges shrieked a tired groan as if disturbed from a long night's slumber. The door leading to the staircase within shut with a thundering slam. The lantern's flame flickered from the vacuum the change in pressure created.

Sunny could make out the black silhouette of windows against the grayness outside. A catacomb quietness filled the air, except for the creaking noise behind her in the hallway. She turned and raised the lantern and shrieked at Nadeen's glowing face before her.

"That was you sneaking up on me! What are you still doing here so late?"

"Late? It's almost seven thirty in the morning."

Sunny turned to the tower room, looking out its windows. The gray mass outside moved, shifting and revealing itself as an early morning fog.

"It can't be," she said, confused. "I've been awake the entire night?"

The fog was clearing up outside, with hulking shapes of poplar trees visible through the foyer's windows. The gloom choked the daylight out in contrast to the interior's rich, warm colors.

Sunny held Rebecca close as she descended the staircase with Nadeen.

"That's when I found this." She held the pendant out. Nadeen looked at it from a distance. "Oh, here," Sunny said, handing Rebecca to Nadeen to unclasp the charm from around her neck.

Nadeen set Rebecca down on a padded window nook, took hold of the medallion, and moved closer to the kitchen's windows. There, she looked it over where the morning light was brighter.

"It looks rather old," she said, gazing over its raised faces with interest.

"There's engraving on the back side," Sunny replied.

Nadeen flipped it over and read aloud, "For my love." She closed her hand around it, thinking a moment. "There's an antique dealer in Alex Bay, a man—"

"You mean Morgan? Do you happen to know anything about Evelyn? She's something else."

Nadeen smiled. "Yes, he's the one." She was about to say more when a car door slammed shut.

Surprised, they turned their attention to the front windows. A Jefferson County Sheriff's Department patrol car was parked at the side of the gate. Even more startling, Sheriff McCullough was already on his way to the front door.

Sunny retreated to the gathering room, out of view of the front windows. "Don't let them know we're here." Her blood ran cold, and she covered a gasp escaping her mouth.

"Becca!"

Her heart went from beating normally to pounding in her chest and ears in seconds. Rebecca was still lying in the window nook. Sunny stepped toward her, then retreated with Nadeen as footsteps thumped onto the porch.

No, not now. Please, not now.

She tried to stifle the growing anxiety by closing her eyes tight before peering around the corner.

McCullough's tall and stout frame appeared before the window. He took his hat off and tossed it onto a porch swing. Then he cupped his hands around his eyes, face up against the hazy window. Unable to see, he huffed breath onto the glass and rubbed some of the grime away.

Rebecca let out a wailing cry that sent Sunny's stomach into cramps. It was a feeling she hadn't experienced since she was pregnant. Yet again, she was helpless and frozen with a decision to make. Either choice could bring this all to an end.

"Hello? Anyone there?" McCullough asked with a raised voice.

Sunny, wide-eyed and her face flushed, turned to Nadeen, who retreated farther. "Aren't you going to answer?"

Nadeen shook her head, keeping an eye on McCullough. "It's the sheriff. My fiancé is good friends with him. If I answer, it will only make matters worse."

"Your car! Won't he see it, though?" Sunny whispered.

"I've feared something like this might happen. That's why I don't park it here."

"I guess I've been too worried about parking my own out of sight to notice."

Rebecca's flailing limbs inched her closer to the nook's edge. Sunny started for her but hesitated with an eye on McCullough moving away from the window. He disappeared out of sight, then the locked front doorknob jiggled.

Sunny took a few paces toward Rebecca, watching McCullough step off the porch. He looked around for several long seconds before lumbering back toward his car. She snatched Rebecca up and held her close, breathing in the precious scent of her baby's hair. "I'm so sorry, Becca," she said through tears, pressing her sweaty forehead to Rebecca's.

Nadeen slipped into the foyer and froze as she looked past Sunny. The necklace and pendant were uncoiled from her hand, dangling as she pointed to the window. "Behind you," she whispered in a cracking voice.

Sunny swallowed her nerves. Not knowing what to expect, she turned to the window.

McCullough was back on the porch, staring right at her.

She stepped back and shifted a crying Rebecca to her other arm, as far away from view as possible.

McCullough put his hat back on, straightened it, and checked his reflection in the window. He returned to his car with one more long look around the grounds. His eyes lingered an extra moment near where her vehicle was parked behind the brush. Satisfied, he climbed into his patrol car, started its engine, and left.

Sunny turned to Nadeen with relief, only to stiffen at her prying eyes.

"How would they have known to look for you here?"

Sunny wept as Rebecca's cries grew louder. "Why won't she stop?"

Nadeen exchanged the pendant for Rebecca. "She senses you're upset," she said, bouncing her.

Sunny sniffled back her insecurities. She couldn't take much more and chose to come clean despite fearing the outcome. "He probably knew to look here from my painting."

"Painting? Of what?"

"This place," Sunny said, the words hanging in a cloud of uncertainty. She knew how it sounded, like everything else lately. "I can't explain it. I've never been to or seen this place before, yet it . . . *haunts* me. I know it sounds unbelievable, but it's why I had to leave."

Nadeen's lack of reaction or judgment unnerved Sunny enough for her to spill more and break an uncomfortable silence.

"They wanted to take Becca from me. Please. All I want is to find some rational explanation. Some answers behind whatever is causing this to happen to me. I'm sorry I wasn't upfront with everything, but I can't go back until I find out what's behind these . . . *things* I see."

Nadeen's eyes roamed around the foyer as if searching for an answer or at least some understanding. "I suppose one day, somebody will learn the truth of whatever happened here. The question is, will anyone believe it?"

Sunny wondered if people here gravitated toward comfortable lies to avoid a rather unpleasant truth. It wouldn't be the first time. It's better to sweep it under the rug and pretend it didn't happen than to live with it knowingly.

Verity and fiction were so entangled. Intertwined. Like the St. Lawrence River on a foggy night, they had become difficult to navigate.

Chapter 25

Later that evening, after more sanding, painting, and cleaning, Sunny left Rebecca with Nadeen to head to Alexandria Bay again. She wanted to see if Second Sight was still in business and to stop by the Antique Shoppe.

It was too much of a coincidence for the woman with the green eyes not to be the young Madame Vanderhill from the diary. The description. The eyes. The talk of seeing shadows. They all pointed to someone who had "seen" something. Something that, like her own experiences, wasn't easily explainable. This person could provide insight into her situation. After all, there could be no shadows without some form of illumination. Or, in her case, enlightenment.

As she entered the village, the car's fuel indicator showed just under a quarter of a tank of gas left. This might as well have been for her too as she was down to a couple of cans of tuna and beans. Losing even more pregnancy weight with her so-called diet wasn't difficult. At least compared to finding clothes that fit.

That was the least of her worries as she passed a village police car. She let out a long, worried sigh. It was about all she could do to relieve the ever-building stress she was encountering. Sooner or later, she would have to do something that would result in upping the ante. That, of course, meant more risk. Returning home wasn't in the cards at this point.

Turning onto Church Street, she looked for any sign that the Second Sight still existed. She passed a couple of old churches before turning onto Walton Street. It seemed off the beaten path—at least for tourists. There was an American Legion on the right, but no sign of what she was looking for.

In the next block was yet another church. This one was made of brownstone with a matching wall around its premise. She couldn't recall ever seeing so many churches in a single village the size of Alexandria Bay. According to the diary's author, she had hung a left onto Miller Avenue, which should come out onto James Street.

Sunny took a right turn and continued eyeing the storefronts. Most seemed like gift shops selling six of one and a half dozen of the other souvenirs. At Lower James

Street, she completed a U-turn before Captain Thomson's Resort and headed back up James.

With no sign in sight, she pulled up to the Antique Shoppe as it started to sprinkle. There, she sat and contemplated whether she should go in and show Morgan the necklace. While she hoped he might know to whom it once belonged, she feared dealing with Evelyn again. That, and the rain, kept her sitting curbside for the moment; there would be no enlightenment with the likes of that black hole.

Inside the store, Evelyn cashed out a customer with her saccharine smile. Morgan entered through the door behind the counter during their exchange.

"Are you going to catch the debate?" she asked the customer, handing him his receipt.

"It seems like forever since we've had one," the customer said. "Right, Morgan?"

Glancing out the store window, Morgan noticed Sunny parking her car. "It always comes down to who has a better reputation," he said. "Right, Evelyn?"

"Stop by again soon," she told the customer as he left with a tip of his hat.

Morgan watched the man exit, then looked perplexed at the space on the wall where he had hung Sunny's picture. "The painting, where did it go?" he asked, glancing out the window as Sunny made her way to the entrance.

"What difference does it make? It was for sale, wasn't it?" Evelyn said with an icy scowl.

The bells over the door announced Sunny's entrance with their familiar jingle. Morgan held his angry eyes on an empty frame behind the counter before greeting Sunny. "See? I told you it wouldn't last," he said, waving a hand to the open spot on the wall.

"You're kidding! I wonder who ... did they say anything about it?"

A rumble of thunder echoed throughout the Antique Shoppe.

"Only that it brought back memories of a particular day," Morgan said. He touched a button on the antique cash register, and its drawer flew open with a ding. He pulled a thick wad of twenty-dollar bills from it, peered over his shoulder at Evelyn, then closed the drawer. "Here's your part of the bargain."

Sunny clasped the wad, surprised. "I wasn't expecting anything, really."

Evelyn cocked her ear to them as she lit a cigarette and opened the newspaper, scanning its headlines. On its back page, a headline read "Authorities Seek Help," with Sunny's photograph beneath it.

"The gentleman who purchased it said he's interested in seeing more of your work," Morgan said.

"I wonder . . . actually, I came here to ask . . ." She searched her pockets for the pendant with no luck. "I must have left it in the car. I'll be right back."

Morgan watched her race to her car in the rain. Evelyn lowered the newspaper.

"Just how much did you give her?"

"What difference does it make? It was for sale, wasn't it?" he quipped back.

Evelyn exhaled a plume of smoke through her nose before she resumed reading the newspaper, turning a page.

Inside her car, Sunny rummaged through her purse, turning it inside out. Then she checked the glovebox to no avail before heaving herself against the back of the driver's seat.

"Where on earth did I put—?" she began to say, looking at the rearview mirror from which the necklace dangled. "There it is," she said, grabbing it.

Sunny slammed the car's door and rushed back toward the Antique Shoppe entrance. On the way, she crossed paths with a dark figure wearing a shawl over their head.

A flash of lightning illuminated Madame Vanderhill's face. Her eyes locked with Sunny's for a moment before she skirted around her.

"Wait!"

The two stood a short distance apart, the drumming of heavy rainfall the only sound between them.

"You've seen me before."

"The other night, at the store," the woman replied.

"No. *Before*," Sunny said, stepping forward and holding up the sun, moon, and stars pendant. "Look. I don't pretend to believe all this horse pucky and shadow shit. I just want some answers."

Madame Vanderhill shook her head. "You don't understand. I cannot interfere. That is my curse, you see?"

She looked past Sunny, who followed her gaze to the amber cigarette glow in the storefront's window. There, Evelyn turned another page, closer to the last. She paused to glare at them, her face obscured by a puff of smoke.

"You will find your answers in time," Madame Vanderhill said warily.

"And then what?"

"And then they will never be able to take your child away from you again."

"But . . . how did you know?"

Madame Vanderhill hurried away, leaving her alone in the pouring rain.

"Sunny two, crazy nothing," Sunny said with some measure of accomplishment.

As she raced back to the Antique Shoppe's entrance, she passed a curbside trash can. Inside it, a crumpled painting bled a river of colors in the rain. The drops flowed down the bent canvas, washing the clouds away and obscuring the moon.

Sunny reentered the Antique Shoppe and brushed her rain-soaked hair behind an ear. "Found it," she said, opening her hand. The necklace uncoiled its length before Morgan's haunted eyes.

Evelyn set the newspaper on the counter, the photo of Sunny and the headline in plain view. Her demeanor changed abruptly upon seeing the pendant. "You must be cold, all wet like that. I'll make some hot tea and fetch you a towel," she said, scurrying away through the door behind the counter.

Sunny handed Morgan the necklace, noting what seemed to be recognition on his face. "If you turn it over, there's something engraved on the back of it."

An uneasiness swelled in Morgan's voice that he couldn't hide. "For my love," he said before flipping the pendant.

"Do you know who it may have belonged to?"

The charm began trembling in his hand before he closed it in a tight fist. "I-I'm sure it meant quite a bit. To someone. Where did you get it?"

Sunny bundled her dark, wet hair and turned her back to him. "Can you help? I want to see how it looks on me in the mirror." She bit her lip, eyes darting between her reflection and the pendant as Morgan drew it around her neck. "The sun, moon, and stars . . ." She stopped, noticing the tremble in his hands as they paused midway around her neck.

A flash of lightning illuminated the room.

Morgan swallowed hard at the reddish oblong birthmark on the back of Sunny's neck. Its size and shape were reminiscent of a rope burn. After hesitating, he locked the necklace's clasp and closed his eyes. The long-delayed crack of thunder rattled him from his stupor as she faced him with the pendant on her bosom.

"You h-have a birthmark," he said with an uneasy smile.

She could see it at that moment. She didn't know what "it" was, but his eyes no longer appeared lost or saddened. Instead, they seemed *haunted*, as if they'd seen too much.

She glanced at the door behind the register and saw the newspaper on the counter. Her throat constricted when she saw her photo and the headline accompanying it. The anxiety struck her hard, but she did her best to stay calm. She was unable to hide it, just as Morgan couldn't conceal his reaction. It was far too late for either to pretend otherwise.

Convinced an awareness or awakening had happened between them just now, she felt the need to leave quickly. She stepped back toward the door with Morgan's eyes fixed on her in a faraway gaze.

"Tell Evelyn . . . tell her I took a rain check," she said and hurried out the door.

By the look on Morgan's face, one might have thought she floated through it, disappearing into the night.

Chapter 26

Windshield wipers sliced back and forth in the heavy rain. Taylor wiped a hand the length of his weary face, from his zombified eyes to a few days of beard stubble. His cell phone rang, prompting him to hit a button on his steering wheel to answer the call as he pulled over.

"George, any luck?"

"The sheriff went up and poked his nose around a bit but didn't see any sign of her, which somewhat puts my mind at ease."

"She wasn't there . . . when he checked."

"He assured me there wasn't a soul there. I don't think it's the type of place anyone would want to spend their time, at least not these days. He said it appeared in better condition than he expected though," George said with remorse. "I didn't know whether the place was still standing, but the sheriff said it's about as occupied as the Bates Motel."

"What made you think she might be up there anyway?"

"Call it a hunch. Like every other one, it led to a dead end," he said with a slight laugh. Then, he explained further, "It used to be a funeral home."

Taylor's fingers danced hopelessly on the steering wheel. "I've tracked accounts and credit cards and phoned her friends. She's . . . disappeared."

"She'll need something sooner or later. The sheriff said he'd put out a bulletin so more eyes should tune in. Where 'bouts you now?"

"About to spend the night in Oswego. Knowing Sunny, she doesn't want to be found, which means not being seen, so I'm checking along the back roads. Watertown looks like a place where people from all over the county might go. I figured I'd stop there tomorrow," Taylor said, not knowing what he would do afterward. He'd already rescheduled some of his patients for later in the week, and every passing day that brought little headway in her disappearance meant juggling more appointments down the road. He wasn't sure how much longer he could manage to do so.

"I'd better be going. Her mother's about to climb the walls now," George said. "I'll check back in the morning."

As Taylor ended the call, he stared at the passenger seat, lost in his thoughts. He could see his wife sitting in it, her feet kicked up on the dashboard while holding her belly and laughing at him.

Relax. Breathe easy. In and out. You're doing good. Everything is going to be OK.

She had said that only a few short months back. It now seemed like something that had happened in another lifetime.

Her favorite perfume, a dark rose elixir with a touch of berries and incense, still lingered in the car. Portrait of a Lady was both beautiful and mysteriously dreadful. A sliver of innocence portending an ethereal existence. It was a singular rose on a black coffin with smoky frankincense burning in the background. It was love and death intermingling as one. It also symbolized, in his mind, their complicated relationship.

She would wear it when they went for a night out on the town. It turned heads, for better or worse, and filled a room with its intoxicating, gothic trail. But here, in the small cabin of his BMW, its lingering traces only managed to serve him with aching nostalgia.

An oncoming car's headlights snapped him out of his memories. Another thought crossed his mind. After all the patients he'd seen, it was only now that he understood what it felt like for those who struggled with having been ghosted.

CHAPTER 27

Sunny sped away from the Antique Shoppe, careful not to exceed the speed limit. The last thing she needed was to be pulled over. That didn't stop her heart from racing as she turned the vehicle onto Route 12. Heading back toward Clayton, her mind analyzed and dissected everything that had happened. What she couldn't shake was seeing the newspaper on the counter.

There was little doubt that Morgan had read it, the way he mentioned his surprise at her having a birthmark. And yet, she couldn't explain the haunted look in his eyes. It didn't seem to fit the nature of discovering her as the one in the newspaper. There was even less doubt that the article about her had mentioned the mark.

Evelyn's reaction was simpler to digest. She had excused herself to go and make a phone call about the missing girl she had just read about. Why else would she have such a sudden change of demeanor?

The two of them together were bringing her closer to an all-out breakdown. If that weren't enough, having her photo in the newspaper raised her anxiety to an all-time high. Now she would need to exercise more caution when she went out. Although she was low on food, she had the good fortune of having sold a painting, which gave her the means to buy more groceries. Alas, that meant going out, which was now all the riskier. Even when she had a small victory, she couldn't win. After all, it wasn't like she could hop on the internet and order something from Amazon Prime. Yet the thought of someone tossing a package over Searchlight's gate and running away drew a smile.

Driving on Route 12 toward the I-81 junction, she noticed the state police barracks on the right-hand side for the first time. She wasn't sure how she had missed it before. It was an innocuous-looking building that could almost have been mistaken for a rest stop. She realized it was the sign she had missed. It was blue with words in white—STATE POLICE—right before the turnoff.

She couldn't recall any patrol cars parked there when she'd passed earlier. Now, she hoped the fact that several were sitting there meant fewer were on patrol. Even so, knowing it was there didn't help ease her anxiety.

As she continued, she passed the bar Morgan had referred to earlier, the Hitchin' Post.

This café and watering hole on the side of the road came complete with a strip of motel rooms that looked like they were from the set of Hitchcock's *Psycho*. Guests were only a stumble or two away from the bar to their rooms, so they had that much going for them.

Sunny turned right onto Searchlight Road, anxious to return to Rebecca and the diary. The thought of Madame Vanderhill crossed her mind as she approached the mansion. She had almost forgotten about her with the ensuing encounter in the Antique Shoppe. The fortune teller hadn't provided any information to explain her dilemma. Her stating that it was her curse and that she couldn't interfere mystified and disturbed Sunny.

Parking near the mansion's gate, she hurried through it and to the porch, unaware of the car parked across the cove, cloaked in the darkness. The glowing amber tip of a cigarette burned bright from within before fading.

Once inside, Sunny changed out of her wet clothes. The rain must have added ten pounds to their weight, and it was a relief to remove them and dry herself off.

Before Nadeen left, she would tell her how grateful she was for helping her with Rebecca. She didn't know what she would have done without her. It was a blessing to stay there and have some much-needed help with her baby.

With Rebecca in tow, she went up the stairs and to her room. Settling the baby, she propped herself up with the diary beside the lantern and read aloud. "October 20, 1994. Another sleepless night." Sighing, she added, "Don't I know the feeling."

A bright light crept across the wall, startling Sunny. She leaped from the bed and hurried to the window. Toward the cove, she saw a pair of red taillights disappearing in the dark.

"It's just Nadeen leaving, Becca."

She slid back into bed and began to read again: "I'm beginning to wonder if people suspect something—" She stopped, the rhythmic tapping interrupting her.

This time, she knew better; the noise was nothing more than water leaking from the ceiling in the other room. After reminding herself to inform Nadeen of the problem, she resumed reading aloud.

"I no longer rent the room out, my stomach twisting at the thought of what is beyond that door . . ."

The crickets are singing their soft lullaby,
While trees sway and murmur, "The time's
drawing nigh."
The clock in the hallway ticks steady and slow,
Each chime marks a moment the dark seems to grow.

Chapter 28

Or could it be something else? Either way, I'm beginning to believe I'm Bogie's secret. Despite promising he would be here today for the big event, I've seen less of him these last few days.

I got up from bed this morning and saw a pink convertible passing through the gate from my window. Streamers fluttered behind as it passed the construction crew placing the new sign at the entrance.

It was the perfect start to what was shaping up to be a beautiful fall day. A slight morning dew on the lawn. Plenty of sunshine. Temperatures were expected to be around 70°, not to mention the scenic St. Lawrence River and the fall season at its peak. All was the icing on the cake for later when a knock at my door stirred me from the scene outside.

Doris entered, beaming from ear to ear. She was all made up, looking prettier than ever. She hugged me and said she would cry, but then she pulled away and told me it looked like I beat her to it.

I took her hands and made her close her eyes— no peeking!—and placed the pendant in them. She giggled and asked what it was and remarked how cold it felt. I told her to go ahead and open her eyes. They grew wide with surprise, and she smiled at the charm. Then, turning it over, she read the inscription on its back: "For my love." She looked at me, smiled, and said, "One day, you'll get married and have 1.6 kids" before trailing off with a concerned look at me.

We had not talked about what happened after Bogie gave me the pendant. Nothing about the out-of-body experience during sex. The trip to the Second Sight. The phantom in the tower room. Yet she must have sensed something from my sullen reaction as she asked if I was sure everything was OK.

There wasn't anything to talk about. I wasn't sure if I was pregnant, nor was I sure of what I saw. Between the two, I wasn't even sure which scared me the most. So I told her I was fine and asked her for help fastening the necklace clasp around my neck.

When I turned back to her, she did what she typically does. She made it seem as though everything were right with the world when, in her cheerful manner, she asked, "Well, are you going to get up and help me tie the knot or not?" Before I could say anything, she pulled me along with her wedding dress. We rushed from the foyer and up the staircase, opening door after door to find a place to change.

There were caterers, guests, wedding planners, and all other types milling about. Finding a room was next to impossible.

She barged in on a couple from the catering crew in bed—how shall I say this?—partaking in extracurricular activities. Doris said it best: "Now there's a prenuptial agreement." Then she closed the door with a laugh and dragged me to the bathroom.

We were cut off by a man who closed the door on us with an unapologetic shrug.

"It's a hell of a time to see a man about a dog," Doris yelled and then giggled.

Grabbing my hand again, she dragged me to the tower room. She commented on the just-painted crescent moon on its door. "I love it!" she said, then asked if I planned to carry the theme throughout the rooms with the sun, stars, and such.

I told her I was thinking about it, but my stomach turned when she opened the door and found the room vacant. I said we should wait for the bathroom to clear, but she wouldn't have any of it. I tried to remain calm on the outside as she tugged me into the room, but my heart was racing as I stood underneath the crossbeam and tried not to look up. From all the windows, we could see the cove decorated for the wedding, and a crowd had begun to mingle.

I began to relax, thinking that the specter I had seen was a figment of my overactive imagination. Then I heard it again. Music, chiming like before. Distant, as if it were traveling through space or time. Doris must have seen my troubled eyes dancing about the room, trying to find its source.

"What's wrong?" she asked, leaving me thinking she didn't hear it.

"I thought I heard music."

We both stood still for a moment. Other than the voices from outside, there was complete silence when Doris broke out in laughter. "They're called wedding bells!"

I was still for another moment, searching around the room and looking up at the crossbeam again. There was no creaking noise, nor a woman or ghost hanging.

I relaxed and agreed with a smile. "Yes, it must have been wedding bells."

Two bridesmaids arrived to help Doris with her dress moments later. I decided to attend to other matters as the big event was almost upon us. One could say that the mansion's interior was "behind the scenes." People rushed about with a frantic, nervous energy, attempting to arrange every last detail. It was like watching an orchestra attempt Beethoven's *Symphony No. 5* but through dance rather than instruments, minus the choreographer.

The scene outside proved to be much different. The guests lined both sides of the stone path leading to the cove. A cobblestone garden bridge led to an elevated gazebo on a small island. There, the wedding party and the groom awaited the arrival of Doris.

It was the first large party we had here but not the first to use the gazebo or, as I like to call it, the wedding chapel. A couple from near Rochester married here a few months ago. They only had a few guests, and they loved the intimate setting it provided.

I kept an eye open for Bogie, but there was no sign of him other than a maître d' with a passing resemblance. Several floated in and out of the crowd, hurrying back and forth to the kitchen. They two-stepped, sashayed, and pirouetted their choreographed moves to avoid spilling their trays.

Before long, a hush fell over the crowd that gathered, heads turning to Doris. Looking as beautiful as ever, she descended the path from the house. The two bridesmaids held up the train of her wedding gown as they marched behind. It was enough to bring a tear to my eye. I was so happy she decided to have her wedding here. It couldn't help but put this place on the map in such a competitive market.

As she passed, she gave me one of her quirky "Yikes!" grins. These were always followed by some comment about jumping off a plane without a parachute.

After a moment, I saw Bogie across the path, having only now arrived. He wasn't alone either. Some raven-haired girl was with him, wearing, of all things, an off-white dress that was too close in color to the bride's. She might as well have held a sign that read "Attention, attention! Desperate need of your attention!" over her head. The nerve. She got it too from a photographer trailing the wedding procession. He snapped photos of the proceedings, left and right.

Bogie could only grin and shrug.

I ignored him, watching Doris and her bridesmaids cross the cobblestone bridge. The guests took to the edge by the water that hugged the little island in the cove. It gave them a perfect view as a minister joined the groom in the chapel—the moment had finally arrived.

As the minister said, "We are gathered here today," a sudden chill came over me. At first, I thought it was only the clouds passing the sun. Everything grew darker, and the shadows of the tall trees disappeared from the ground. An uneasiness remained in the air.

I looked at the sixty or seventy guests, smiling as they watched the ceremony. Standing there with my hand on my belly, I was nauseous. My heartbeat pounded in my chest. Before long, it exploded in my ears like fireworks on the Fourth of July.

It was as if time slowed, and the world had fallen silent. The only audible noise was my heart's panicked beating in my ears. Even the minister's lips moved unnaturally slowly. I couldn't hear anything other than the same musical chimes as earlier. I can't imagine what extent of "disturbed" I appeared to portray when Bogie stared at me with concern.

As I looked away, I finally heard the minister say, "Congratulations, you may now kiss the—" when the sun appeared from behind the clouds, forcing me to turn and shield my eyes. At that moment, the image of the hanging woman in the white dress appeared through the large windows of the tower room.

Horrified, I drew a breath so loud that the proceedings stopped.

One by one, the heads turned my way like dominos falling. There were a few rumbles of nervous laughter and a loud, dissatisfied groan. The buzz of confusion and necks craning, eyes staring, and mouths murmuring grew as I stood there in shock.

As I looked back to the tower, the sun shone off its windows, and the woman was still visible. I pointed to her with my arm shaking. "There! Don't you see her? The lady in the window!"

Just then, the wedding photographer snapped a photo of the tower and turned toward the crowd with a shrug. *Poor Doris*, I thought, seeing her covering her mouth in dismay. Her newly anointed husband spun away, his hand on the back of his neck as the confused chatter grew louder.

I stepped away, looking around the crowd of guests as they whispered to one another, eyes firmly on me. I backed into Bogie, who had approached me from behind to save this damsel in distress.

"What lady?" he asked.

"There, in the window. The ghost!" I said, pointing to her again, but she was gone. "Didn't you get a look at her? She was inside, hanging!"

Bogie stepped closer, raising his hands to calm me. I continued to back my way toward the mansion as Doris approached. I wish I could have vanished into thin air after ruining her wedding. But, of course, I couldn't, and I ran into the house and locked myself in my room instead.

There was no need to listen to the whispering after that. The looks on their faces spoke louder than any words.

She's crazy.

Chapter 29

"What are you talking about?" Morgan asked Evelyn gruffly, his face flushed red.

"She knows!" Evelyn searched his stone face for a reaction before he turned away from her. "Where do you suppose she went after she left here?" She circled to face him again. "The painting. The necklace. Do you believe they're just coincidences?"

Morgan shuffled to the painting of the bed and breakfast on the wall, his voice sullen. "How I've longed to see her again."

"Have you gone mad yourself?" Evelyn asked.

"You know damn well who she is," he said, hoping it would strike more fear in her than she was showing, but not too much.

"And every girl who's entered this place over the last decade or so with a passing resemblance draws the same look from you. Don't tell me that's not true, because I've seen it. And for what? You believe she's come back to haunt us?" Evelyn scoffed and stuck a cigarette in her mouth. She lit it and took a deep, therapeutic drag. "I warned you all those years ago at that wedding. I warned you to avoid her and that madness she displayed." The smoke seeped out as she seethed, "But you wouldn't listen."

She focused her attention out the front window, rubbing the cigarette between her fingers. "You better not wait to find out what else she'll dig up next." She paused, giving him a moment to reply. "Rest assured, if you don't do something, I will."

Storming out the door, she was a black hole on a collision course with the sun, the moon, and the stars.

Chapter 30

Sunny wandered along the cove, small, choppy waves slapping its shore. A lone seagull cried in the distance, adding to her isolated feeling. Afraid to go anywhere for fear someone might recognize her, she was a prisoner inside her head and a slave to the anxieties that percolated there.

The last day's events left her full of dread. Yet she continued to believe there was some rational explanation for everything. These problematic beliefs were like her shadow, always with their twisted logic. They snuck up behind her at unsuspecting moments. There was never anywhere to run, for her shadow would always be right behind her.

She had come outside to clear her head and see firsthand where the wedding had occurred. Amid the knee-high grass near the river's edge, she touched its golden-brown tips swaying in the wind.

The path was still there, but dead weeds crept between the stones, many of which were cracked or broken. Like the house, Sunny wondered what effort it would take to make the lawn presentable.

Added to the list was the cobblestone garden bridge. From what she could tell, it appeared to be in good shape, albeit obscured by more tall grass. The wooden gazebo on the little island it led to was a different story. Its posts were wooden canes, keeping its skeletal frame standing. The whole thing slumped forward as if suffering from spinal stenosis.

Time and the elements hadn't been kind to Searchlight. It was hard to imagine the place teeming with people as it had been nearly thirty years before.

That day had started with so much hope, and the owner had worked hard to make it a big success. Events unfolded that derailed the wedding ceremony. The future of the bed and breakfast suffered as a result. Whatever happened here was nothing short of tragic. But it also left Sunny wondering what precisely the diary's author had seen. Then she remembered that a photographer had been present. It must have been Steven's father.

Her memory had been improving, but she remained fuzzy on the events since her hospitalization. Still, she recalled Steven's father being horrified to see a female in a white dress visible in a tower window in one of his photos. For whatever reason, he hadn't noticed her when he took the picture.

Based on the diary entries, the story Steven had told in class now had some validity. There were so many people here that day. Did someone wander into that room right at that moment? And what were the odds that they happened to be wearing white?

Sunny also recalled that Steven's father never spoke of it to anyone else for fear of being ostracized. His description of the sounds going silent and the moonlight disappearing also mirrored the author's experience.

It's as if you can still see her there in the window.

Sunny figured she was standing near the same spot the author had been during the wedding. She eyed the gazebo, then turned and looked up at the windows. Gauging the distance to the house, she backtracked a few steps and turned to look up again.

A leaf from a nearby maple tree spiraled in a free fall, its path crossing her view of the windows. Her eyes suddenly fixed on the tower, and she shuddered. The ghost of a female was staring at her—no, seemingly *through* her—as if she didn't exist.

Sunny's motherly instincts had her sprinting to the side door leading up to the tower, fearing for Rebecca's safety. She raced up the narrow staircase and entered the second-floor room, where Nadeen was admiring the freshly painted crescent moon on the door.

"Where is Becca?" Sunny cried, startling Nadeen.

"Why, sleeping. Where she was but ten minutes ago when you said you were stepping outside for some fresh air."

Sunny looked at the windows in the tower room, confused. "I . . . I thought . . . I saw something in the window."

"Something? Or someone?"

"Someone," Sunny replied.

"That was me. You were down in that overgrown yard. You looked a bit lost, staring at what was left of the gazebo. Then you looked up here."

Sunny rubbed her temples with a confused grimace. Her reaction proved somebody in the window could have been mistaken for someone else, especially if earlier thoughts or associations primed it. In other words, instead of seeing Nadeen, she saw the ghost in white.

And now here she was, feeling silly. Her face blushed crimson for a moment. Then a rhythmic tapping punctuated the growing silence.

Tap. Tap. Tap.

"I forgot to tell you. There's a leak here." Sunny pointed to the stained ceiling in the hallway. "Can you hear the water dripping?"

Nadeen stepped forward and looked up at the big brown spot. She appeared more concerned with Sunny though. "You seem very anxious. Are you sure everything is OK?"

Tap. Tap. Tap.

"Aside from getting very little sleep, yes. But that constant drip is driving me . . ." She dared not complete the sentence, groaning in frustration instead.

A rainbow of hazy, multicolored daylight bled through a stained-glass window onto a trapdoor that opened into the attic. Sunny placed her flashlight on the floor and hoisted herself up. A layer of decades-old dust billowed, sending her into a coughing fit.

She crouched as she meandered about a series of turns. Whoever built this place must have loved mazes. She followed a path she hoped would lead her to where the stain originated. After another turn, she pursued a streak of liquid on the floor. It cut through the thick layer of dust before fading away.

Beyond the next corner, the attic appeared brighter. She found an open area with a window casting more hazy daylight into the space. As her eyes adjusted, she picked up the liquid trail on the floor again, leading to a sight that gave her goose bumps.

A burial casket with a white cloth hanging from underneath its lid rested on the attic floor. She couldn't tell if the liquid was coming from the coffin, but it was pooling underneath it. Even so, the sight of the white cloth caused her heart to flutter.

"Oh, for Chrissakes, you've got to be kidding me."

She reached for the casket's lid, her hand trembling as her fingers fumbled around its edges. She unlatched it with a loud click. The coffin opened with a creak of its long-dormant hinges. As she held up the lid, she recoiled with a shriek—not from what was inside it but from what was *outside*.

Blurry figures gathered around the coffin: silhouettes against the golden light from the window. They were, in fact, shadows—or that was the best way she could describe them in her panic-stricken moment. Blurry shadows gathered around an open casket. She crept closer for a look inside.

It was a pale female corpse that seemed to be *her*, yet it was not. It had darker hair and a rope-like burn around its neck that remained visible despite a mortician's best effort to cover it up.

As she stepped closer, the attic grew darker. Clouds dimmed the hazy sunlight through the window. Then, like a magic trick, the shadows and the corpse in the casket were gone. There was nothing inside except a white burial dress, part of it draped over the coffin's side.

Sunny stared in disbelief, then confusion, holding her chest as her heart raced. Was it real? Or was the sun casting shadows, preying on her heightened anxiety and imagination? With a palm to her face, she wondered again if she was losing her mind. In a stupor, she found several paintings stacked against the wall behind the casket. One was of the old entrance sign described in the diary—NADIR BED AND BREAKFAST.

Tap. Tap. Tap.

She followed the sound of water dripping to a stack of items covered by a grimy plastic sheet. Indeed, the water was leaking from the roof and directly onto this. The tapping noise reverberated through the open part of the attic.

"Well, at least that noise has a rational explanation," she mumbled aloud. She grabbed a handful of plastic with her free hand and whisked it back, stirring more dust into the air. Ducking away from it, she covered her eyes and nose for several moments. Finally, she held the light to the items underneath.

One that drew her immediate interest was an old wooden cabinet. Or at least that's what she thought at first, but it was too short and had a lid. On the side facing her were two doors, and above them was an intricate design carved in the wood.

She pulled the plastic off, exposing a crank handle on the cabinet's right side. The lid had water damage, but the name Sonora was still legible in flaked gold print. As she lifted the cover, her eyes lit up. A warped record rested on an otherwise well-preserved antique turntable.

She moved the flashlight to the side and turned the crank several times. Then, she played with a few switches on the turntable before it began to spin. She placed the heavy arm on the spinning record. The scratchy sound of a muted piano played the beginning of "Dream Sweet, My Darling." Her eyes widened with joy at the familiar melody before she closed them, humming along for a moment, lost in its spell.

Dream sweet, my darling, the moon's shining bright,
She watches your window, and whispers, "Goodnight."
The stars weave a blanket to cradle your sleep,
While shadows stretch closer, their secrets to keep.

Sunny grinned as the song played through the first refrain without flaw. Her eyes roamed among several boxes, one with "baby stuff" scrawled on its side.

The record skipped, repeating the refrain three times—"While shadows stretch closer, their secrets to keep"—then continuing to the next verse. The needle tracked over the warped section of the record, distorting the sound. It now played with a sense of foreboding and dread, and the grin on her face flatlined as she stared at the boxes.

Hush now, don't stir, for the night's here to stay,
It carries your worries so far, far away.
But hold to your breath if the wind starts to call,
For not every voice means you're safe after all.

She was standing in her parents' house again, Becca fast asleep as she hummed the same tune. Boxes stacked near the closet caught her attention, and her father's muffled voice drifted through the register.

I can't say I wish to be around when she realizes what's happened. She'll probably end up with another stay at the center.

The record continued playing the haunting lyrics as Sunny reached for a box. She half expected to find Rebecca's clothes inside—the déjà vu was that strong.

The crickets are singing their soft lullaby,
While trees sway and murmur, "The time's drawing nigh."
The clock in the hallway ticks steady and slow,
Each chime marks a moment the dark seems to grow.

The needle repeatedly skipped back to "The dark seems to grow" as the warped music and lyrics slowed to an agonizing crawl before stopping.

The top of the box opened to a string of cobwebs with fuzzy pink baby pajamas clinging to them. She set the lid aside, dug into the box, and found a framed photo of a baby cradled next to a bosom. At last, she spied a clue: the pendant she had found earlier rested beside the baby's head.

Sunny flipped the frame over. Her manic fingers fumbled to undo the latch and remove its backside. Her heart sped up in anticipation as she slipped the photo out. She turned it over and found four words written on the back that shattered her entire reality:

Sunny, eight months old

The glass slipped from her hand, shattering into broken shards—part of the puzzle of the fragmented memories that haunted her. Sunny slumped against a wall and slid down it like a peeling, yellowed piece of wallpaper—she suddenly felt as abandoned and empty as this old mansion.

She drew her legs inward to her chest. Her teary eyes latched onto something gleaming in the corner. Something light, covered in part by plastic: a white crib.

Her mind spun as a new reality had come to light, resulting in more questions than answers. It also pushed her closer to the brink of a long, dark chasm. On one side was sanity, on the other . . . madness. Between was the fantasy that had been her life up until now.

Don't go squandering it worrying about the future. And don't waste it dwelling too much on what's happened in the past.

How could she wish to spend as much time as possible in the present when her current reality was a nightmare? She grabbed her hair on both sides of her shaking head and did the only thing she could do.

She screamed.

CHAPTER 31

Sunny apologized to Nadeen for not feeling well and withdrew to her room in shock for the rest of the day. While Nadeen understood, she expressed concern, having heard Sunny scream.

Stealing a page from the diary, Sunny said a bat had swooped down at her in the attic. After all, it wasn't an unusual occurrence here on the river. Had she told her the truth, however . . .

As she lay in bed, she thought about George and Martha not being her birth parents. This, of course, was what they meant by not even being honest with themselves, let alone Taylor.

Her emotions ran the gamut—anger, betrayal, sadness— all dovetailing into a growing numbness. How could she feel anything if she didn't even know who she was? Tears slipped from the corners of her eyes and down her cheeks. She thought about the conversations she could remember before all this happened. The rest were still locked away in some synapses in her brain. There they waited for a stimulus to bubble them back into her consciousness.

She had expressed concern about her father's amputation and wanted to know if it was hereditary. He'd snapped at her with a resounding no, knowing that if she'd inherited anything of concern, it was from her biological mother. Most likely, she'd been born here; that must be why the place seemed so distantly familiar. It also meant her parents might have known the owner or what had happened to her.

The other conversations that struck a chord in hindsight were the ones she'd had with her class about how our beliefs are often framed by those closest to us. Kyle had alluded to deceptive ideas parents use, such as Santa Claus. The irony both saddened her and made her want to laugh.

She had found a rational explanation for half her troubles. In her case, "Like mother, like daughter" didn't bring the comfort she wished. Quite the opposite. Adding to this, she didn't know who she was anymore. She might very well end up with another stay at the psych center after all. What she needed to do now to earn a free trip back was to start laughing and never stop.

Fortunately, there was more to this story. She knew she didn't have to look very far—the answer to whatever happened had to be in the diaries. One thing was certain:

her adoptive parents had been hiding something. As it turned out, Sunny was the skeleton in *their* closet. But she suspected Morgan and Evelyn had secrets they were keeping too. Other than the cryptic Madame Vanderhill, somebody in this town had to know something.

Before Nadeen left that evening, Sunny told her she felt better. Unafraid of what she might find, she made another trip into the tower room. After all, what could be worse than this? She took the flashlight and retrieved another diary, blowing out the candles in the hallway on her way back.

After tucking Rebecca in for the night, she was determined to get to the bottom of what had happened here. She knew that finding the truth would help her avoid returning to that place.

Hush now, don't stir, for the night's here to stay,
It carries your worries so far, far away.
But watch for the dreams that come knocking tonight,
Some bring only peace, and some never leave light.

Chapter 32

June 3, 1995

Business has suffered a significant drop-off recently. It started soon after the wedding last October, and it wasn't unexpected. That is when the tourist season shutters for the season. But still, I had held out hope that traffic would remain near the same level as last year.

I can sense the negative energy directed toward me whenever I visit Alex Bay. There is less of it in Clayton, and I can only guess that's because the news hasn't spread in that direction . . . yet. It's disheartening to dedicate so much time and effort to a business only to have your aspirations shattered by every whisper and stare. It's gotten to the point where I hardly leave the house, but that's not unjustified since I now have a child.

Since I first informed Bogie about my pregnancy, he has increasingly withdrawn from me. His behavior remains unchanged despite my reassurances that Sunny cannot be anyone's child but his. He disappears for extended periods, and I have caught him in the company of the woman with the dark hair. He tells me I'm either overreacting or imagining things when I confront him, as if I'm not already questioning my judgment enough as it is.

As Sunny gets older, he's been visiting more. He does bring gifts, hoping to make up for his earlier absence. One was a doll—an old, eerie porcelain doll. I don't understand why someone would gift such a hideous object to a baby. It's far too heavy for an infant, and the porcelain head makes the doll look sickly.

Moreover, this doll "speaks," reciting a nursery rhyme. It's so sinister that it sounds like it's from a horror story. I threw it onto the bed, and its sound was just as unsettling as its appearance. Hearing it the first time, I couldn't help but wonder if giving it to Sunny was an intentional effort to drive me insane. This thought arises because I fear he may be up to something more than just bonding with the baby. He could be looking for evidence to take her away from me. I can't imagine what else he could be after, except this house. After all, he has already had me.

It's not only the doll either. At night, I've been hearing noises coming from outside. Hushed voices in the darkness. I'm unsure whether I'm more disturbed by the thought of it being pranksters or not knowing the source at all.

And then there was what happened last evening. I make it a habit to keep my bedroom door locked after the sun goes down. I was sitting here rocking Sunny to sleep and humming her favorite song when footsteps came up the stairs.

These were no ordinary ones either. Heavy and plodding, they were the type a man makes, staggering after too many drinks. No guests were staying, and I wasn't expecting any late arrivals. The doorknob turned slightly, as it was locked, and made little noise. It then rotated in the opposite direction.

Then it was still, as if the person on the other side couldn't figure it out before wrestling with it for a few seconds. It caused such a commotion that, had I not known better, I'd have thought it possessed.

This was no ghost, at least not one hanging in the tower room.

Sunny began crying, and I did my best to hush her, faintly singing her favorite lullaby. The doorknob remained still. After a while, I got up with her in my arms, opened the door, and peered down the hall both ways; whoever it was had disappeared, but not without leaving a trace.

I caught the scent of the cologne I gave Bogie for his birthday: a fragrance of lemon, lavender, and vanilla mixed with the pungent aroma of bourbon. Aged bourbon, left to saturate in an old oak barrel. It smelled of somebody, three sheets to the wind.

I could envision Bogie, bottle in hand, shirt unbuttoned, and a black tie hanging loose from his neck as he stumbled down the hall. When I asked him this morning if he had stopped by last night, he said he didn't know what I was talking about.

The thought of an apparition hanging in one of these rooms is horrifying. But, it's nowhere near as terrifying as Bogie taking my sunshine away.

Chapter 33

For most of the night, Sunny lay awake, watching over Rebecca. When she wasn't doing that, she was reading and somehow lost track of time. There wasn't any sense in working herself up until she called her parents and got the truth out of them. Although she felt like she already knew the answer, she needed validation. She needed to hear from them, in their own words, what they knew of the situation. Then, and only then, could she tackle the questions about what she had read.

What bothered her most was whether the diary's author was her mother, and whether her suicide was the result of Sunny being taken from her. The overwhelming thoughts that came with this idea kept her awake until just before dawn. Then a nightmare woke her, leaving her in a cold sweat.

She dreamed she was back in the attic, walking through its maze with the lantern. Her shadow was behind her with every turn, threatening to catch up and overtake her. She tried to move faster but kept returning to the same place and repeating the pattern. The shadow remained right on her heels. Then she turned around and ran into somebody in the dark. As she raised the lantern to the mysterious person's face, she realized it was herself. She looked tired, older, cold, and haunted. That's when she awoke with a startle.

Though always fascinated with dream interpretation, Sunny did not like this kind. She had had her fair share of odd ones while pregnant with Rebecca, but she never tried to decipher them. This, however, seemed like an amalgamation of several things, not the least of which were Madame Vanderhill's comments: the older we are, the more we look back. The younger we are, the more we look forward.

It was also surreal, echoing, to some degree, her father's words of wisdom: don't squander time living in the past, and don't waste it worrying about the future. Of course, there were the shadows. Had her shadow caught up to her in her dream? Or had she become her shadow? She wasn't sure. Finally, there was what Madame Vanderhill had said about Nadir being the house of shadows, telling us what we fear. What we're afraid to feel.

Sunny pondered what "the end of matters" meant as she lay awake with the sun shining through the window.

It was all some metaphysical-existential nightmare bound to bring on a headache.

After some time in bed, she considered the consequences of making the phone call, realizing that there would be no turning back once she did. They would know her location, which could trigger events she wasn't prepared for. With a sigh, she recalled her father's voice drifting through the register again.

Damned if we do, damned if we don't at this juncture.

For only the second time since sneaking off in the middle of the night, Sunny wished she had kept her cell phone. "I need to make a phone call home," she told Rebecca. "But that means going into town, and there's only one place I know with a phone that has one with a little privacy."

It was time to go and paint a picture of the fear she was afraid to feel. But, in her sweeping strokes, she would need to bite her tongue. As much as she wanted to, avoiding using colorful language to express her feelings to her parents would be best.

Chapter 34

As Sunny approached James Street, it occurred to her that she didn't have a backup plan. Just because there was an old phone booth on the corner in front of the Antique Shoppe didn't necessarily mean it worked. She didn't recall seeing anybody using it, nor would she have expected to. Leaving anywhere without your cell phone nowadays was akin to going outside naked. She couldn't remember the last time she had used a landline.

The other thing she hadn't thought about was change. All of $1.25 in quarters jangled in her pocketbook. Fortunately, she remembered she was driving her father's car. After pulling up to a parking space farther down the street, she checked the ashtray. Quarters spilled out as she opened it, making her feel like she'd hit the jackpot.

Sunny walked down the block from the car to the phone booth. She shivered in the crisp October air invading the region as she reached the booth and looked around. She didn't want to look like an idiot if it wasn't in working order. Making this call was stressful enough without her looking as if she were crazy. Satisfied that no one was watching, she entered the phone booth and closed the door. Much to her relief, a dial tone was audible when she lifted the phone and placed it to her ear. A dead fly lay on the booth's small counter. Although harmless, it conjured the nightmarish sounds of loud buzzing.

Feeling it coming on again, she closed her eyes. "No, please, not now," she whispered to herself. The greenish feet with purple toes dangling above the floor flashed through her mind's eye.

Tap. Tap. Tap. The larvae fell to the floor. The sound of buzzing flies grew to a crescendo before stopping. When she opened her eyes, everything had returned to normal. A few people were strolling across the street, but nobody seemed to be paying any attention to her.

After she dialed the number, an automated voice instructed her to deposit one dollar for a two-minute conversation. The first quarter she attempted to put in the slot slipped from her trembling fingers, clanked off the counter, and bounced to the bottom of the booth. She glanced around the neighborhood again. After the next four quarters found their mark, she curled her hair behind her ear and waited for the call to be picked up.

"Hello?" Martha's weary voice answered.

"I want the truth," Sunny said in an even, determined tone. Judging from the momentary silence, she had caught her mother off guard.

"Sunny? Oh, thank heavens! Where are you?" After receiving silence in return, Martha asked, "The truth? About what, honey?"

"I was born in Alexandria Bay, a small village in the Thousand Islands, wasn't I?"

Cliff swept the sidewalk in front of his store down the street and briefly made eye contact before waving to her.

"The woman who gave birth to me owned a bed and breakfast in the area." She glanced back at Cliff, who appeared puzzled before he went back to sweeping.

"I-I . . ." Martha hemmed and hawed.

"It's true, isn't it?" Sunny cried out. "It's why this place feels so familiar. I must look like her too!"

"Sunny? Sunny, please . . ."

"All this time, you've lied and kept this from me. Why?" Sunny's soft sobs made Martha's voice crack. "Oh, Sunny. We wanted so much to have a child, but we were told I was . . . *broken* and would never be able to."

Composing herself, Sunny added several more quarters to the phone. She reached into her pocket and dumped a handful on the counter. Several rolled off onto the floor. She stacked the rest into columns of four.

"It was our first wedding anniversary, and we made reservations for late in the season. In October, at Searchlight Bed and Breakfast. Only when we got there—"

"You found its name had changed."

"Yes. It was odd. We didn't make much of it though. Your father assured me the owner remembered us."

"What was her name?"

"I don't recall, Sunny."

"If you adopted me, it would be on the paperwork."

"This was almost thirty years ago, and the lawyer handled it. Miss Dudley, if I remember correctly. We couldn't find anybody when we entered. Then we heard a faint noise from upstairs, like a faint knock. So we went to investigate, not knowing what to expect."

Sunny surveyed the neighborhood again, her eyes falling on the Antique Shoppe. Its storefront window, where Evelyn typically roosted, was empty, thank goodness.

"Halfway up the stairs, we were hit with a foul odor that led us to the end of the hall. I begged George not to go any farther. It was horrible, and the air was full of buzzing flies."

Sunny's heart thumped quickly as she looked at the single dead fly on the counter.

"A distant lighthouse's beam shone under the door, and shadows were moving from inside the room. We could hear the floorboards creaking, or so we thought."

Sunny's eyes widened at the mention of the lighthouse. "There was a crescent moon on the door, wasn't there?"

"Yes," Martha answered softly in a distressed voice. "She was inside the room. We couldn't make her out at first, with the lights off and everything. But the lighthouse's beam passed in short intervals through the windows, revealing little details each time. It was horrible. So horrible."

Sunny closed her eyes, trying to keep the images from haunting her. The yellowish-green feet. The purplish toes dangling above the floor—larvae dropping onto it, one by one. "She was hanging. And she had been for some time. That's what sounded like the floor creaking, isn't it?"

"Like I said, Sunny, it was horrible."

"What . . . what about me?"

"Your mother wasn't in the room alone. That's where the knocking was coming from, like a grim SOS. We looked toward the sound, and when the light came back around, we saw a white crib in the corner of the room."

Sunny deposited another two hours' worth of arcade games into the phone. Shaking her head, dismayed, she covered her ears, not wanting to hear what would come next.

"There was a wheezing sound coming from it. The stench in that room . . . we were overcome by it. If you hadn't uttered a soft cry . . . I don't know if we'd be having this conversation now."

Sunny closed her eyes again and swallowed hard. "What. Happened?"

"You were under a blanket. And the blanket was covered with flies. When I pulled it back, you reached up to me. A fly landed on your hand while your other hand kept hitting the wall."

Tap. Tap. Tap.

"We rushed you to the hospital. You weren't responsive when we got you there. But, by God's grace, you made it."

Sunny squeezed her eyes tight as if it would somehow stop her from hearing these words. "I don't understand."

"We were allowed to adopt you when nobody claimed you as their kin."

Sunny braced herself and asked what she had feared most with a dreadful quake in her voice. "What about my mother? She wouldn't have just left me like that."

"We never told you about her because we didn't want you to know she was sick."

"So now you think I am too," Sunny said through soft sobs.

"We didn't know what to think when all this started happening until—"

"She wouldn't have left me! I was all she had!" Sunny cried, letting go of the phone. Sliding down the booth's interior as far as possible, she held herself with the phone in her lap. Quarters rained down from their toppled stacks on the counter.

"Sunny? Please come home, baby."

Sunny got to her feet and left the booth. The phone swung back and forth, inches above the dead flies that littered the floor.

"Sunny?"

CHAPTER 35

While in Watertown, Taylor posted the missing person flyer in the local mall. Like so many others in the modern era, it looked deserted. Strolling through it left him wondering how the stores could afford to stay open. When he approached the food court, he realized many couldn't. There were more boarded-up storefronts awaiting new businesses than there were tenants themselves.

A cineplex and the mall's main entrance were at the far end of the food court. Posting a flyer here seemed the best option for foot traffic, as people still went to the movies. He taped one near the "Now Showing" posters on the wall and hoped for the best.

The next stop was downtown. There, he hung a few more around the public square. He then headed up a street, finding an intriguing building that appeared out of place. Greek Renaissance columns. Twin marble lions guarded its entrance. A large green dome. It all looked far too grand to be the public library, yet that's what it was.

Taylor entered and found himself staring at the artwork painted in the rotunda and the dome's interior. A bust of Governor Roswell P. Flower sat in the center of the room. A plaque stated that the library had been built in his memory by his daughter, Emma Flower Taylor. A library of this grandeur must have a reasonably decent research center. After milling about for half an hour, Taylor found what he was looking for on the second floor. Over the next two hours, he searched for information on the bed and breakfast in the newspaper archives.

It had opened in 1994, but further mention was limited to the subsequent year. The place had had several owners over the past two decades. Most had only owned it for a few years. It had sat vacant for long stretches before returning to the market. Before that, it was, as George had stated, a funeral home.

What caught Taylor's attention was its proximity to water. This was something Sunny had mentioned under hypnosis. He had taken her description to mean the psychiatric center, but both had "many rooms where people stayed for short periods."

He was about to seek assistance locating a photo of it when his cell phone rang with an incoming call.

"George?"

"Taylor, she is up around the Thousand Islands. She just called—"

"Wait, do you know specifically where?"

"No. She just called and spoke to Martha."

"How do you know she's up there then? You said the sheriff checked that place . . ."

There was a moment of hesitant silence before George continued. "There's something you should know. Something we didn't want to believe ourselves."

"I'm listening . . ." Taylor answered.

"We adopted Sunny as an infant," George said. Taylor could hear the tremble in his voice as he continued, "Her mother . . . she had issues right after she was born."

"What kind of issues?"

"I'm not exactly sure. They were psychological in nature, and she took her own life."

"Jesus," Taylor exclaimed with a sigh. "Do you have any other information? A name? Anything?"

"No, we knew the mother only as Miss Dudley. I don't know what happened to the adoption papers. We got married there the year before, when it was called Searchlight Bed and Breakfast. The following year, it changed to something else. We never knew if she had been married before having Sunny or not. We hired a lawyer for the adoption, but we didn't know much. Nor did we want to, considering the circumstances we found her under. Whatever you do, don't bother wasting time coming back here."

"I won't," Taylor said after a long pause. "George, I hope we're not too late."

CHAPTER 36

Evelyn was busy putting the final touches on a large banner. Covered with red, white, and blue stars, it read, "REELECT MORGAN ARBOGAST, VILLAGE OF ALEXANDRIA BAY MAYOR." The chimes over the door suddenly clanged, announcing someone's entrance. She looked up with surprise as Cliff strolled into the shop.

"What brings you here? I hope it's not to inform me I'm wasting my time with this banner and that you're withdrawing from the election."

"No, not quite," a sheepish Cliff answered. "I couldn't help but notice the gal coming over here the last few days."

"Who? That Rebecca?"

Confused, Cliff rubbed his chin. "Hmm. Maybe it's not her after all."

"What are you flapping your gums about?"

"I thought it was the same one," Cliff said, confusing her even more. "The missing girl."

"What missing girl?"

"In the newspaper. Didn't you read it? There was a story about it just the other day."

Evelyn dropped her thread and needle. She lifted the fabric and checked underneath before moving to the counter. After a bit of searching, she found the newspaper under some clutter.

"It was on the back page."

Evelyn flipped to the back of the paper. Her eyebrows perked up at Sunny's photo. "So it is." She read for a moment. "It says her name is Sunny. Why would she lie?" she asked rhetorically, continuing to read. "It says here her family is 'concerned for her well-being.'" She scoffed at the last bit.

"She was asking questions about that old funeral home out at the point, upriver. I thought perhaps you might know something."

Evelyn gave Cliff a sharp look before scuttling to her purse. She dug through it and found a cigarette. "I certainly know trouble when I see it waltzing in." She lit the cigarette and inhaled. "Though she's more the 'tripping' type if you catch my drift." She exhaled a plume of smoke in his direction.

"I should go and contact that number in the paper. I needed someone to verify it's the same girl."

Evelyn picked up the phone on the counter. "Don't trouble yourself. I'll have it called in before you're back to your store."

"Oh, that's very kind of you," Cliff said, opening the door.

"It's the very least I can do. Oh, and Cliff . . ." She waited for him to turn and acknowledge her. "Best of luck at the debate."

She set the phone back down as he exited. She picked up the newspaper again, and, as she read further, a devious smile spread. "And so it is."

Chapter 37

Sunny had never been as numb as she was driving away from James Street after the phone call to her mother. Yet a couple of blocks later, her shaking was so severe that she pulled onto a side street. She struggled to push the notion of inheriting a mental illness out of her mind altogether.

Her thoughts ran rapidly as she reviewed the discussion with her mother. Her parents had kept the truth and her identity from her all this time. And for what? Because they didn't want her to know that her birth mother was supposedly "sick?" That was ridiculous in and of itself. It only convinced her more than ever that something malicious had happened. There was no way her mother had committed suicide. And there was no way she left her child behind in a crib to be infested with maggots and flies as the days passed. Yet she couldn't deny that, other than murder, it was the only other plausible explanation.

First, her mother's pregnancy had been unexpected. Then, a psychic had warned her about seeing "shadows." Nobody appeared to know about that part. So when she started encountering something she couldn't explain, word quickly spread. She must be crazy. Furthermore, nobody understood she was fearful her baby would be taken from her. Nor did they know she had reason to believe she was being . . . "Gaslighted," Sunny said aloud.

Her mind rewound. Nobody appeared to know about her seeing shadows other than Madame Vanderhill. But how could a young teen be involved with something like that? The only other way anyone would know was if . . . "Someone had read her diary," she said to herself.

Saying that and *gaslighted* aloud put everything into a context she hadn't considered. One big problem still existed that was hard to overlook. She'd have to accept that tarot cards and psychics had some validity to come to this conclusion. That was asking a lot. One thing she didn't question: there were no such things as ghosts . . . except the ones that dwelled inside our heads. That much she was sure of.

This situation, however, called for having one problematic belief disprove another. If that were to happen, the first would prove to be unproblematic as a result. Despite some unexplained experiences, she wasn't ready for that leap of faith. Like her experiences, the tarot-related paranormal stuff would have to take a back seat and remain unexplained, at least for now.

As she drove away and turned right onto Route 12, it was already festering in the back of her mind. Regardless, it gave her something to think about rather than being abandoned. That had caused her all sorts of grief and unanswered questions. Coming to terms with the potential of never knowing what had happened or why would be one tall task.

Farther up the road, she passed the state police substation. Only three police cars were parked there. "That's three fewer on the roads," she muttered. That didn't ease her stress, knowing her doomsday clock had already started ticking. It might as well be two minutes to midnight as she slowed the car and turned into a parking lot.

There was one last place she wanted to visit before the proverbial clock struck midnight. Morgan had intimated that this place might be full of BS and tall tales. But it would be worth the risk if she found one pearl of truth among the suds, shots, and stories within.

CHAPTER 38

The neon sign in the window flickered THE HITCHIN' POST as Sunny approached, but that wasn't what caught her eye. It was the Halloween decoration on the entrance door—a ghost staring back as if taunting her. She rolled her eyes, though grateful there weren't any jangling bells over her head upon entering.

Save for some hazy sunlight from the windows, it was dark inside. As her eyes adjusted, she saw only three customers. Two were sitting at the bar, and the third was shooting pool alone in a corner. A bevy of bats and ghosts were hung throughout, not to mention a witch on a broom chasing ghosts on the blades of the ceiling fan.

Approaching the bar, she passed the two older men sitting along its short end. They looked like they'd come straight from fishing on the river, minus the poles. She sat on a maroon barstool at the bar's main stretch and glanced back at them. They stared at her a moment before whispering to one another. As she curled her hair behind her ear, the two men stood up. One tipped his baseball hat and yelled, "Catch you later, Sam," before exiting as if the building were on fire. The other gave one last mystified glance at Sunny on his way out.

"Take it easy now, you fellas," Sam, the bartender, who had a salt-and-pepper buzz cut, said. He turned to Sunny, sizing her up.

"Did I interrupt something?" she asked.

"You ever hear the one about the pretty gal who strolled into a bar and the two dirty old men who hightailed it out of there before she could even order herself a glass of the giggle juice?"

Sunny shrugged and shook her head. "Should I be worried?"

"Not unless you came in expecting a glass of fruit punch and a four-course meal," Sam said with a smile.

She could tell he wasn't quite sure what to make of her. "Have you ever been led to believe something, only to learn your entire reality is one big lie?" she asked.

"Miss, no offense, but all day and night long, my reality is helping other people escape from theirs. So what'll it be?"

Sunny managed a small smile. She looked beyond Sam to a tapestry of old newspaper clippings and headlines about local events on the wall. Searching for a list of brews, she found one on a chalkboard, but she couldn't read it from where she sat and gave up.

"I'll have a tall glass of your finest reality escaper then, please."

Sam's eyebrows raised, surprised. He picked a pint-size glass and showboated with a twirl of it as he walked the length of the bar. There, he poured a thick-headed, dark, and chewy beer. Its foam took a good minute or so to settle before he topped it off, returned, and placed it in front of Sunny.

She sniffed it before taking a small sip. "Mm. Imperial stout. Stone Brewing?"

By the look on Sam's face, his eyes wide and his jaw hanging open, she could tell he was impressed. "Not bad. Close, but still, not bad. Xocoveza imperial stout. Stone Brewing."

"Must be the Tres Leches edition," Sunny said with a smirk.

Sam threw a towel over his shoulder and walked back to the far end of the bar to check the tap. "Well, I'll be. You sure do know your shit."

"Blame my husband. He deals with people's reality all day long. This is his favorite way of escaping."

"Oh? What's he do?"

"He's a psychiatrist."

"Interesting. Of course, it doesn't help when people escape a little too far either."

"Tell me about it," Sunny replied with a knowing laugh.

"Bert, one of the guys here a moment ago, was out doing a little fishing on the river last night. Near the point, opposite the old funeral home. He said he saw 'the ghost' through the windows, roaming around inside, carrying a lantern and a child."

"The ghost" caught Sunny mid-sip, sending the stout down the wrong pipe. It was more like Choke-oveza. With a deep cough, she blew the foam off the top of the pint glass. This was yet another example of priming and the rational bias that came with it. There was no doubt that fisherman Bert had heard the ghost stories floating around town over the years. So, when he saw her in the window with Rebecca, he believed she was a ghost—much like she had when, in reality, it had only been Nadeen. *This will be interesting*, she thought.

"Yeah. You know what I mean," Sam said, seeing her smirk as he wiped the bar clean.

Sunny coughed a few times into her hand, clearing her throat. "You don't think he saw something else that could have given him that impression?"

"Sure. The bottom of—oh, about five too many pints of that stuff," he said with a nod to her beer.

"What if I told you he saw *me* in the window?"

Sam stopped mid-wipe and looked at her with utter shock. "I'd probably ask what on earth would possess you to go and do a thing like that?"

"I can't help what someone thinks or believes. Let alone what they think they see," she said with a slight laugh. "It's like with the owner and her supposed suicide—"

"I was there for that wedding at that bed and breakfast. Saw it with my own eyes."

"Saw what? A ghost?" Sunny questioned, catching Sam looking at her like he was checking her out.

"Saw her freak out. It's like she took her own life to prove she wasn't crazy. In my book, ya gotta be nuts to do something like that."

Sunny chuckled at the idea that Sam had a book. "You don't think there was any foul play involved?"

Sam looked as if she had just spoken a foreign language. "You mean murder? *Here?*"

"A little easier to swallow than some silly ghost story, right? Don't tell me that goes down smoother around here than a genuine mystery."

She caught him again, not looking at her so much as through her.

Sam's face flushed a deeper shade of merlot with every breath. "That sort of business doesn't happen here. No, ma'am. This community is respectable, with respectable people who raise respectable families."

"Of course, that's what you believe. You're part of that very same community." She punctuated her remarks by miming the look of disbelief being wiped from her face.

"And a fine community it is at that," Sam said. He distanced himself from her and went to the register, where he checked paperwork.

Sunny took another sip of her beer. "So why didn't anybody help her? Isn't that what respectable people in respectable communities do? Instead, she was ostracized and made to feel crazy and shunned in the process."

As Sam walked by her, he gave her a sideways glance. That he wasn't making eye contact was driving her up the wall. "If murder happened around here, people would have other things to discuss, is all."

Sunny kept an eye on him as he paced to the other side of the bar and made his way back. "Why would anybody make up some ghost story in the first place?" she asked as an epiphany struck. "Unless to cover up the truth?" She drank a big gulp of beer and slumped against the stool's backrest, wondering how she had missed that. Looking up at Sam, she caught him staring awkwardly at her bosom.

"Say, this might sound a little odd, but . . . my mother used to have a necklace like that."

Sunny looked down, realizing he'd been checking out the pendant she had forgotten she was wearing. "*Your* mother?" she asked in disbelief. The world had just turned upside down right before her eyes.

"Yeah. I got in trouble playing with it once. Trust me—it's hard to forget what it looked like after that. My pop spent a small fortune on it; at least for him it was. Even had it inscribed with something on the back."

Sunny's head was spinning. This wasn't making any sense. "What did it say?" she asked, not wanting to know.

"Gosh. That, I don't remember. Pop fell on hard times after she passed away. She was cremated, so he sold it at an antique store over there at the bay."

Sunny's spinning head came to a complete halt. It snapped up; the roller coaster ride she'd been on the last week had just slammed its brakes. "To Morgan?"

"Yeah, that's his name. The mayor. He's been collecting stuff since dirt was clean."

A sudden anxiousness swept through Sunny. The revelation landed like a roundhouse punch to the head. She could feel the color running from her face. The roller coaster was now speeding in reverse, giving her a bad case of whiplash.

It all made sense now. His behavior toward her, right from the start. His reactions to her repeating the phrases from the diary. The way he paused with a haunted look in his eyes when he helped her put the necklace on and saw her birthmark. *He knew.* And despite this all making sense in hindsight, she still found it hard to believe. Could it be true? Her stomach was now twisting into knots, and she could feel a cold sweat breaking out.

"Speaking of ghosts, you look like one snuck up behind you and tapped you on the shoulder," Sam said, concerned. He snapped his fingers. "'My dear' or 'my love.' Something like that on the back. Is it the same one?"

Sunny shook her head no as she attempted to avoid his eyes.

"Huh. I could have sworn . . . Anyway, it was years ago. The noggin here doesn't quite work as it used to."

"Tell me about it," Sunny said, finding it hard to swallow at the moment. She felt lightheaded and sick to her stomach. The purple toes. The lighthouse and its flashing beam. The flies. All these thoughts swarmed her mind and stung her heart.

"You know, I have an article about that woman somewhere . . ." His voice trailed off as he turned, eyes flicking over the wall, searching. Seconds stretched, thick and heavy, before he suddenly jolted. "Here!" His fingers landed on a brittle, yellowed clipping. He pivoted toward the bar—but Sunny was gone.

The front door eased shut with an almost deliberate finality. In her place: a near-full beer, beads of condensation slipping down the glass, and a ten-dollar bill resting beneath it. Sam stood frozen, breath shallow, heart pounding against the walls of his ribs. It was as if he had just seen a ghost.

A chill coiled around his spine, urging him to return to the article. The headline stared him down like an accusation: Inn Owner Found Dead, Leaves Orphaned Infant Behind. To the right was a grainy photo of Searchlight Bed and Breakfast. Sam's breath froze. A woman in the photograph's foreground bore an uncanny resemblance to Sunny. She had the same piercing eyes. The same quiet intensity, but her hair was dark. Beneath the image, a name.

Nadeen Dudley.

Chapter 39

Sunny spent the three-minute ride up Searchlight Road to the bed and breakfast with her mind traveling far faster than the thirty miles per hour her vehicle did.

She pulled up to the front gate and sat in the car for several minutes thinking. Not only trying to process all this information but also figuring out a plan. Part of that entailed anticipating what might come next. If there were ever a time to visit a psychic, now would be it.

There was little doubt of Morgan's involvement now. Though still uncertain what role Evelyn might have played, she didn't doubt her participation either. It seemed more likely that her mother had been someone on the side and Evelyn found out. Still, the gaslighting angle made sense. Sunny's connection to Morgan now casts his behavior in a new light, revealing a darker, more mysterious side. Not to mention the many more questions that arose with it.

She rubbed her temples, trying to remember if the diary's author had mentioned the ghost having dark hair. She assumed that Evelyn was the woman with raven hair in the off-white dress at the wedding. It was all starting to come together. But she still didn't know the answer to perhaps the most essential question: Why?

Why was she left behind in a crib with death buzzing around her?

Sunny looked around at her surroundings. She didn't want to park in the same spot after that close call with the sheriff's visit. When Nadeen had left the other night, she had parked on the opposite side of the cove. Her car couldn't be seen from the road there, at least not with most of the leaves still on the trees. But Sunny couldn't recall seeing a right turn anywhere from the road that would lead there.

She drove back from the front gate toward Route 12 and found a fork in the road within the first hundred yards she hadn't seen before. This was probably because the road to the right wasn't paved. There wasn't any apparent reason someone would go down that way. It was bumpy and shrouded in a canopy of apple trees. There were no turns or adjoining roads either. It led straight to the small clearing where she'd seen the car leaving the night before.

Parking here left her with just a short stroll to the bed and breakfast on what remained of a once well-worn trail.

During the walk, she began concocting a plan. By the time she reached the mansion, it had become something else altogether: a trap. She didn't have all the details yet, but it would require another trip to the dark labyrinth of shadows.

Guided by her flashlight and the waning daylight, Sunny didn't find the attic as challenging to navigate this time. Even so, it was no less shuddersome than the previous trip. She had found a couple of old sheets in one of the room's dressers. She rolled them up and tied their ends together, hoping their musty fabric hadn't become compromised and could bear some weight.

She reached the white crib, and an overwhelming sadness struck her. It was here she had been abandoned and left to die. She couldn't imagine anyone doing such a thing. Then she thought, *What if something happened to me? Would Rebecca face a similar fate?*

She pulled the remaining plastic off the crib. Pointing the flashlight's beam at it, she feared she might find its bedding covered with dead flies. Or, worse yet, still-squirming larvae. To her relief, nothing ghastly was there.

Once she reached the casket, she placed the flashlight on its lower half and averted her gaze as she lifted its lid.

She didn't want to risk witnessing anything unsettling there either. The white burial gown was still inside, and she grabbed it, letting the lid drop with a resounding slam. She picked up the flashlight and inspected the dress. It appeared to be in good condition.

Satisfied, she set it inside the crib, which fortunately had wheels so she could maneuver it to the trapdoor. Hesitant, she put her free hand on the crib's rail. She realized she was touching something that had been a cross between a prison and a crypt when she was an infant. Now, its wood was covered with dust. The moisture from humidity and the heat in the attic over the years had made it grimy to the touch.

As Sunny pushed it, the long strands of cobwebs clinging to it stretched to their breaking point. After she maneuvered the crib to the trapdoor, she removed the mattress and tossed it down into the hallway below. Then, tying one end of the bedsheet to one of the crib's legs, she lowered it. As it neared halfway, she noticed Spook looking up from the hallway floor.

Surprised, she felt the flashlight slip from her hand. It bounced off the crib and smashed onto the floor, scaring the black cat away. "Shoot!" she said, watching the light dim to a faint glow before going out. She descended the pull-down ladder and grabbed the flashlight, attempting to turn it off and on again. It appeared dead or broken.

She shook it, then banged it against her thigh to revive it with no luck. "Great."

After pushing back the ladder, Sunny looked down the hall and called out the cat's name. "I guess I spooked Spook away," she said and proceeded to her room. There, she quietly checked on Rebecca, sound asleep on the bed. She held her hand out to brush the whispers of dark hair from Rebecca's forehead, then pulled back at the last moment. Though not superstitious, she didn't want to touch her baby after handling that filthy crib.

"Dream sweet, my darling Becca. Mommy needs to clean this crib and move it into the other room along with the bed. That way, Mommy can watch out the window and not worry about waking you up. How's that sound?"

Of course, there was more to her plan than that, but she still had to work the details out and get some supplies. And she needed to move fast before anybody else came snooping around.

First things first, though. After setting up the tower room, she wanted to read more of the diaries before turning in for the night. The more she knew, the better prepared she would be to lay the perfect trap.

The World's fast asleep, but there's more to be told,
Where whispers grow colder and stories grow old.
So close your sweet eyes, and drift into sleep,
Where lullabies linger and shadows still creep.

Chapter 40

October 24, 1995

What a difference a year makes. I used to love fall. The cool, crisp mornings displacing the hot and humid summer days. The scents and sights of the leaves turning. Their crunchy sounds underfoot when taking long walks around the point here. It all marks a season of change.

It's saddening to think it was only twelve months ago that Searchlight had its finest hour. It seems unreal that it's been that long since Doris was to have her big day here. It was a change of season for her, representing a moment when everything seemed possible. It was true for me too, with my first child on her way. Whether Bogie was to continue to be a part of it remained to be seen.

Everything was going as perfectly as it could be that day, but the wheels fell off.

A year later, I'm haunted by the sights and sounds of some maligned spirit and the surroundings I once loved. Looking over to the cove, I can still hear the children laughing before the wedding ceremony. They had chased one another around, crossing the stone bridge and back, teasing all the while. The only noises present now, at least during the daylight, are the cries of the seagulls. Those and the waves crashing on the shore might very well be the loneliest sounds on earth.

The cool, crisp fall mornings now make the ground feel as cold as the touch of a tombstone on a winter's day. And what of the fallen leaves? Their bright reds, oranges, and yellows decomposing into brown nothingness. Even the trees appear lifeless after last week's windstorm. The gray October skies mourn the passing of another season with continuous rain.

The daylight dies a little earlier every day, darkness arriving and snuffing it out. Soon, the cold, wet, dead leaves and ground will lie in state until they're buried under a cocoon of snow and darkness.

There, life will wait to be reborn with yet another season's passing.

The end of another season brings the slow death of a dream; I hold its cold hand with every grasp of the front doorknob. Bitter heartache felt with every twist I make, each bringing me closer to the last. At some point, the doors will be closed for good. What will become of this place? Will it be reborn as something else?

I should have continued its use as a funeral home. Of course, one doesn't worry about building a clientele with those.

In the last month or so, I've lost twelve pounds. Getting a good night's sleep is only a dream. When I manage to sleep—or should I say, when Sunny allows me to—I'm startled awake by nightmares. The deceased who used to lie in wake here had more restful nights than I have these last few weeks. Judging by the brown, leathery handbags under my eyes, I'm sure they also looked better.

And then there's the sudden death of romance itself. How strange that it started so innocently and then fell apart, going through its own cycles. A seed planted during the fall resulted in new life late this spring, becoming the glue that keeps me together. Sunny is the beacon in my life who keeps me grounded. She helps me see through all this darkness and stormy weather during these changing seasons.

October 25, 1995

It's beginning again—the voices at night, whispering in the dark outside. I heard footsteps on the front porch but didn't dare look out the window. Instead, I grabbed Sunny and held her tight most of the night with my eyes on the bedroom door. Even though Bogie doesn't come around as much, he still has a key. I fear his returning in another late-night drunken stupor and what it may result in.

I sat on the bed for what seemed like an eternity. With Sunny in my arms, I repeated, "I'm not crazy, despite what they say; please don't let them take my baby away." Whenever she fussed, I hummed "Dream Sweet, My Darling" to settle her down.

Then, when she fell silent, I tried not to think about the noises I heard. They seemed to be coming from outside and down the hall in the tower room.

I never once contemplated calling the police. As if they aren't aware of the public's perception of "that lady out at the point." The one who rarely leaves her bed and breakfast despite claiming it's haunted. How would I address the situation? Tell them I hear things? That they should come and check them out? I would be writing myself a one-way ticket to some institution. Or, at the very least, giving Bogie ammunition to take Sunny from me. I can see him now, requesting that I be held for observation and taking her.

When I awoke this morning, I went outside to investigate the night's noises. Standing in the thick fog, I read "crazy" spray-painted in red across the front door. The paint had dripped onto the porch's floor in long trails resembling blood as if to scare or intimidate me.

CHAPTER 41

Sunny read the diary aloud, sitting on the edge of the bed, now relocated to the tower room. A lantern with a melted candle and its flame clinging to life sat on the floor while sunrise bathed the room in an orangish-pink glow.

"Though I have no proof of who did it, I know he thinks I'm crazy by how he looks at me. I've debated whether to call, invite, and have it out with him. The only thing that stops me is Sunny and an indescribable sensation in my gut. I can't help but believe something horrible will happen when he's near."

Sunny tossed the diary onto the floor in disgust. It landed with a dull thud, its pages fanning in the air as it lay on its spine. "They did something to her," she said, hovering over Rebecca in the crib. "And then covered it all up with lies nobody questioned."

Something to the right of her field of vision caught her attention. Turning, she realized it was just her reflection in the mirror on the other side of the room. She eyed herself in it, her voice dreamy. "But then I showed up." Her gaze dropped to the pendant on her chest. "And *I've* been haunting them ever since."

Her head snapped to the windows as a thought struck her. She touched a pane of glass, struggling with a memory from Steven's retelling of his father's story. A student had asked a question, but what was it? She closed her eyes and rubbed her temples with a grimace.

So ... who was in the window?

Sunny's eyes snapped open, searching outside and landing on the fog-covered cove.

My father swore it was the woman who passed by him that night.

"It was Evelyn," Sunny said aloud. "It was Evelyn in the window. It was her on the road too. And it was Evelyn I saw leaving in the car the other night. She suspects I somehow know, and now she's ..."

Sunny slumped her shoulders and lowered her head. "But that sounds like I'm being paranoid, doesn't it, Becca?"

"No. It doesn't."

Nadeen's voice startled Sunny.

"How long have you been—?"

"Long enough."

Sunny flipped a strand of hair behind her ear and bit her thumb, considering it for a moment. Finally, she heaved a defeated sigh. "But who's going to believe me?"

Nadeen picked up the old porcelain doll next to Rebecca in the crib and brushed its hair back. "They will . . . if you give them proof."

"I have a plan, but I need some help."

"As you know, help can be hard to come by around here . . . unless you know just the right person," Nadeen said, flashing a vindictive smile.

Later that morning, Sunny searched her grocery bags and found the midnight black hair dye. The instructions noted to start at the roots and apply the color mixture to dry, unwashed hair. That was perfect, except it needed rinsing after twenty-five minutes.

Searching the second floor, she found a bucket in one of the bathrooms. She strolled to the backyard and filled it with ice-cold water from the river by the cove. "This will be one hell of a shock to the system," she said.

Back inside, she squeezed the contents of one of the tubes into the bottle provided. Then she shook it until the color was well blended and applied it all over her blonde hair. Finally, she worked it from the roots up and through to the tips.

While waiting for her hair to be ready to rinse, she took the other canvas she'd started at the hospital and set it against a window. She stared at *"Lies"* scrawled at the bottom for a long moment. Then she dipped her paintbrush into some syrupy red paint and added the word *All* before it in quick strokes. For good measure, she added an exclamation mark at the end and watched the color run down the canvas.

When she stepped back to eye the painting, Sunny caught a whiff of the dye in her hair.

"Oh lord, this stuff stinks like rotten eggs!"

A moment later, Rebecca began fussing in the crib. Sunny looked through her suitcase and found the bottle of her favorite perfume. She spritzed her neckline and wrists a couple of times. A cloud of dark roses, spicy cinnamon, tart berries, and gothic incense enveloped her in moments.

"Don't worry, Becca; I won't spray you. You're much too delicate for this. I'm just going to give Ms. Carmella here a little dab."

After spraying the porcelain doll's fabric, she picked it up and set it against the opposite end of the crib. There, it worked its magic on Rebecca, casting its spell and settling her down.

Turning back to the painting, Sunny dipped the brush into the paint and worked on the canvas. In quick, aggressive strokes, colors splattered off the surface and onto the floor. Stepping back again, she eyed her work.

Van Gogh had only cut off one of his ears. But Sunny wanted this frenzied piece of fairy tale turned nightmare to look like its artist had lopped off both. She dipped the brush into the red paint again, splattering it onto the canvas. Her arms flailed like a priest throwing holy water during an exorcism.

She cracked a devious smile at the added effect.

All Sunny needed to do now was wrap the picture up and polar-plunge her hair. Then she would visit the Antique Shoppe and give them something to squirm over. Her smile grew as she imagined their reaction. Then, suddenly, Spook, in heat, shrieked one of the baby-like cries that still managed to send a chill down her spine.

She turned to the cat in the doorway, knelt to it and said, "Hey, girl," as she rubbed its neck. "Play around with ghosts, and you're bound to get spooked."

CHAPTER 42

Sunny drove down Church Street and into the village, taking the same route as before. She used the side roads to enter James Street from Miller Avenue, making it feel as though she was in the middle of a sneak attack.

There were few people out and about on the crisp late-October afternoon. Nothing but a few fair clouds fluttered in the sky on an otherwise typical fall day. A slight wind stirred a pile of leaves, sending them down the sidewalk toward the Antique Shoppe. From there, they inexplicably blew in a different direction and across the street as if fleeing it.

Sunny parked the car in front of the Gift Zone, a shop two doors down, and tilted the mirror to check herself. Her hair, now a bewitching black shade with a midnight-blue sheen, had dried. It gave her a moody look and complemented her perfume's gothic edge. They'd be able to smell her coming a mile away.

Satisfied, she slid the mirror back into place and smiled at Rebecca's reflection in the rear car seat. After a steadying breath, she stepped out of the vehicle. She retrieved Rebecca first, threading one arm through the car seat handle so the baby faced her. With her free hand, she pulled the seat's visor down as far as it would go, then grabbed the wrapped-up painting.

The 130-foot distance to the Antique Shoppe was like walking a plank in high heels. Blindfolded. Her nerves were on edge, much as they had been before her high school basketball games. In those days, she'd spend ten minutes in the bathroom before tip-off. While her stomach always tied itself into knots, she was all business come game time. This, however, was different; it would take more than just putting her game face on to see this through.

Though a short distance, time seemed to slow as the wind blew the leaves past her. It was one of those moments full of little details she knew she would remember for the rest of her life—her anxiety spiking as she approached the store. The leaves tumbled down James Street. The long October shadows stretched before her on the ground. The scent of a wood-burning oven wafted in the chilly air. They were all specific sensory moments combined to mark a significant event in her life, yet to be played out.

She didn't know how it would end, but she didn't doubt it would never be forgotten.

The cozy aroma in the air would have been almost enough to relax her had she not been heading straight for the black hole's lair. The smoke from that beast's lungs would not be pleasant. As she approached the white picket fence in front of the Antique Shoppe, her stomach sank at the sign hanging on it: REELECT MAYOR ARBOGAST—DEBATE MONDAY NIGHT, OCTOBER 25, 6:30 PM.

"That's tonight," she said. That put her plan in doubt. Maybe she should stop, but she knew she was running out of time.

It was too late. Evelyn had seen her through the window.

"I don't know if she recognized me, Becca." She looked around the neighborhood, biting her lower lip. "Nadeen will be back in a bit, though." She sighed. "It's now or never. Damned if you do, damned if you don't. Damn straight." She strode down the sidewalk to the entrance. She struggled to open the door with the painting and Rebecca in her arms. Once she was inside, Evelyn's icy, shocked glare greeted her before changing like a chameleon.

"Who did you bring to see us today?" Evelyn asked, sounding cheerful while angling to see inside the car seat. "Oh, isn't she adorable?"

Sunny spun Rebecca away from her view. "Is Morgan here?"

"No, not right this moment." Evelyn looked away toward several customers milling about the store.

"That's all right. I thought I would drop off another painting."

Sunny placed the covered canvas next to the counter, hoping to make this visit brief and unnoticed as possible.

Evelyn lowered her voice, eying the customers warily. "Why don't you just leave him alone?"

"I beg your pardon?" Sunny asked loudly enough to draw a few curious glances. Evelyn's smile flickered into place—forced, plastic, like the lighthouse's beam signaling: *warning, danger ahead.*

"If I were you, I would pack my bags and leave this town before—"

"Before what? I intend to hang around here for some time to come."

Evelyn clenched her jaw as more heads turned. She waited for them to mind their damn business.

"I know what you're trying to do."

"And I know what you've done," Sunny said, her voice rising like a flare. Now every customer was watching. "Yes, it's a shame he's not here. Anyway, I must run along."

"Don't you mean run away?" Evelyn pushed the newspaper on the counter toward Sunny; the prying eyes fell on her now. "They're looking. Only a matter of time, a sick girl like you."

Sunny took an anxious step back, nodding to the wrapped painting. "I added some personal touches to this one. I hope you both enjoy it and have a place to hang it," she said before hurrying past the whispers and stares.

"Give baby Rebecca a kiss for me, won't you, Sunny?" Evelyn said, her smile withering as her eyes fell on the covered picture.

Sunny hurried to the phone booth, reaching into her pocket for loose change. She set Rebecca on the small counter and dialed a phone number. Evelyn was perched in the Antique Shoppe's window, glaring back at her.

She put two dollars' worth of change into the slot and waited for the call to connect.

George's calm voice answered on the other end. "Hello?"

"Dad, listen to me," Sunny rushed frantically. "She believed she saw a ghost, and everybody thought she was crazy."

"Sunny, calm down. Where are—?"

"He wanted to take me from her. She thought she was being gaslighted and was afraid for her life!" She paused, listening to a commotion on the other end before Martha spoke.

"Honey? You have us so worried."

"Mom, listen! If people believed she was crazy, nobody would suspect a thing if it looked like suicide."

"Sunny, you're scaring us."

"I don't have time for this!" With a sigh, she started again in a softer voice. "I know you wanted to protect me from what you believed to be the truth, but it was all a cover-up." Sunny looked up and saw an elderly couple approaching with curious eyes. "Everybody bought it, including you and Dad."

Martha's tear-stained words pleaded, "Sunny, Taylor is looking for you. Please call him. Please come home to us."

As the elderly couple passed by, Sunny spotted Madame Vanderhill on the opposite side of the street, looking directly at her and holding her gaze.

"If something happens, know I would never abandon Rebecca like that. Ever!"

Madame Vanderhill nodded to her, then made her way briskly down James Street.

"Honey, please—"

Sunny hung up the phone, giving Evelyn one last look in the window. She then watched Madame Vanderhill turn down a narrow street opposite where she parked.

She hurried out of the booth with Rebecca and headed to the small alley. Sunny looked down what appeared to be a fire lane, but there was no sign of the fortune teller.

It was just as well. Everything was set in motion, and she couldn't afford to let the sands of time slip away. She needed to get back to the mansion and finish what she'd started with her trap. They wanted people to believe this ghost nonsense, and she was determined to give them one in return.

CHAPTER 43

The black BMW pulled up to a tavern off Route 12. Inside, Taylor stared at a stack of missing person flyers on the passenger seat. Unshaven and with dark bags under his eyes, he looked like a man who hadn't slept much in the past week.

Earlier, he had found the location of the bed and breakfast George had spoken of. However, there was no sign of a car in its vicinity, nor anyone there when he peeked through the porch windows. The only thing to note was tire tracks near the gated entrance, which could have been from the sheriff's visit.

He'd spent the afternoon driving along Route 12 between Clayton and Alexandria Bay. Along the way, he stopped at gas stations, convenience stores, and everywhere in between. He shared the flyers and asked if there had been any sightings, with no luck.

Moments ago, he had received a phone call from an upset Martha, who had just spoken to Sunny. She was upset and frightened by some of Sunny's words about a murder cover-up made to look like a suicide.

Taylor wasn't surprised. This had begun during her pregnancy and continued with more frequency through therapy. He pulled his little cassette recorder from his satchel, hit the play button, and listened.

I've just learned that I'm pregnant.

Have you any fears about becoming a mother?

Not knowing what to do, feeling helpless. Overwhelmed. Not bonding with my child.

Let us go to a time when you're afraid. A time when your current symptoms are present. Can you tell me where you are?

Taylor hit the stop button, rewound, and pressed play again.

Let us go to a time when you're afraid.

Stop. Rewind. Play.

Let us go to a time.

He stopped it again, frowning. Something about the passage didn't seem right, but he couldn't put his finger on it. Shaking his head in frustration, he fast-forwarded the tape and pressed play.

I'm not crazy, despite what they say; please don't let them take my baby away.

He stopped the tape and shoved the recorder into his pocket, defeated. He grabbed a flyer and headed to the tavern's entrance. A neon sign flashed on and off in its window: Hitchin' Post.

Taylor approached the bar with the flyer in hand. Sam sized him up before asking, "What can I get you, friend?"

"Mind if I hang this in your entrance window? It's for a missing person." He handed Sam the flyer. "It's my wife."

Sam looked at it and set it down as if it were cursed.

Taylor recognized his body language. She had more than been there; she had made an impression that left him shaken. "You saw her."

Sam hesitated as he glanced at the flyer, his voice shaking as he leaned forward. "Ever hear the one about the pretty gal who strolled into a bar and the two dirty old men who hightailed it out of there before she could even order herself a glass of the giggle juice?"

Taylor shook his head, confused.

"That's because it was no pretty gal they saw. It was a ghost."

Chapter 44

We don't have time for this," Evelyn insisted with a glance at her watch as Morgan stood before the wrapped painting. She flipped the sign on the entrance to read CLOSED and turned back to him. They were both wearing their Sunday best clothes for the debate. "We are running behind. Before long, the only thing left to debate will be your absence."

Ignoring her, Morgan grabbed one corner of the wrapping and peeled away a strip. Evelyn stomped to his side and ripped the rest of the paper off in two manic tears. Morgan stumbled back, mouth agape.

Blotches and streaks in the crudely expressionist painting portrayed a woman hanging. She wore a white dress, and the tower's windows were recognizable in the background. It was a portrait of madness, as if a six-year-old had painted the nightmare that had kept them awake the night before. Even the woman's limbs were a gross exaggeration. Her black hair was nothing more than long, frantic strokes over her face. Between the strands of hair were large, bulging eyes staring straight back at them.

Below the hanging corpse was the accusing phrase, dripping in blood red: "All Lies!"

Evelyn gasped and stood frozen for a moment. Coming to, she looked around and found a long antique iron candle holder. She grabbed and attacked the painting with it, gashing the canvas with several blows, then sent it tumbling down an aisle with one swift swing.

She gasped to catch her breath. Her tight bun of black hair had come loose; long, straight strands fell over her face. Had she looked in a mirror just then, she would have mistaken herself for the image in the painting.

Morgan trudged to the safe behind the counter and pulled out the satin box. Mumbling to himself, he shuffled to the door like one of the living dead.

Evelyn cut him off, flashing the newspaper article in his face. "It shouldn't surprise you to see she's sick," she said, each subsequent word louder. "Just like her mother!"

The sorrow in Morgan's eyes turned to pity. "It's never been about me, Evelyn. It's always been about you, hasn't it? What *you* think. How *you* look. It was my life that changed forever that night, not yours. Or maybe it's that you never had one of your own to begin with."

"She is going to ruin you!"

"That's it, isn't it?"

"Say what you will of me. Can't you see what she's doing?"

Morgan stared at the painting of the inn, the anonymous donation received years ago. Hanging on the wall, it was an eternal reminder that held him a prisoner to the past. An everlasting curse that had had him under a foggy spell ever since. "I see what you've been doing to me all these years ... and you'll never let me forget it, will you?"

"You wouldn't listen. You should have stayed away from her!"

Morgan attempted to brush by Evelyn. She halted him with a maniacal smile, her voice crackling with euphoria. "We can do it again. It will be perfect!"

Morgan unleashed a slap to her face that echoed through the empty store. She stood in a shocked daze. A sudden, wailing cry segued into unhinged laughter, unnerving him.

"What have you done?"

"I'm only trying to protect you as I've always done!"

Morgan looked her over from head to toe, unsure what to make of her. "You're the one who's crazy," he seethed, opening the door. "As am I, for having listened to you in the first place." He punctuated his exit by slamming the door on his way out.

Evelyn gazed at him through the window, the newspaper shaking in her hand. She ripped it down the middle of Sunny's photo and shredded it further and further into oblivion in a fit of rage.

Chapter 45

Sunny parked at the gate, hurried upstairs to the tower room, and placed Rebecca in her crib across from Miss Carmela. The doll's fabric still wafted a dusty gothic rose from that single spray. Sunny inhaled, the incense-heavy elixir soothing her nerves. The scent would undoubtedly stay on the doll and its fabric for months, making it a lovely room freshener. It overwhelmed any remaining smell of the hair dye in the air; that was certain.

She looked out the tower's windows facing the half-circle driveway. The sun cast an orange glow through a row of maple trees, their tops a mixture of fiery yellow and red as the sun set. Their shadows had grown long, covering most of the ground leading up to the gates. Soon it would be dark, and this lonely road had no streetlights. Any vehicle would need to have its headlights on, helping her spot them in advance as they approached.

Like grains of sand falling in an hourglass, the waning light outside was the only harbinger of time. It reminded her to place the remaining candles on the sconces between the windows in the tower room. She hoped these, along with the rising Hunter's Moon, would be enough to offset the impending darkness a bit.

After placing and lighting the candles, Sunny paced the room, looking out the windows every few moments. She alternated between wringing her hands and tucking a strand of her dyed hair behind her ear. Her growling stomach prompted her to struggle to recall the last good meal she'd eaten. Unfortunately, her hunger, like everything else, would have to wait.

The white burial dress and tied-together sheets were where she had left them on one of the windowsills. It was now her time to wait; she settled into a chair and looked out the window. There, she waited for the show to begin, or so she hoped. She wondered if Morgan and Evelyn had seen her gift yet.

She'd opted to call the painting *The Truth Hung by a Precarious Lie*. Even though she liked *Portrait of a Hanging Lady* and the brevity of *All Lies*, she found the first more fitting. She liked the idea of a lie unraveling after all these years under the weight of the truth until it all fell apart. This was her goal, but it was another take on the dichotomy of things. As with shadow and light, it painted vivid imagery in one's mind. It also spoke to the weight of the burden on those who knew the truth but chose not to tell it.

Suddenly, Sunny heard what sounded like the old organ playing. She followed the slow, melancholy tune down the hallway, down the stairs, and into the gathering room.

Nadeen sat at the organ. She stopped playing when Sunny entered the room.

"I didn't know you were even here," Sunny said. "I passed through only moments ago." She moved closer, concerned by Nadeen's disheveled appearance. Her sweater hung open, exposing dark green, gray, and purple bruises around her neck. "What happened?"

"He . . ." Nadeen began, her gaze drifting off. She then looked at Sunny, her eyes filled with a distant sorrow. She attempted a smile but turned away instead. "I always wanted us to be together, but I never thought it would end like this, despite seeing it coming."

"Your fiancé did this to you?" Sunny asked, angered. "Does he know about this place yet? All the work you've put into it?"

Nadeen rose from the organ, searching around the room as if she were breathing it all in for the last time. "None of that matters any longer. He'll be here soon enough," she said. "The truth will come out then, and this will all be laid to rest."

"Truth?" Sunny asked, confused; she couldn't comprehend what had transpired. Was it because Nadeen had been spending so much time away from him, fixing this place up? Then she thought of her situation. She knew full well what might transpire if and when Taylor were to arrive here.

Just then, a car door slammed.

Sunny opened a curtain to peer outside, realizing the room didn't offer a view of the mansion's front yard. She turned to Nadeen and looked in the direction of her gaze, toward the foyer and the front entrance door. Heavy, plodding footsteps thumped onto the porch. A shadow materialized through the door's frosted window moments later.

"I'll make him see how wrong he is," Sunny said, charging the door, determined to set Nadeen's fiancé straight. She wouldn't let him get away with mistreating her.

When she opened the door, she stood surprised at the man barely recognizable before her.

"Taylor?"

Chapter 46

For the briefest of moments, Sunny's anger subsided at the sight of her husband. With his baggy eyes and sunken cheeks under a week's beard growth, he looked like a contestant on *Survivor*. From the confusion on Taylor's face, it seemed he could scarcely identify her as well, with her golden locks dyed black. They both might as well have been wearing Halloween costumes.

"I was wrong," Taylor acknowledged as he cautiously entered the foyer and looked around. "I shouldn't have tried taking Rebecca from you." His eyes searched the floor as he shook his head, genuine in his remorse. "I know that now, but it's time to let go so we can all move on."

Sunny covered her ears and closed her eyes with a grimace. "I didn't deserve to be treated like some lunatic and kept in that hospital!" Her voice trembled with hurtful anger. "To have my memories wiped completely away. Do you have any idea what that was like?"

Taylor took another step forward. "The world you're living in . . . it's not reality."

Sunny laughed. "Reality? Do me a favor and define that for me. Because you must mean waking up one day and discovering you're not who you thought you were. That you weren't born where you believed you were. Or your parents aren't who you thought they were and have kept the truth hidden from you all these years. You must be talking about that reality, right?"

"I know," Taylor said, raising his hands. "George told me about your past. Your mother. He also informed me of her illness."

"She didn't kill herself any more than she saw some ghost." Sunny looked toward the grand room's entrance. "Ask Nadeen. She'll tell you."

Taylor followed her gaze, eyes falling back to her as he desperately pleaded, "Sunny, come with me. Please."

Nadeen crossed to the foot of the staircase and rested her hand on the railing's finial.

"Women are more at risk of developing peripartum psychosis if there is a history of it in the family." He inched another step closer.

"As you can see, I did a good job making this place up too. The door with the moon on it upstairs. The—"

"Because you've been here before!" Taylor snapped back, pursing his lips before taking a deep breath.

"That's right. Relax. Breathe easy. In and out. You're doing good," Sunny taunted as she looked out the window. The full Hunter's Moon was now ascending above the treetops. "I don't have time for this."

"Hallucinations. Insomnia. Paranoia. Delusions." Taylor inched closer. "You've stopped taking your medications," he said, taking another step. "And now you're experiencing all these, aren't you?"

Sunny rubbed her temples with another grimace. Then she turned and watched Nadeen as she went up the staircase.

"You've created this fantasy to justify the world as you want it to be."

"Like you believing that I have some psychosis justifies taking Becca from me, right?" she asked, matching his progress with a step back toward the staircase.

Taylor held up the mini-cassette recorder as she retreated and pressed play. Her voice recited the repetitive chant, sounding paranoid.

I'm not crazy, despite what they say; please don't let them take my baby away.

Sunny covered her ears.

"Don't you see what everyone's afraid of?" Taylor asked.

She shook her head, betrayed.

"You're already at the edge," he warned, reaching into his blazer and withdrawing a syringe.

Tears streamed down Sunny's cheeks as she groped her head at the foot of the staircase.

"You refuse to hear that—"

"Please don't do this," she pleaded, reaching for the railing behind her.

"—what you're searching for is the very thing you're running from."

Her hand found the post's decorative marble finial and took a firm hold of it. Her voice quivered. "You're not taking her from me. I will count from ten, and you'll feel something hit you like a ton of bricks." Her voice rose to a scream, and she swung the loose finial at Taylor as he lunged for her. "And you will sleep like a motherfucking baby!"

The heavy marble ball connected with the side of his head, making a dull thud and dropping him to the floor like a bag of bones. "Ten," she said softly, standing over him, heaving deep breaths.

A pool of blood spread from his head as he lay face down. The finial fell from her hand, landed next to him with a thunderous bounce, and then rolled to a stop.

CHAPTER 47

It seemed like minutes, even hours, passed before Sunny gasped with a hand to her mouth. She kneeled beside Taylor, cradling his head.

"What have I done?" she asked herself as she looked around. Somehow, this all felt eerily familiar. She was sure this had happened at the hospital, or so she thought she remembered. It had been all too real when it happened before, and it only made her more confused that it had happened again, like an echo in time.

For a moment, she thought of taking Taylor's cell phone and . . . and what? Calling 911? Doing so would surely end all this, right here, right now. Her chest heaved as she took deep, panicked breaths. Here she was, in a life-and-death situation, and she had access to a cell phone. A wave of guilt splashed over her as if she had a choice. She'd face the consequences and return to that place rather than leave him here like this, wouldn't—?

The faint illumination of headlights crawled across the gathering room's wall.

It's too late. He's here.

"Nadeen?" she called out to no answer.

The headlights grew brighter; the vehicle was getting closer. Sunny bolted to her feet, alarmed.

"He's coming!" she yelled, calling out for Nadeen again. She stood still. The only noise was the car's engine as it neared. Her eyes dropped to Taylor, her hand rubbing her brow as she pondered what to do. His mini-cassette recorder lay on the floor several feet away, catching her attention.

"Nadeen?"

There was no response. She picked up the recorder, rushed up the stairs and down the candlelit hallway. She slowed as she came to the tower room, finding its door closed. A blood-red sunset shone through a neighboring room's windows and onto the door's crescent moon.

"Nadeen!"

Sunny placed a trembling hand on the freshly painted crescent moon. She pushed the door open and gawked at the bloody handprint left behind as her arm fell to her side. She stood in a stupor before raising her blood-soaked hand and examining it with a shudder.

Something isn't right here.

Again, the queasy thought of her dream about the attic maze came to mind. Her shadow kept catching up no matter how fast she tried to move. It was as if she were reliving a nightmare, or her shadow had finally caught up to her. Both left her feeling lightheaded and sick to her stomach.

She glanced over her shoulder when she heard the car's door close. "Nadeen!" she cried out again, desperate for a response.

The hourglass in her head was almost empty. The last grains of sand careened down as she rushed into the tower room and closed the door. Wherever Nadeen was hiding, she had Rebecca with her to prevent Taylor from taking her. That meant Sunny no longer had a witness at hand. However, she did have the mini-cassette recorder to capture the events as they unfolded.

She was quick to change into the white burial dress. Then she pressed the record button on the cassette recorder and slid it into her undergarment. Taking hold of the tied-together bedsheets, she looped one end into a noose and knotted it before slinging it over the crossbeam. Next, she pulled it some length downward, the loop swinging back and forth just above her head. Finally, she took the other end and tied it to one of the legs of the bed.

All she had to do now was wait. It then occurred to her how similar and applicable Nadeen's words were to her situation. Other than a gut feeling, she didn't know for certain who was approaching.

He'll be here soon enough. The truth will come out then, and this will all be laid to rest.

Sunny was already lightheaded, and the thought conjured a warmth in her belly. It didn't take long for it to spread to her head and her legs to turn to jelly. Soon came the soft tapping—tap, tap, tap—and the quick flashes of larvae falling to the floor followed.

"Oh, dear God. Please. Not now," she cried.

She put a hand on her belly and fell to the floor on her knees. Now, it was a matter of which would come first: this horrible nausea's passing or Morgan's moment of reckoning.

Either way, the weight of the truth, hung by a precarious lie, was about to break free. The question was, how hard would it land? And more importantly, where would it lead her?

Chapter 48

As Morgan approached, the car's headlights cast shadows of the gate onto the mansion. The darkening evening sky had set the wispy clouds ablaze with orange, pink, and crimson. He hadn't been sure what to expect, but the two vehicles near the gate were the least. He pulled his car off to the side of the road and parked. There was Sunny's automobile, but the other was unfamiliar. He turned his headlights off and sat in the car, noticing the glow of light inside the second floor's tower room.

Perhaps this wasn't a good idea. He hadn't the foggiest idea what he would say, and it was doubtful Sunny would even want to listen to him. But, as hard as it was, she should know the truth after all these years. Most of all, he was concerned for her. Any redemption would come from preventing her from falling into the depths of her mother's mental illness.

Evelyn was furious with him, and he understood why. Missing the only debate before reelection would surely result in many questions. Most, he was sure he wouldn't care to answer. It wasn't like him, but he wouldn't let this situation haunt him for the rest of his life. Failing to be reelected was nothing in comparison to letting what had happened years ago continue to plague him any further. Listening to Evelyn then had only managed to turn him into a host for her parasitic tendencies. And here he was now, a shadow of the person he'd once been.

Morgan grabbed the satin cloth-covered box on the passenger seat and got out of the car. He lumbered through the gate, stopped, and looked up at the tower room's windows. He half expected to see Nadeen standing there, looking down at him again.

Fortunately, the window was empty, save for the faint glow of light flickering within.

The past had haunted him at every turn for the last twenty-eight years—most recently, with a figurative ghost. His only child, who resembled her mother in many ways, from her eyes right down to how she curled her hair behind her ear, haunted him more than any literal ghost ever could. The worst was when she used the same phrases as her mother, like "the sun, moon, and stars." It was one thing to resemble her. But her saying those same words left him feeling like he was being visited from beyond the grave.

As he approached the front entrance, he wondered if it was best to knock first or just enter. He realized he was overthinking it, a sign of the nervousness he had often dealt with over the years. With a simple twist of the knob and a push against the door, he overcame his anxiety and stepped inside.

For the second time in a few short minutes, Morgan encountered the unexpected. A man's crumpled body lay on the floor. His head rested in a pool of coagulating blood. A large marble ball, no doubt the weapon that had sent him sprawling, lay on the floor several feet away.

Who was this man? What was he doing here? Who did this to him? Was he dead?

A growing dread overcame Morgan. Any hope for redemption seemed shattered like the skull of the man lying motionless before him.

The answer to one of his questions came almost immediately.

The man's sudden moans startled Morgan as he kneeled on the floor. He attempted to stir the man further; he was alive but remained unconscious. Morgan pulled his cell phone from his pocket, pressed nine and one, and paused, his finger hovering over the one. He canceled the call with a heavy sigh and slid the phone into his suit's pocket.

Of course, he'd have to explain everything if he were to call for help. What was he doing here? He was supposed to be at the mayoral debate right now. A tidal wave of questions would follow. They would pull him into the undertow and threaten to drown him. He hadn't come here to risk all that happening for somebody he didn't know. Not to mention the fact that it was likely Sunny who'd done this to him.

A clatter from above broke his train of thought.

Morgan noticed drops of blood leading up the winding staircase. He started up the steps, his legs numb from the weight of nearly three decades of secrets, horror, and guilt. With each step, he relived the night he'd come here to have it out with Nadeen and force her to get help.

It had been a late October evening, as it was tonight, the same sky in its dying throes of daylight. The same scent of dried leaves had filled the air outside—so too the sweet, smoky smell of burning wood in the distance. Seeing the place in its current state, with flaps of ugly, aged wallpaper uncurling down the walls, left him morose. The hopes, dreams, and vivacity that had once filled this place were long gone. In their place was an air of fear, dread, and anxiety—all emitting from him.

Time was cruel like this. It was supposed to heal all wounds. Yet, climbing the stairs again for the first time in decades, all the good memories had faded away. The only ones left now were the stained ones. Rather than healing, time had become the salt in those still-open wounds. They had become more painful with every tick-tock of the clock and drumbeat of his heart.

His hand trembled with each grasp of the railing. As he climbed, he could have sworn he heard his daughter crying. He followed the dim candlelight down the hallway to the tower room's closed door. He was expected presently, but the past overcame his mind. His daughter's cries subsided, followed by her mother telling her that Mommy wouldn't let him take her away. Then there was that awful chant.

I'm not crazy, despite what they say; please don't let them take my baby away.

The past was never too far behind. It was always there in his head, following him wherever he went. Had he only followed his heart instead . . .

As he inched closer, he saw a patch of sheen on the door. His heart nearly stopped. It was a fresh bloodstain from a handprint on the old crescent moon decor. Drips of blood were still running down the door. He feared the worst.

With bated breath, Morgan pushed the door open.

That it was unlocked was a minor surprise. At least, compared to finding the man on the floor at the bottom of the stairs and two vehicles parked outside. Yet nothing could have prepared him for what he would see next.

CHAPTER 49

Sunny heard footsteps shuffling down the hallway toward the door. It didn't surprise her that he knew exactly where he was heading. He stopped outside the door, most likely noticing the bloody handprint. The doorknob jiggled and turned, then opened to reveal Morgan. Wearing a dark suit, he was barely visible against the faint candlelight from the hallway behind him.

Nor was she surprised that he looked stunned to see her wearing a white dress with her hair dyed black. The foreboding noose hung between them and gave the effect she'd sought as she held a lantern up. Her resemblance to her mother was eating away at Morgan . . . almost as if he'd seen a ghost.

"Sunny, please . . ."

The sight of her was hitting the depths of his despair.

She heard the desperation in his pleading voice as he advanced a step toward her with arms wide open. All Sunny could think was what her mother, Martha, had told her about how her tiny arms reached out, much like his now, as flies swarmed her crib.

The lantern's flame flickered and went out from a draft passing through the room. Only the dying daylight, the rising moon outside, and several lit candles remained.

"Don't come any closer," Sunny said as she set the lantern on the nightstand. Tearful anger rose on her moonlit face, her skin pale as porcelain. "It wasn't her sanity she was afraid of losing most. It was me! And what did I mean to you? Was I some dirty little secret? A pawn in some sick scheme?" She gave him a moment to respond before crying out, "Or both?"

A woman's voice echoed from outside the room, startling them.

"Go on, Morgan."

Sunny's eyes darted to the door to the staircase that zigzagged down to the outside as it creaked open. A ghostlike figure appeared, dark and barely visible in the shadows.

"What are you waiting for? This is your chance to tell her the truth."

"I t-tried t-to help her, Sunny," Morgan stuttered. "It tore me to see her deteriorate the way she did. Always distant . . . always talking of 'ghosts' and things that weren't there. I told her she needed help, that she wasn't well."

"Of course, she wasn't," Sunny snapped at him. "You were driving her crazy."

"That's not true."

"She was having a nervous breakdown because she was afraid you would take me from her."

"I came that night to beg her to seek help before it was too late. She screamed at me not to go near you while you slept in the crib. She couldn't see what she'd become, that she was sick. She said . . ." Morgan paused, gathering himself. "I approached her, and she said—her exact words were—'Don't! Or you will regret this moment for the rest of your life.'"

He sounded convincing. But Sunny wondered if he'd ever truly regretted abandoning her, not to mention never trying to find her. It had taken her a trip through hell to find the answers to keep her daughter from being taken from her. Why couldn't he have bothered to do the same?

"It sounded like a threat to me," Morgan said. "I asked if it were meant as one. She said, 'For the love of God, it's a warning. Before it's too late.'"

"And you didn't listen," the voice said from the shadows. "Did you?"

"I couldn't stand by and watch her like this, Sunny. So I rushed toward the crib."

"You were! You were going to take me from her!"

"She was sick! She pushed me back and kept going until we were in the hallway. I grabbed her, trying to get her to settle down," Morgan said, on the verge of tears. "I-I . . . I spun her away, but she slipped out of my grasp and teetered against the railing. She lost her balance and . . ." He choked up, sobbing, the last three words a whine that sounded like a single word: "She fell over!" He gathered himself and spoke as calmly as he could. "The last thing she said to me? 'Mark my words, so help me.'"

His face was twisted, anguished, still trying to comprehend what had happened.

"It's all lies!" Sunny yelled.

"She screamed as she fell over. When I looked down below, she was lying motionless on the foyer floor."

Sunny shook her head, defiant. This was more than a lie; it was pure malicious manipulation. Morgan was telling her this, having just come through the lobby and seen Taylor on the floor. She didn't believe her mother had hanged herself. And now she refused to believe she had died as a result of some accident.

Something sinister was in the air, and the dish he served up, instead of the truth, was too hard to swallow. Besides, this didn't explain how her mother was found. He was trying to throw her off by manipulating the situation. Her mother dying where Taylor might lie dead, by her own hands no less, was just too much of a coincidence to fathom.

"I didn't know what t-to do, so I called Evelyn. When she saw the body, she said it would be perfect." Morgan whimpered with another round of sobs and buried his face in his hands.

Sunny caught a movement in the shadows of the doorway to the side entrance staircase. A flame as a match was struck, then drawn to a cupped hand. A cigarette's tip began glowing a bright amber before the flame was shaken out.

Evelyn stepped out of the darkness and into the tower room. She paused, took a long drag from her cigarette, and exhaled a plume of thick smoke toward Sunny.

"This place even smells like a funeral home. Go on, Morgan, tell her. Tell her everything."

CHAPTER 50

Sunny hadn't anticipated Evelyn showing up as well. From what little she had seen so far, she could tell that Evelyn and Morgan were not on the best of terms. She wondered if her painting had something to do with it. Either that or it was the truth coming out after all these years, though Evelyn seemed a little too eager to have it told. One would think she'd be spinning a web of deceit instead.

While she had little doubt of Morgan's manipulativeness, Evelyn was on a different level. Her presence and eagerness left Sunny assured of her involvement. Either way, being here alone with them wasn't a good idea. Where had Nadeen disappeared to with Rebecca? The cassette player was recording, but she didn't know if she was close enough for it to capture their voices. Also, she wasn't sure how long the tape was; she couldn't recall ever using one before in this digital age.

"It was Evelyn's idea to hang her," Morgan said. "With her notoriety and financial problems, it would be much more believable. Everyone knew of her situation. A fall like that would only raise questions." He wiped his brow, continuing, "So I carried her limp body up the stairs to this room. Evelyn found a long enough piece of rope and made a noose . . . and then—"

"You're not skipping the part about poor, pathetic Morgan? Don't you remember what I asked you?" Evelyn asked. "You were going to sit there and mope. It was your mess, and you couldn't be bothered to get your hands dirty and help clean it up." She stalked along the room's outer edge.

Sunny withdrew to the center, near the noose.

Evelyn approached the nightstand, her gaze firmly on Sunny. She took a candle from a wall sconce and relit the lantern with it. Holding the candle up to her face, she blew it out and flashed a malicious grin.

Sunny stumbled over the diary on the floor as she backed away. She glanced at it; her eyes ping-ponged between Morgan and Evelyn until Evelyn retreated. The lighthouse's beam made its first pass of the early evening, momentarily casting Sunny's shadow onto them. Seeing the light pass above the crib gave her a sudden chill. The warmth from her belly spread to her head again, accompanied by the sound of buzzing flies.

"And then what happened, Morgan?" Evelyn asked, sounding like a teacher prodding her student to learn his lesson.

"As I tried to hold her limp body up, Evelyn tied the noose around her neck. It was perfect, except . . ."

"Except what?"

"Except she may not have been dead." Morgan's shaky hand raised to cover his mouth. "Her arm. It jerked forward. It may have been only a reflex. I don't—I don't know." He turned to Sunny, dropping his gaze to the floor. "The lighthouse's beam went by again, and you began to cry when her shadow fell over you in the crib."

"He'd been seeing her for some time, but I didn't know about you," Evelyn said, turning to Sunny. "That wasn't the only secret he'd been keeping. I saw the necklace he'd given her, snatched it off her neck, and threw it. God only knows where it landed. But after all these years, it appears you found it," she said, focusing on the pendant around Sunny's neck.

"It was hanging from the crossbeam, snagged on a nail," Sunny said. Her wary eyes followed Evelyn's every step as she began circling her, like a shark sensing blood in the water.

"How appropriate," Evelyn cackled. "What would people think? Morgan, with a child out of the blue? Surely there would be questions with a young mother dead by suicide while her child was missing." She dropped her cigarette butt to the floor and smothered it with a heel twist. "So he left you for someone else to find. And why, Miss Sunshine, would he do a thing like that?"

Sunny's voice was soft. Distant. *Crushed.*

"Because. He didn't care."

Evelyn flashed a triumphant smile and turned her back to them.

CHAPTER 51

An overwhelming sense of nausea struck Taylor. He attempted to push himself up from the floor, but the world had been spinning around him since he opened his eyes. Adding to his dilemma, he didn't know where he was.

His head was throbbing, and he could taste something salty and metallic in his mouth. As he raised himself, he saw a pool of liquid he could only assume was his blood. Crimson bubbles protruded from his nostrils then retracted with every shallow breath.

He could hear voices coming from somewhere. As hard as he tried, he couldn't tell what they were talking about. But he recognized one of the female voices; it was his wife. That's when everything started coming back to him.

I will count from ten, and you'll feel something hit you like a ton of bricks.

He opened his eyes again, trying to make out the blurry object a couple of feet away from his face. Blinking several times brought the image into focus. It looked like a softball made of marble. The blood streaking across it looked like red stitching.

That's what she must have hit him with. He could make out the syringe about ten feet away from him on the floor.

He tried to stand, but his entire body seized, and he crashed back to the floor again. He still heard the distant voices but could not decipher anything until a man's voice yelled, "That's not true!"

For the first time, Taylor began to think his wife was in danger from someone other than herself. And yet, all he could do now was listen as he faded in and out of consciousness.

Chapter 52

I'd just lost your mother!" Morgan pleaded to Sunny. "I was in shock. I came here to save her, not to lose her—or you, for that matter. The truth is I've never let you go. I've held on, hoping, all these years, that I would see you again one day."

"But you never even tried to find me," Sunny said, heartbroken. "The lengths I've gone to to keep my baby from being taken from me. To prove I wasn't crazy. Only to find the opposite was true for me as an infant. That I wasn't worth the effort."

"That's not true either," Morgan said as he inched closer. "I was afraid that something like this would happen if I did and that you would reject me. And how could I blame you? You still have your whole life in front of you. Mine has been squandered on regrets."

Something in his words chipped away at Sunny's disbelief. Little by little, she started believing him, partly due to what he said, echoing George's advice. Plus, the things he was saying were making sense.

At last, she had what she'd come for; perhaps that was enough. She could provide their confession to the authorities and let the chips fall where they may. Then, she remembered the last words from Madame Vanderhill, about how they would never be able to take Rebecca from her again and felt a sense of peace.

"You must have been desperate to listen to your wife like that," Sunny said after a long pause.

"Ha!" Evelyn scoffed, carrying the lantern into the hallway. She lit another cigarette with its flame and took a deep drag. "What did I tell you, Morgan? She's crazy. Just like her mother."

A twisted frown spread across Morgan's confused face. "M-My wife? Evelyn?" He glanced at her in the hallway. "Evie is my sister."

"If she's your sister, then who . . .?" a befuddled Sunny began to ask before her mind rumbled off the tracks.

"The only woman I have ever cared about was your mother, Nadeen."

After Evelyn lit her cigarette in the hallway, she thought she heard a moan echo from below.

Pivoting to the short railing overlooking the foyer, she held the lantern up. Shadows danced in eerie rhythms as its flickering flame stretched into the dark. As her eyes adjusted, she could see what appeared to be a person on the floor.

She walked the length of the hall, holding the lantern out as she passed the second railing to get a better look. As she descended the stairs, her heels echoed through the foyer. When she reached the bottom step, her hand glided over the space where the finial should have been. She held the lantern closer, noticing its absence.

The candlelight revealed the marble finial on the floor. As she approached it, she noticed a pool of blood leading to a man struggling to sit upward.

"Sunny?" he murmured, confused and barely intelligible. "Help. Please."

"Wait there," Evelyn said. "I'll find something to ease the pain." She marched down a hallway, a jittery silhouette against the lantern's glow.

She suspected Sunny's husband had found her, much to his detriment. In the kitchen, she pulled drawers open. One by one, she rummaged through them with a crazed determination.

Inside one, the lantern light reflected off the blade of a medium-sized carving knife. She picked it up, turning it over before something else caused her eyes to widen with menacing delight. She pulled on a black handle buried under a clutter of silverware. Out came a stainless steel chef's knife, the blade at least nine inches long.

She wrapped her spindly fingers around the handle, savoring its heft.

This will do the trick, she thought, glancing toward the foyer.

Sunny froze with shock, a silent scream of "No!" falling from her hushed lips as the whisper of Nadeen's words surrounded her.

He'll be here soon enough. The truth will come out then, and this will all be laid to rest.

"I fell into a depression afterward, and Evelyn cared for me," Morgan confessed.

Sunny shook her head, her eyes wide with disbelief.

"It's . . . it's a lie!"

"Evelyn wasn't about to let anyone know the truth about Nadeen and me. Not with her illness and what people thought of her."

Sunny closed her eyes tightly and gripped the side of her head, Taylor's voice tearing through her mind.

You refuse to hear that what you're searching for is the very thing you're running from.

She knew Taylor was referring to the truth, but this was a lie. It had to be. "There's no such thing as ghosts," she sobbed defiantly. "Nadeen is the one—"

"Nadeen is dead," Morgan said firmly.

"No!" Sunny cried. "She's the one . . . she's the one who's been watching Rebecca."

"She is dead!" Morgan thundered.

CHAPTER 53

Evelyn didn't care for rats. They didn't necessarily bother her; everything had its place in this world, after all. But there was a large one out in the foyer with big ears that may have heard too much already.

One thing she was sick and tired of, however, was cleaning up after Morgan. If people only knew the trail he'd left behind, starting with that Nadeen. Morgan knew nothing about the others, but she was only the beginning.

When the coroner had doubted Nadeen's cause of death because of other injuries from the fall, she had to take care of that too. He had a well-known drinking problem. He also had a penchant for speed in his sports car. It had been no surprise to see his love of the bottle result in a cocktail-fueled fiery crash.

"How tragic," people said, usually followed by "Like I didn't see that coming."

The coroner's replacement, a two-timing sleazeball who took bribes to support his drug addiction, hadn't fared any better. Evelyn had been more than happy to assist him in kicking the habit. He showed up one day going through withdrawals and demanded more "or else." She said she couldn't give him any more money but could get him the fix he was after.

Three days later, he was found dead from an overdose of mixed prescription opioids. Again, nobody was surprised. If anything, they were left wondering how he got the job in the first place.

That was nearly thirty years ago. It had been the last of the doubts until little Miss Sunshine walked into the Antique Shoppe not quite a week ago.

As for Evelyn, she had long given up having meaningful relationships with people. Her brother, Morgan, had a natural gift of gab and a warmth that drew people in. She knew she was as cold as ice, but she had a talent for reading others and exploiting their weaknesses. So when Morgan wouldn't leave well enough alone, she wasn't against using him as a pawn to checkmate Sunny.

Stepping back into the foyer, knife in hand, she looked toward the man in the pool of blood. The plan was already unfolding, and she could see how it would play out in the newspapers.

Oh, it would be shocking. But it too would come as no surprise.

Her crooked smile returned, and her high heels echoed down the hall as she went to fulfill her promise. Despite everything she had done, she never once considered herself a painkiller—until now.

CHAPTER 54

A nauseous feeling rose through Sunny from her stomach to her chest. It was a tidal wave coming to wipe away whatever calm waters remained and all the sands of time left on the shore, uncovering an ugly truth in the process. When it finally struck, it did so with such force that it left her shaking by three simple words: "She is dead!"

Sunny looked to the crib as the lighthouse's beam made its way around and flashed in her eyes.

"Becca's not . . ." She paused, confused, as the light flooded the room. It exposed the crib and Miss Carmella, resting in its otherwise empty corner.

"My baby isn't . . ."

Try not to mix the stories with reality. As you said, many don't want to hear any differently despite what they know and see. They fear it will destroy the illusions they cling to.

"Don't you . . ." Sunny began again, stepping toward the crib. "She's just sleeping."

The fragmented memories. Those lost to the darkness of electroconvulsive therapy. They all came rushing back, with each wave crashing and receding on the seahorse-shaped part of the brain, the hippocampus.

We're fine, really. I bet you get that all the time with babies crying in the back seat. Kind of ironic, huh?

"Don't you tell me my baby's . . ." She stopped to watch Morgan as he approached the crib and picked up the old porcelain doll.

"Sunny? It's the doll I gave you when you were a baby."

She took Miss Carmella without so much a glance. "I-I know. But Nadeen has Becca. She came upstairs when Taylor arrived. We were arguing . . ." She turned toward the door, calling out, "Nadeen! Where are you?"

Morgan covered his ears as his face twisted. "Why are you doing this to me?"

Sunny ignored him with an expectant look to the doorway. Doubt crept in with every passing moment as the waves continued to pound the shore.

I can't say I wish to be around when she realizes what's happened. She'll probably end up with another stay at the center.

Sunny's tearful voice cracked. "Where is she?"

Why? Why are you doing this? I just want to see Becca.

"Nadeen?" she sobbed, staring at the empty doorway.

It's time to let go so we can all move on.

Sunny reached for the picture on the nightstand. She was holding Rebecca just after her daughter's birth. The Hunter's Moon shone on it through the windows as Taylor's voice hit her with an uppercut.

What happened at the hospital?

CHAPTER 55

Along with the overwhelming headache, Taylor felt an unbearable dread swelling. He didn't know who the woman was who had told him to stay there. He tried to sit up, his hand groping the floor before he attempted to place his weight on his forearm.

He heard a man roar from upstairs, "She is dead!" Then the voices died down into an unintelligible conversation again. He pulled his knees up underneath him and rested for several moments.

The woman was rummaging through something in a room off the foyer. It sounded like cutlery banging together. What was she doing? Was she looking for something to help with his head?

Did it matter? His wife sounded distressed and in trouble.

A strand of coagulated blood dripped from his jaw to the floor. He arched his back up, swung his hips around, and sat upright. Then he tried to use his arms to keep himself from collapsing back to the floor, but they buckled under the pressure.

While catching his breath, he heard his wife scream, "I am never going back there!"

For the second time, he thought these people might be there to help, and the gentleman may have been a doctor. He saw the syringe swirling on the floor through his double vision and tried reaching for it.

The click-clack of high heels grew closer as the woman returned. It stopped behind him as he grabbed the needle. His shadow fell over the floor from the lantern light behind him. Just then, he saw the green eyes of a black cat staring at him from the darkness beyond the syringe.

A commotion drew his attention to the staircase. He failed to see the cat look up and beyond him. Nor did he see it scurry into the darkness when the woman behind him raised the knife.

Upstairs, a door suddenly clapped shut like booming thunder. It slammed so hard, Taylor thought for a split second the sharp, piercing pain was his eardrum rupturing from the sound.

And then the pain was no more.

Chapter 56

The last wave to crash finally struck Sunny. Taylor's attempt to get her to remember what had happened at the hospital eventually flooded her memory, receded, and revealed the missing piece. Her fingers trembled as she reached for the photo of herself and Rebecca. Although it had only been a few months before, it seemed like forever. Much of that time had been spent lost at sea and struggling through rough waters to find her way here.

How ironic, she thought, as the lighthouse's beam cut through the darkness, making its rounds again. Not only had it appeared in her fragmented memories, but it also symbolized her search for the truth. All she had to do was look deep within herself. But even then, she would have found only the repressed truth of her Jungian shadow. That dark part of herself that she kept outside her light of consciousness.

She had arrived about a week ago in a fog, literally and figuratively. But now, she stood quite clear with a full moon rising while the lighthouse's beam still warned of danger. Taylor was right: the thing she was searching for was the very thing she had been running from.

"They didn't save you in time," she whispered through tears as she touched the photo. "You strangled on the umbilical cord. Your father yelled, 'She is dead!' And then he took you from me when I wouldn't . . ."

She stumbled, her voice cracking and the floodgates opening.

"*Let go.*"

Understanding what had happened at last, the last voice she heard was her own.

Ah, but why do we deceive others? Or, better yet, ourselves?

How could this happen to her? The realization that her husband had been trying to help her all this time sank in.

There it was again, an allusion to the sands of time. When mixed with water, they created quicksand. But, unlike hazardous shoals, there were no lighthouses to warn wayward souls of personal pitfalls.

And so it was in quicksand that her heart now sank with thoughts that she might have killed Taylor. And for what? Choosing the shadowy illusion of a comforting lie over the illumination of an unpleasant truth?

Or was there another possibility? One that made all the pieces fall together more meaningfully, as hard as it might be to believe?

She could no longer tell which was which, now thinking she might have had them backward all along. Perhaps the science of psychology was the illusion that cloaked an uncomfortable reality: there is more than just the physical, natural world that can't be readily explained.

Sunny knew she had heard, held, and hugged Rebecca. She could even smell her. But she also didn't believe in ghosts. Yet there was also Nadeen, who couldn't have been some figment of her imagination. In some strange way, she could *feel* that Nadeen was her mother; they shared some of the same characteristics and tendencies. More so, anyway, than she ever had with George or Martha. She could also see the resemblance now, with her hair nearly the same color.

This was the stress between the pull of two simultaneously held yet contradictory beliefs. It left her dazed and confused, unsure of what was up, down, inside out, or outside in anymore. It was cognitive dissonance in all its uncomfortableness, and she now understood it was much easier to teach than to experience firsthand.

Sunny pulled her finger from the photo, her mind threatening to tumble over the edge into the chasm.

She turned to Morgan, who approached with his arms open again.

"I don't understand. If she's dead . . ." she began to ask as he came forward with a cautious step. "Then why do I still see her?"

Morgan's arms fell to his side in defeat, searching futilely for some comforting explanation no amount of light could ever reveal. "Sunny, whatever illness your mother had—"

He stopped, bracing himself as she suddenly charged him.

"I am never going back there!" she screamed.

Morgan retreated with his arms up, ready to defend himself. "Sunny, please. You need help," he pleaded, in the same situation as with Nadeen years ago. He stumbled into the hallway, wary of events from the past repeating themselves. Only this time, the heavy door boomed like a fired cannon as it slammed in his face.

CHAPTER 57

"I'm not crazy, despite what they say; please don't let them take my baby away." Sunny chanted this, not knowing what else to do as she searched the dark room, wide-eyed. "Nadeen?" She held Miss Carmella closer, asking desperately, "Where are you?"

She dropped the old porcelain doll into the crib. It landed with a dull thud followed by a long, eerie "mama." Its cry sounded like an old phonograph recording from the late nineteenth century in all its creepiness.

"Spook?" she called out in desperation, fearing everything was as Taylor had said. "I know what I've seen is real." Sunny covered her ears as Morgan banged on the door. "Nadeen? Why didn't you tell me?"

"Because you weren't ready to *hear* the truth."

Sunny spun toward the voice from the middle of the room, stumbling over the diary on the floor. A faint smile grew through her tears as Nadeen stood before her, holding

Rebecca. But her excitement was quick to wither. "I can never go back there."

"You don't have to. This is your home. It always has been and always will be. I was afraid they would take you from me. It was me they took from you, but you've never walked alone in your journey."

A cloud of doubt hovered over Sunny.

She understood the mountainous challenge before her. Trying to escape the same label as her mother would not be easy—particularly considering what she'd done to Taylor, who was most likely dead now. It would offset all the proof incriminating Morgan and Evelyn. And for what? Covering up an accident? It would no doubt come down to their word against hers.

The lighthouse beam came around again. In passing, it superimposed a shadow of the noose on Sunny's own shadow on the wall.

"But no one will believe . . ." she said, cornered, defeated, and fearing one last wave was yet to come. Its tide would carry her up the river, across Lake Ontario, and back to the psychiatric center. There, she would spend the rest of her life painting portraits she would never finish. They would also provide her with the finest reality escapers, chased with complimentary shots of electricity. Even knowing Rebecca was dead, they would continue trying to take her from Sunny until even her memories were no more.

"Make them," Nadeen said with a chilling smile as she eyed the noose. "And stay with us . . . *forever.*" The last word echoed as if spoken by a thousand voices traveling through space and time.

Sunny knew the connection between mother and daughter was immediate. A child was born tethered to the mother's heart and bound by something more than love. A bond so strong a mother's heart would tear from her chest long before the tether ever broke. It was a connection strong enough even to follow a child into death.

It all seemed so clear now.

Sunny was once a child, and that tether still existed between her and Nadeen. Knowing no bounds of space, time, or dimension, it was what had brought her here.

It was what had brought her home.

CHAPTER 58

Morgan slumped on the other side of the door, confused about what had just transpired and how he had ended up in the hall. He had started to suggest that whatever illness her mother had was present in her. And, like her mother, she cracked. It ended there, at least for the moment.

Fortunately, there had been no pushing on Sunny's part that might have resulted in her meeting the same fate as her mother. Yet Morgan was still concerned for her well-being. She acknowledged the death of her child at birth, which, for better or worse, was a step in the right direction. The next step, however, would be the most important: getting help.

Placing his ear to the door, he struggled to hear what was happening inside. It sounded as if Sunny were repeating some familiar phrase. Though indecipherable, he recognized it from the cadence as the same chant Nadeen had spoken.

Alarmed, Morgan banged his fists on the door but to no avail until he remembered what he had brought in his pocket. He pulled out the satin-clothed bundle, undid its string, and unwrapped an old black box.

He lifted its top. A small, beautiful, and elegant carved box of black and gold sat inside. Its lid was engraved with the sun, moon, and stars. Its sides were etched with zodiac signs in exquisite detail.

He carefully removed it, holding it in one hand as he knocked on the door with his other. "Sunny? Your mother would've wanted you to have this."

In the bottom of the outer box was a key that he retrieved and used to wind the mechanism on the inner box's underside. Although the box dated to the early 1890s, Morgan had long ago found someone who custom-made a drum for the unit.

He set it on the floor and waited for its seventy-two-note rendition of "Dream Sweet, My Darling." But the only sound that filled the air was silence. Disappointed, he placed his ear to the door again and listened.

Sunny hummed the tune, then sang its second verse.

The world's fast asleep, but there's more to be told,
Where whispers grow colder and stories grow old.

So close your sweet eyes, and drift into the deep,
Where lullabies linger and shadows still creep.

Morgan had never paid much attention to the song's lyrics. Hearing them now, in this context, gave him goose bumps. Then, Sunny suddenly stopped.

"Sunny? Sunny, please." He waited for a response; the silence was unnerving. Evelyn's high heels click-clacked up the stairs, startling him. But it was nowhere near as much of a startle as when he spun and saw her.

She held the lantern in one hand; its light revealed a large, bloodied knife in her other.

"Evelyn! What have you done?"

Morgan dashed to the railing overlooking the foyer. Below, he could make out Taylor in a motionless heap at the bottom of the stairs.

Evelyn made no effort to answer as she continued up the stairs. Click-clack, click-clack, her heels echoed on every step until she reached the top.

The wind had begun to pick up outside, whistling through the corridors, its drone interrupted by something heavy falling to the floor in the tower room, followed by a gasp.

Morgan flashed a wary glance at Evelyn as he stepped toward the door. He could not determine what the noises were as all was silent now, save for a slow creaking from within. His gaze lowered to the floor. There, moonlight through the windows cast shadows that moved back and forth beneath the door.

"Sunny!" he cried in desperate, rising horror, grabbing the doorknob and shaking it madly. He then leaned his shoulder into the door's heft, repeatedly ramming it with all his might. Finally, it burst open, splintering the frame at the latch. In stumbled Morgan, who sprawled onto the floor.

Looking up wide-eyed, he was in the shadow of death itself.

Chapter 59

The lighthouse's beam passed through the windows, making a silhouette of Sunny's hanging body. Her arm shot upward with her hand reaching out, grasping the air.

Morgan looked up from the floor with a horrific scream. "Sunny!" Stumbling to his feet, he raced to her, kicking aside the chair she stood on before tipping it over.

Sunny choked, her labored breath wheezing oddly like the wind whistling down the hall. A gurgling noise came from her throat like she was drowning. Then, bucking and trembling, her eyes rolled back in her head.

Morgan attempted to hold her up, alleviating the noose's stranglehold on her neck. "Help me! Please!" he begged Evelyn as she stood, a passive observer in the doorway with the lantern. Her only response was to step farther back into the hall and watch.

Morgan spun Sunny around in a circle, desperate to save her in a father-daughter danse macabre. Unable to hold her up, he knew this first and last dance was coming to an end all too soon.

The last wave to strike seemed to have pulled Sunny under for good.

Morgan began to sob, pausing as he heard her attempt to speak. Her faint yet euphoric voice whispered with an unmistakable smile, the words choking, with long pauses between them as she struggled with every breath.

"I ... can ... still ... see her!"

Within moments, she stopped moving.

Swaying back and forth, suspended from the beam, she appeared to be floating freely in calm waters.

Evelyn stood in the doorway, shocked for but a single moment. Not that Sunny had done this to herself. Instead, shocked at how all too easy it seemed. She dared to think it for a moment: she was almost disappointed, having expected more of a struggle.

She stood by and watched as Morgan collapsed to the floor. So pathetic, as always. It was not like he ever knew her, for crying out loud.

She had tried to warn him in the preceding days as she had years ago. Sunny was crazy, just like her mother, and this outcome was inevitable. It shouldn't come as a surprise to anyone, least of all Morgan.

Evelyn had known it when she read the article in the newspaper. Her family was concerned for her well-being after she had lost her child during birth. This had been written in the stars for her. That's how she wanted all this to look, at least for everyone else. Then she remembered she was holding the bloody knife and realized there was still much work to do.

So here she was again, cleaning up Morgan's mess. Now she had to figure out how to remove them from the equation.

She searched the room for something she could use and spotted Sunny's suitcase. She opened it, grabbed a random shirt, and wiped the suitcase clean. Then she wiped the knife's handle clean and forced it into Sunny's hand, squeezing her limp fingers around it. Using the shirt to keep her hand from touching Sunny's, she tossed the knife onto the floor.

From there, she wiped down the doorknobs and picked up the cigarette butts from the floor. She paused—what to do with the ashes?

There had been a hand broom and dustpan downstairs. She needed to return there anyway to erase her prints from everything she'd touched. The drawer handles. The staircase railing. The tower room staircase and door. Everything. There would be no signs of their having been in the house for anyone to discover by the time she finished.

She considered asking Morgan if he was going to sit there and mope or get up and help, but decided against it. He was bound to slow her down, if not create more work than necessary.

"Why don't you just wipe your tears and snotty nose all over her and leave more evidence you were here in the process?" she said, heading down the hallway. "And for God's sake, don't touch anything else while I'm gone."

CHAPTER 60

Morgan rose from his hands and knees for the second time, unable to take his eyes off Sunny's limp body. A range of emotions ran through him, from anger and sadness to guilt and depression.

The wind moaned steadily through the tower room, coming up the staircase through the door below. It whistled as it escaped through the broken window, leaving a noticeable chill in its wake.

A glint of candlelight reflected off Sunny's chest. Morgan moved closer and saw the sun, moon, and stars pendant dangling from her neck. That and her dyed hair brought back images of Nadeen from years ago as the hem of Sunny's white dress fluttered in the breeze.

He reached out to touch the pendant and saw the pages of the diary on the floor flipping from the draft through the room. One of the candles blew out, and the necklace inexplicably fell onto the open journal with a thump.

Morgan was afraid to look at the book on the floor. He could make out Nadeen's elegant handwriting by the silvery moonlight on the pages. He bent over and picked it up, carefully removing the necklace and pendant from its crease. Using a penlight he pulled from his blazer's pocket, he fanned through the pages beyond the crease. The light revealed them all to be empty.

The charm had fallen onto the page with the last diary entry.

This was no coincidence, and it left Morgan frozen with terror.

A cell phone rang in the hallway, snapping him from his stupor. He thought for a moment it was Evelyn's, but it was going unanswered. The ringing had stopped by the time he realized it most likely belonged to the dead man at the bottom of the stairs.

He turned his attention back to the diary, flipping the pages back to where he saw the date of the last entry. October 26, 1995.

His lips quivered.

That was the day Nadeen had died.

He turned his back to Sunny to avoid seeing her still swaying corpse. It didn't work; the lighthouse's beam cast her shadow onto the wall before him as it passed.

Morgan's eyes stumbled along the page, leaving his mouth agape.

After several moments, the music box in the hallway sprang to life with slow chimes. "Dream Sweet, My Darling" crept into the tower room, the discordant notes warped and haunting.

As she descended the staircase, Evelyn rubbed the handrail clean of fingerprints. She worked her way down, pausing at the bottom to survey the man's body.

It occurred to her to check for drops of blood on the staircase; then she realized it didn't matter. Sunny would have carried the knife up the stairs before committing suicide. That's why she'd tossed it onto the floor. She had been concerned with the direction of the blood spatter, but that would only matter if she'd been carrying the knife down the stairs.

The devil was in the details. She knew the importance of forensic evidence and how one careless oversight could help crack a case when things didn't add up.

She then moved down the hallway to the kitchen and cleaned all the drawer handles. It might have seemed like overkill, but chances were they hadn't been cleaned in years. Cleaning one and not the others might draw more suspicion than cleaning them all.

She saved the drawer where she touched the other knife for last. Opening it and wiping the carving knife's handle clean, she dropped it back inside and slid it closed. Then she went over its exterior surface, rubbing out any potential fingerprints.

After thinking, Evelyn returned to the hall and paused again in the foyer. There, she looked toward the front door. Morgan would have entered there. She marched to it, opened it, and cleaned the exterior doorknob. This was precisely why she didn't want Morgan to touch anything else.

Closing the door, she did the same to the interior knob and returned to the staircase. While staring at the finial on the floor, she went through the long checklist in her head.

The sudden ring from a cell phone startled her.

It was coming from the dead man's blazer, and as much as she wanted to know who might be calling him, she wasn't about to touch it. But it crossed her mind that they might be in trouble if somebody was expecting him. What if whoever was calling knew he was coming here? What if the caller was letting him know they were on the way?

Evelyn's calm, chilly, and methodical demeanor faltered for the first time. She quickened her pace up the stairs, wiping the other railing along the way. When she reached the top, she hurried from room to room, checking for anything unusual.

In one room, she found a painting of the mansion that Sunny had completed, but there was a white stain on it. Several leather-bound books were on the floor.

Just then, she heard the discordant chimes playing from the hallway.

One note kept striking every few moments, stuck in a repetitive pattern of ding, ding, ding. Other notes carried a broken melody around it. The repetitiveness brought a growing tension thick with dread. It was like a doomsday clock ticking to its final countdown, hastening her pace.

She took another quick look around the room. The heavy, sour, floral smell of a funeral home was present there too, as if it were following her around. After a few moments, she couldn't think of anything else that would incriminate herself or Morgan. Satisfied, she followed the doomsday clock's ticking back to the tower room.

She stood in the doorway and looked at Morgan. With eyes strained and mouth agape, he was reading a leather-bound book with his penlight. The book trembled in one hand; the penlight shook in the other. Finally, he looked up, his face blanched and void of life as the diary slipped from his grip to the floor.

"Morgan? What is it?" she asked, not wanting to know.

Chapter 61

Unresponsive, Morgan attempted to pocket his pen with its light still on, only to have it fall to the floor. He walked past Evelyn into the hallway and picked up the music box. Its single stuck note slowed the ghoulish countdown as he proceeded to the staircase.

"Morgan?" Evelyn sighed in exasperation, picking up his penlight. "What are you doing? Don't go down that way!"

Morgan continued down the hall, then descended the stairs.

Evelyn threw her hands in the air and raced behind him. He grabbed the railing; she wiped away his fingerprints all the way down to the bottom. There, she waited to see if he would continue unabated and trudge through the pool of blood. He would have had she not pulled him by his arm and guided him around the crimson pond at the last moment.

"What has gotten into you!"

She let go of his arm and watched him continue to the door. Charging ahead of him, she grabbed its knob with the shirt rag and opened it for him, baffled as he passed by.

He continued to the edge of the porch, sat down on the steps, and stared straight ahead. The music box was still in his hand, the repetitive ding, ding, ding having slowed to a death crawl.

Evelyn shook her head. "Fine. Sit there. I'll be back in a moment."

She returned inside, closed the door, and took a deep breath, wondering what had gotten into him. She strode through the foyer and up the stairs, heading straight for the tower room.

Her thoughts tumbled with doubt about him keeping his mouth shut. This was the first time he had been aware of her taking such drastic actions. She thought she'd done the man in the foyer a favor by putting him out of his misery. If nothing else, at least she'd kept her word.

But would Morgan, her flesh and blood, now become a rat? She took some measure of comfort in his comatose state in the present. She also feared he would become a liability before long.

Underneath Sunny's hanging corpse was the book he had been reading. It had the same leather-bound cover as the others she saw. She picked it up and flipped through its pages, then closed it with a thump, realizing it was a diary. Looking around, she found two more on the bed beside the crib.

Once again, Evelyn found herself frozen with indecision. None of this was according to any plan. If she had one, she could work backward from the intended result. Instead, she felt stuck and needed to build a bridge to the ending: one plus one equals murder-suicide. Nothing more, nothing less.

Looking at the lantern in her hand, she determined it was the perfect place to start. After wiping its handle, she forced it into Sunny's hand, closing her fingers around it as she had done with the cloth and the knife, and set it on the floor several feet away, careful not to touch it with her bare hand. She watched as the candlelight thrashed in its own danse macabre, soon to burn itself out.

Satisfied, she hurried back down the hall to the other room. She picked up the diaries and gave thought to the painting, deciding to use it to carry the books on.

Back in the tower room, she grabbed the diaries from the bed and gave the room another cursory glance. Satisfied, she carried the book-laden painting and headed to the stairway door. She turned and faced Sunny's corpse, then looked at the candles between the windows still aglow. "Don't forget to turn the lights out."

Evelyn opened the door and shivered from the cold draft. Just as she was about to descend the first step, an audible click stopped her dead in her tracks. A slow creaking and a fluttering noise followed it.

With an apprehensive look over her shoulder, she saw something white moving from the corner of her eye. The lighthouse's beam passed as she turned around, casting Sunny's shadow onto her. All the candles were out except the lantern on the floor. The curtains on the broken window flapped in the breeze, and the swaying body caused the beam to creak.

"The wind blew them out," an anxious Evelyn told herself aloud, looking at the candles on the wall. But that didn't explain the click. It was a familiar sound she had not heard for some time.

Her eyes pressed into every nook and cranny, finding nothing that could have made such a sound.

Then it dawned on her. It had come from Sunny. She set the painting and books down and cautiously walked back into the room.

Approaching the corpse, Evelyn caught a whiff of her gothic perfume. Using the cloth to pat her down, she felt something small and hard beneath her dress. Reaching under it, she found a mini-cassette recorder stuffed into Sunny's underwear. She pulled it out with a disgusted grimace. In the light of the Hunter's Moon, she could see that the tape inside had come to the end of its reel and stopped.

She looked up into Sunny's dead eyes, her pupils large as black holes, and smirked.

"Nice try."

She picked up the painting and the books, stepped through the doorway, and closed the door.

The change in the room's pressure created another vacuum, snuffing out the lantern's flame. Its smoldering left a small plume of billowing smoke in the moonlight beneath Sunny's dangling feet.

CHAPTER 62

When she rounded the corner to the front of the mansion, Evelyn found Morgan on the steps where she had left him. Careful not to step on the grass or in the mud, she took the sidewalk between the gated fence and the house.

A baby's sudden cry startled her, the unexpected sound sending a chill through her as she stopped. It sounded as if it had come from inside.

There was no child inside, was there?

She dismissed it as her mind playing tricks on her from when they'd left Sunny to die in that same crib. If only she had taken a pillow to her that night. But she couldn't do that. Not to Morgan. Besides, it would have deprived her of the irony of knowing Sunny survived only to return and take her own life here. In the very same room, no less.

That irony quickly turned to dread; she could partially see Sunny when she looked up at the tower's windows.

From that angle, she was unrecognizable as anything other than a white . . . *blemish.*

The Hunter's Moon shone through the windows. Evelyn gawked at the sight. Her grip on the painting slackened, and one of the books slid off to the ground.

Her gaze drifted downward at Sunny's painting in her hands and the white blemish on the tower. A figure of a man sat on the porch, just as Morgan was, and a full moon hung in the starry sky overhead.

It's not . . . finished. There should be a moon here and a gentleman sitting on the steps here.

Evelyn's incredulous eyes blinked from the blemish to the windows and Morgan sitting on the porch. She shook her head in disbelief, the ding of the doomsday box returning her from her dreadful trance.

She picked the diary off the ground and rushed to Morgan, setting the painting and books beside him.

"Listen to me and listen carefully," she barked.

There was no response. He continued to stare off into the unknown.

Without warning, she slapped him across the face. His cheek blanched first, then a redness came as the blood flowed, followed by a sudden bout of fresh tears.

"Listen to me!"

He finally acknowledged her with a dazed nod.

"You are going to get into your car, and you are going to drive down the entrance here with your lights off. Then you will pull off to the side of the road right before Route 12 and wait until no cars are coming. Do you understand me?"

Again, he nodded, the music box's ding joining in.

"Wait until you see no headlights approaching from the bend in the road about half a mile. Then turn left with your headlights off. Only turn them on after you've passed the bar on the corner. It will be a matter of seconds once you make your turn."

Evelyn wasn't wasting any more time explaining why. It should be evident to him that she didn't want anyone to see a car turn off from that road. If someone did, they could provide details of it to the authorities. But Morgan wasn't exactly in the right frame of mind, so she asked again if he understood. He nodded. She watched as he took the music box, got into his car, and drove away, leaving his headlights off.

She was grateful that the road leading up to the mansion was paved, unlike the side road she had taken to park at the cove. It shouldn't have surprised her that, as Morgan pulled away, he went onto the dirt around the other cars. Although she was one step closer to being home free, the most challenging part of the night remained ahead.

First, she'd take care of the tire tracks he left behind. Once she was finished and back in her car, she would drive it to the edge of Route 12 and park off to the side. From there, she would go back and painstakingly remove all signs of her vehicle's tracks from the dirt road. That would remove both herself and Morgan from the equation altogether.

One plus one equals two dead from a murder-suicide.

She looked at the tower's windows one last time. The beam of light passed through and exposed the silhouette of Sunny's body hanging inside.

Though the coincidences of the painting and the scene before her were uncanny, it was all behind her now. Looking ahead, she could see the headlines in the paper already—"Missing Woman Found Dead in Apparent Murder-Suicide."

Despite there being no other witnesses, nobody would have any reason to believe otherwise. Evelyn couldn't help but beam a crooked smile at the irony.

It was simply the truth.

Anybody who couldn't see or believe that must be crazy.

Dream sweet, my darling, the moon's shining bright,
She'll hold you in silence till first morning light.
But if in the morning, the sun doesn't rise,
You'll rest safe forever in night's tender ties.

CHAPTER 63

October 26, 1995

Before turning in last night, I was compelled to paint a picture of the bed and breakfast. I didn't quite finish it as I couldn't remember the number of windows in the tower room. I believed I had it correct, but I decided to walk down the hall and peek inside despite my fears.

I don't know if it was a dream or something else, but the events that transpired shook me worse than any other. I'm still trying to process them as I sense my time is slipping away. I can't explain it other than by mother's intuition. I continue feeling in my gut that something will happen to Sunny when Bogie is near.

I packaged the painting and sent it to the Antique Shoppe this morning with a note. I told them it was an "anonymous donation for your collection." I don't know why I would do such a thing unless, as odd as it sounds, I'm sending it to be seen by someone in the future. I will also hide this diary, along with the others, in case something should happen to me.

I know this sounds unbelievable. Even writing it seems surreal. I didn't open the door to the tower room, at least not at first. Instead, I stood a few feet away, contemplating whether I should or not. As I did, I felt a chill, like a shadow had fallen over me from behind.

When I turned, the apparition that haunts me appeared clear for the first time, hurrying toward me. Though she wasn't dressed in the white gown, she wore the same pendant as I. Stranger yet, she seemed to be me with long, dark hair, but she wasn't.

Even so, the specter didn't slow as she approached. Anxiety washed over me as she ran through me, stopping in front of the door and looking back—not so much at me, but through me as if I weren't there at all. Perhaps someone was coming after her. She seemed desperate and yelled my name.

She then turned and touched the door near the crescent moon. When she removed her hand, she looked at it in disbelief, having left a bloody handprint on it. After that, she disappeared through the closed door. Yes, I know how that sounds, but it happened.

I stood in shock for several moments before hearing my name yelled from the other side of the door. When I finally opened it, I saw her in the white gown hanging from the crossbeam as I had seen several times before. There was no doubt it was the same girl I had seen only moments prior.

Though off-kilter, the strangely distant music that played whenever she appeared was finally recognizable too. It's the lullaby I sing to Sunny.

I can only hope to put the pieces together as I now fear the worst when Bogie is near. This ghost, this shadow I see—could it be a premonition?

Chapter 64

A frazzled Evelyn read the diary with the eyes of an insomniac.

Wisps of her straight black hair peppered with gray strayed every which way from their bun. Her mouth hung open. Though bloodshot, her eyes moved across the page at a feverish pace. They widened with horror as they passed over the final words of the entry.

She tossed the book into the wood-burning stove as if its leather-bound cover were a corpse's cold, withering skin. It landed next to the charred remains of the other diaries, necklace, and pendant.

Evelyn fixated on the last passage as flames danced around its edges.

> But if it's not of my death,
> could it be Sunny's?

The page blackened as the heat bled through and burst into flames.

Evelyn nudged the book deeper with a poker. Then she took the small cassette and yanked its tape until it lay coiled on the floor in a bundle. She picked it up and tossed it into the stove. Some hung over the edge, and she used the poker to loop it and flick it into the fire.

Then she eyed Sunny's painting of the man sitting on the porch steps. The white blemish shaped like a ghost in the window caught her attention. She hesitated, not wanting to touch it. Looking at it was enough to make her skin crawl. Finally, she bent and stuffed it into the stove.

It burned for a moment on its own, then she poked it several times as if it were about to crawl out of its funeral pyre. She pulled the poker back with relief and hung it on the metal rack next to the stove.

After watching the remaining items burn to ashes, she turned her attention to an unkempt man. It was Morgan, sitting in a chair and staring out the window. He had only moved a few times in the last week. She looked him over with a shake of her head. A thick stubble had grown on his catatonic face. It was as gray and lifeless as the early November sky outside.

A fly buzzed by her. She watched it land on Morgan's cheek and crawl closer to his open mouth. Unaware, he stared out the window as it scurried over him like he was already dead.

"Morgan?"

He continued staring, lost in whatever little world he was now in.

She felt a bit guilty, hoping he'd keep quiet about what the newspaper reported as a murder-suicide. But she did not intend for him to be like this. Cleaning up this mess and now having to watch over him had made the situation even more stressful. He was clearly still in some sort of shock.

She had only managed this long through denial and the stories she told herself. For all she knew, Sunny had written those diaries and planned this all in advance. That's what crazy people did. You saw them daily on the news, doing crazy things with their crazy beliefs.

"All I've done is try to protect you, Morgan. Didn't you see it in her eyes? Didn't you hear it in her voice? And the things she said?" She tried her best to provoke Morgan into showing some sign of life. He only sat still, eyes vacant. And that fly crawling all over him . . . it made her shudder.

She watched through the window as a car pulled into a parking space in front of the Antique Shoppe.

"Who could that be? Don't they know we're not open on Sundays?"

She again checked the remnants of the diaries and other items in the stove. Then she perched behind the register in the Antique Shoppe and waited for a knock at the door.

CHAPTER 65

Two dark figures loomed behind the entrance door's frosted glass, their outlines distorted, spectral. Evelyn had been expecting them. Yet, when the knock finally came, she flinched.

She smoothed her damp palms over her skirt, steadied her breath, and unlocked the door. Sheriff McCullough stood before her, his broad frame backlit by the heavy morning sky. Beside him, a lean man in a trench coat—face carved from stone, eyes unreadable. His hands remained behind his back, an instinctual tic of control that sent unease curling through her. She didn't trust people whose hands she couldn't see.

"Morning, Evelyn," McCullough greeted, his voice grave. "This here is Detective Carmichael. He's with the New York State Police's Bureau of Criminal Investigation."

The man offered only a curt nod. His gaze remained fixed on her, unblinking.

"Do you mind if we come in?"

Evelyn kept her expression open, unbothered. "Not at all," she said lightly, stepping aside. "What's the occasion?"

McCullough barely looked at her as he crossed the threshold. "We heard the news about Morgan," he said, his tone too even. "How's he doing?"

"News?" She forced a confused frown. "Oh. Yes. I'm afraid he still isn't much better. It was sudden . . . came out of nowhere."

Her fingers worked through her hair, an automatic attempt to fix something—herself, the moment. Anything. From the corner of her eye, she glanced at Morgan, seated in his chair by the window. His back remained to them, still as a painting. He didn't even seem aware of their presence.

"Is there anything I can assist you two gentlemen with?" Evelyn asked, regaining composure. "Unfortunately, we're not usually open on Sundays."

McCullough followed her gaze to Morgan, lingering on him for a beat too long.

"I'm sad to say, this isn't a social visit," he murmured. "We have a few questions about the murder-suicide."

Evelyn stiffened.

"I'm sorry," she said, eyes widening. "Murder?"

McCullough didn't answer immediately. Instead, he picked up a delicate porcelain figurine from a shelf, turned it over in his thick fingers, then set it down in the wrong place. Evelyn's skin crawled.

"I'm sure you've heard?" he prodded.

"Oh, why yes, of course," she said, schooling her voice into something neutral. "It just sounds so . . . strange—foreign even. You know, here, in the Thousand Islands. I don't understand who could do such a thing. What the hell is this world coming to?"

McCullough's gaze flickered toward the empty spot on the wall, where the original painting of the mansion had once hung.

"Is it just me, or did there used to be something hanging there?"

"H-hanging?" Evelyn's throat went dry. "Oh. Yes. There was a painting."

McCullough hummed low in his throat, then shifted his attention. "A woman believed to be suffering from—what was it?" he asked his partner.

"Postpartum psychosis," Carmichael answered, monotone. His eyes never left Evelyn.

"That's it. I knew it was postpartum something or other." McCullough sighed, rubbing his chin. "Her baby was stillborn. The mother had some . . . trouble, you could say. The family feared what might happen when she ran off. When her husband found her, she killed him. The family's worst nightmare became reality, and she took her own life." He exhaled sharply. "The funeral was a couple of days ago. Small gathering. From what I heard, the mortician did the best he could..."

Evelyn swallowed against a rising tide of nausea. *This isn't real. This is just a conversation. Just words.*

"How terrible," she uttered. "And the death of a child ... I can't even imagine. How did she—?" She stopped herself, pressing her fingers to her lips. "Well, it's none of my business, of course."

McCullough studied her. "She hung herself at the old funeral home, of all places."

A low, slow breath. A steady grip on the counter.

"Well," Evelyn said, forcing a small, regretful smile. "As you said, she wasn't in the right frame of mind."

She stepped back, grabbed a pack of cigarettes, and retreated to the doorway.

"That's a possible explanation," McCullough said. "But not the only one we're exploring."

Something in his voice put her on edge.

"Oh?" She held up a cigarette and a matchbook. "Do you mind?"

McCullough shook his head.

"We have a witness," he continued. "Of sorts."

Evelyn struck the match but failed to light it. She faltered. Outside, through the glass, a woman sat in the back of their unmarked car.

A woman in a shawl.

Evelyn's breath hitched. The woman lifted her head, and those eyes—those unnatural, light-green eyes—pierced her very soul. As their eyes locked, Evelyn heard an unmistakable ding. She tried to place the woman in the car. She knew she had seen her before but wasn't sure where.

A chill came over her as her eyes wandered to the wood stove.

The diaries.

Ding.

The sound jolted through her.

Her hand trembled as she struck another match. It snapped in half.

McCullough continued speaking, but Evelyn barely heard.

"The woman's adoptive parents said she feared something might happen to her, to cover up a murder there years ago." His voice carried from far away. "That person, who was believed to have died by suicide years ago, was her mother."

Ding.

"Well, as you said, she wasn't in the right frame of mind," Evelyn repeated, glancing about the room. "It must run in the family."

"Right, but our witness corroborated their story and provided more details. And then we found an item in the house. It turns out it is part of a rare antique collection."

Evelyn's strained eyes darted around as she tried to maintain her composure. She couldn't find the source of the noise. The cracks were showing.

Ding.

"I don't believe we're missing anything if that's what you're—"

"It was registered by Morgan a few decades ago, number 139 of 250. The girl's adoptive parents recognized it as well."

Detective Carmichael followed Evelyn's eyes.

"D-do you hear that?" Evelyn asked, continuing to look with a madness growing in her eyes.

The two paused, listening.

Ding.

"It's music. Playing," she said, losing her grip and withering under their gaze. Her face then soured. "That smell! It's her." She looked about wildly. "She's—she's here!"

The sun burst through the clouds, drenching the room in a sudden, blinding light.

The world tilted. Sound melted away, except for the broken music box's eerie chime.

Evelyn's sleep-deprived eyes darted back to the detective.

And then—she appeared.

Sunny in the white dress, aglow from the sunlight. Its rays revealed her ethereal presence, a phantom stepping out of time. She had an eerie smile and appeared to move supernaturally slow, holding Rebecca out as she approached, as if to suggest Evelyn kiss the baby herself. Her last gurgle-choked words between shallow breaths echoed.

"I . . . can . . . still . . . see her!"

Evelyn's scream ripped from her throat. She stumbled back, hands clawing at her face, shielding her eyes. She slid down the doorframe, collapsing in a heap.

The music box's warped tune grew louder.

Flies. A drone of flies.

And then—silence.

Cold. Dark. Lifeless silence.

A single fly crawled across Evelyn's hand. She jerked. It took flight.

Carmichael's voice cut through the hush.

"Ms. Arbogast?"

Evelyn's bloodshot eyes locked onto the antique porcelain doll in his hands. The fly landed on its face.

Ding.

Morgan sat in his chair, staring through the window. The music box in his lap.

Slowly, methodically, he wound it up.

The off-key tune began again.

Evelyn staggered to her feet, her body leaden.

"You'll have to forgive me," she whispered, lips trembling. "I haven't been feeling . . . quite . . . *myself* . . . of late."

Ding.

Carmichael stepped forward. "Is there something you would like to tell us?"

Evelyn flicked her cigarette between her lips. Struck a match.

It caught. A small victory.

McCullough drew closer.

"Ms. Arbogast?"

She brought the flame to the cigarette's tip.

And then—a breath that was not her own extinguished it.

Ding.

Her breath hitched.

Her gaze dropped.

The cigarette tumbled from her lips.

She exhaled, the raspy, hollow sound of a smoker's cough.

"Sheriff," she started, staring at nothing. After a long moment, "Do you believe in ghosts?"

Sheriff McCullough gave an uncertain look to the detective. "No."

"Neither did I," said Evelyn as the cigarette fell from her mouth.

"I do believe there are some things that defy explanation," a wary Sheriff McCullough added. "To be honest, we're here because we don't know *what* to believe."

Evelyn shook her head and looked up at them with haunted eyes. Her words sputtered out of her mouth as if she hardly believed them herself.

"I can still ... *see* her."

Detective Carmichael's face blanched as he looked back at the sheriff.

Ding.

Evelyn twitched at the music box. Her lips parted in something between a smile and a sob as she covered her ears.

"Our witness said you'd say that," Sheriff McCullough declared.

He wiped the doubt from his face before letting his hand drop to the handcuffs on his belt and clicking them open.

THE END

About the Author

James P. Barker is a multiple award-winning writer whose work spans screenwriting, historical research, and essay writing. He graduated with high distinction from the University at Buffalo with degrees in Psychology and Media Study (with a concentration in interpretation).

His writing explores the haunted intersections of memory, narrative, and the human mind. His essays on the science and art of storytelling have been cited in academic and creative circles around the world.

The Fourth House draws from a unique synthesis of narrative theory, philosophy, and neuroscience—blurring the line between literary architecture and lived experience.

Visit him at www.jamespbarkerwriter.com.